Born in Liverpool, Abbey Clancy balances her home life with her career as a model and TV presenter. She is an ambassador for many of the UK's top brands and has designed her own clothing and jewellery lines as well as launching a range of baby products. Abbey is married to Premiership footballer Peter Crouch and has four small children. *I'll Be Home for Christmas* is her second novel.

I'll Be Home for Christmas

Abbey Clancy
with Debbie Johnson

MILLS & BOON

This novel is entirely a work of fiction. The names, characters and incidents portrayed in it are the work of the author's imagination. Any resemblance to actual persons, living or dead, events or localities is entirely coincidental.

Mills & Boon
An imprint of HarperCollins*Publishers* Ltd
1 London Bridge Street
London SE1 9GF

This edition 2019

1
First published in Great Britain by
Mills & Boon, an imprint of HarperCollins*Publishers* Ltd 2019

With thanks to Debbie Johnson

A catalogue record for this book is
available from the British Library.

ISBN: 978-1-84845-681-5

MIX
Paper from
responsible sources
FSC™ C007454

This book is produced from independently certified FSC™ paper to ensure responsible forest management.

For more information visit: www.harpercollins.co.uk/green

Printed and bound in Great Britain by
CPI Group (UK) Ltd, Croydon, CR0 4YY

For you, Mum.
Love you loads. Don't know what
I would do without you.

Chapter 1

There are many aspects to the world of social media that I find confusing. Embarrassing. Overwhelming, even.

Like when someone snaps a picture of me the morning after the night before, and sticks it up on Instagram without even a measly Willow filter. I mean, we've all been there, right? Your mouth feels like it's been vacuum packed with a decomposing ferret, and your hair has gone full-on *Walking Dead*, and you know you're just going to die unless you get immediate access to a paper bag full of McDonald's hash browns?

Yeah. Well, imagine in that precise moment, someone incredibly chipper bounces over, grinning from ear to ear at the sight of you, and wants nothing more than to snap a picture of you together, no matter how grey your skin is or how far down your face your mascara's slipped. Not good.

But – and I get this, I really do – it's all part of my job. My job isn't an ordinary job. It's being a pop star – Jessika – to the world at large. Not very long ago at all I was the person who would have been bouncing over and asking for the pic, so I can't complain. Not very long ago, I was scraping a living singing Disney covers at kids' birthday parties, working as an intern at a record label, and filling in my lonely nights waitressing at glamorous showbiz events I wasn't good enough to actually get invited to.

So I get it. I understand that it's all part of my brave, weird new world – and that I have a responsibility to suck it up, smile for the camera, even if I really, really don't want to.

I also understand that people will comment about me, and to me – posting everything from sweet compliments on my music through to borderline-stalker psycho abuse. I know everything I say and do will be analysed, twisted, churned up, chewed up, and spat back out by the media. I have help with that, in the form of my scary PR manager Patty, and I'm sensible enough not to take the nasty stuff seriously. I've worked hard on developing a thick skin, and coping with the demands of being famous.

One thing, though, I don't think I will ever get used to is this: my mother is currently trending on Twitter.

To put this in context, my mother is a tiny Scouse powerhouse in her fifties, with dyed black hair, strong opinions and endless energy. I'd say she has zero per cent body fat, 200 per cent work ethic, and loves nothing more than her family, which includes my nan, who is officially ancient, my dad Phil, my older sister Becky, me and my little brother Luke (or The Knobhead, as he's known to everyone who's ever met him).

She is also totally in love with her first ever grandchild – Becky's baby Ollie, who is now four months old and rules the world from his bouncy chair like a benign Jabba the Hutt. He's one of those fat babies with rolls of flesh everywhere, and his eyes completely disappear every time he laughs. Which is a lot.

So, Mum is a family woman. Her life isn't glamorous, or

that interesting. She spends every spare minute looking after us lot, and still works on the tills at the local Asda, even though she doesn't really need to any more. She's extraordinary, but ordinary, if you know what I mean – one of those salt-of-the-earth-women you could build an empire on the back of.

All of which begs the question: why is she trending on Twitter? When did she even join Twitter? *Why* did she join Twitter?

I scroll down the pages – literally endless pages – and see that every pic on there has the hashtag #jessikasmum. It looks like the whole of Liverpool has popped into the supermarket to pick up a packet of crumpets, a bottle of Prosecco, and a selfie with my mother. There are hundreds of them – all featuring complete strangers, gurning like idiots, and my mum, happily posing alongside them.

My mum has described herself as 'daughter, wife, mother, grandmother, and lover of all things Michael Bublé'. I suppose I should be grateful that the great crooner himself hasn't also called in with a selfie stick in his hand.

'Fab time at Asda with mummy diva', says one tweet. 'Jessika's mum is awesome', says another. 'Forget Jessika – her mum needs her own reality show!' on one more. 'Why's she still working?' asks a random girl who, according to her profile, loves knitting, cats and visiting S&M clubs. Hopefully not all at the same time.

Mum's still working, of course, because she wants to. Not because she's skint, or because I haven't offered to give her anything she needs – but because she is who she is. She's my mum, and she'll probably be going into Asda when she's eighty, popping her false teeth back in for photo calls.

I close down the screen, and take a breath. Tell myself there's no harm done. That it could be worse – my dad could be on Twitter, and then the world as we know it would collapse in on itself.

My life is insane. Nobody warned me being a pop star would be quite this crazy.

#passmetheproseccoplease

*

I used to think my life was complicated when I was younger. I was sharing a scummy flat with my old school friend, Ruby, running our marginally successful Disney princess party business, feeding my body with a steady diet of cheap packet noodles and feeding my soul with a vision of becoming a singer.

I suppose I was a typically star-struck girl from Liverpool who was a chasing a dream – a dream of becoming a pop star, of making it big, of hanging framed platinum discs on my toilet wall and playing to sell-out crowds in stadiums across the globe.

In some ways, all of that has come true. Sort of by accident, if I'm honest. I was singing at a birthday party in Cheshire, soaked to the skin and 'Letting It Go', when I was 'spotted' by a music mogul called Jack Duncan.

When you read that in newspapers and magazines – 'spotted' – it always sounds like stardom happened magically overnight. Like the tall skinny geeky girl was shopping for a new pencil case in Paperchase one minute, and strutting her stuff on the Paris catwalks the next. And maybe, in some cases, that's what happens, I don't know.

With me, it was different. After I was 'spotted', Jack whisked me away to a new life in London – but it was a new life that didn't exactly start out brilliantly. I was working long hours as the office intern at Starmaker Records, slaving for the PR team by day and perfecting my craft by night.

Well, that's not quite accurate. Some of those nights, I'd spend with Jack Duncan – who'd spotted my talent in more ways than one. I still cringe a little inside when I think about Jack. I can't say he exploited me, but he didn't exactly behave like a knight in shining armour either – because while I was gullibly falling in love with him, he was part-time shacked up with my friend Vogue as well.

It all came out in the wash, and we got our revenge – revenge that involved handcuffing him to a bed, taking obscene pictures of him in embarrassing positions and, more importantly, walking out on Starmaker to form our own record label – In Vogue.

Still. Cringing inside, even as I speak. I have a trusting soul, and that isn't always a good thing in show business – because the Jack Duncans of that world are literally swimming through its waters like seductive sharks, guzzling up tiddlers like me for breakfast.

I went from being me to being a new and not-so-improved version of me – featuring on a number one single with Vogue, on the pages of all the bikini-body celeb-style magazines, even on the telly for a live Christmas Day broadcast.

Between the glamour and the parties and Jack and the

sheer wondrous hard work of it all, I lost my bearings a bit though. I forgot who I was. I left behind Jessy, the nice girl from Liverpool who loved her family and kept her feet on the ground, and embraced Jessika, who, possibly as a result of some kind of toxic poisoning from all the fake eyelashes and fake tan she used, could be a bit of a bitch.

I'm not proud of some of the things I did back then, but I am proud that I pulled it back. It's not easy to get any kind of balance when your entire life is a crazy carousel of lunacy, but I did.

I didn't do it alone, though. I did it with the help of my family, bonkers as they are. I did it with the help of Vogue, who might be a diva but has a heart the size of a planet. I did it with the help of Neale, my stylist and the most fabulous and best of friends.

Mainly, though, I did it with the help of Daniel Wells – the love of my life.

*

Daniel Wells is my real hero. He's Han Solo and Jack Bauer and Barack Obama all rolled up into one. He doesn't look or act like any of those people – I'm just trying to convey how brilliant he is. To me at least.

Daniel and I have known each other since we were toddlers. He used to live next door to us on our quiet terraced street in Liverpool, and there are, I believe, photos still in existence of us playing with rubber ducks in the bath together when we were two. We still sometimes take a bath together, but things tend to end differently these days.

Daniel was a geek before it was remotely cool to be one. Overweight, over-haired, over-pimpled and over-shy, he spent his teenage years locked away, writing songs, fiddling with tech, and, it turns out, pining over me.

We lost touch for years when his family moved down South, but he miraculously appeared back in my life just when I needed him most. I had recreated myself as Jessika, and he had recreated himself as Wellsy – the coolest record producer of his generation. But while I embraced the madness of public life – I was always a much bigger show-off than him – he'd become a hermit, setting up his studio in the wilds of the countryside, his anonymity and lack of showbiz neediness somehow making him even more desirable within the industry.

He'd not changed a bit – he still knew me inside out, upside down, and standing on my head. He still understood me, warts and all, and loved me anyway. In fact, the only thing that had changed about Daniel was the way he looked – time had been kind to him, good genetics allowing him to blossom into a taller version of Leonardo DiCaprio. Cute Leo – like *Catch Me If You Can* Leo, not the Leo covered in blood and drool like in *The Revenant*.

I don't think I'm exaggerating when I say he saved me. Or, at the very least, he made room for me on his life raft as the *Titanic* was sinking – unlike that cow Rose.

And now, we're together. So together it's unreal. In public, we might be Wellsy and Jessika, but, in private, we're just Jessy and Daniel. Loved-up in a way I've never known before. He has his career, I have mine, and we both have each other. My time with him is precious and perfect and utterly satisfying in every possible way. He's the kind of man you can watch a box set of *Happy Valley* with one minute, and have Olympic-level sex with the next. He doesn't care if I look like crap, or accidentally leave my hair extensions hanging on the back of the bathroom door like a skinned cat, or fall asleep at 8 p.m. because I'm exhausted. He understands my lifestyle, and he understand me. Frankly, I can't believe how much I lucked out – in many ways, but mainly with Daniel.

It sounds simple. Idyllic, even. But, of course, it's not that straightforward – nothing ever is. Because I still spend a lot of my time in London, for work, and he's still based at his farmhouse in Sussex. Because I'm living in the public eye so much even my mum gets approached for selfies, and he values his privacy.

Mainly, at the moment, because I have a brain tangle about what will happen next. Part of me just wants to run away to the countryside and snuggle up with him for the rest of our lives. We could raise chickens and sheep and maybe even add to my mum's adorable grandchild collection. I'm sure we'd be happy. Super-happy, in fact.

I could eat more carbs and grow a muffin top and I'm pretty sure he wouldn't mind, and we could go for long walks and have long baths and turn into one of those couples who don't even own a telly. Maybe I'd even forget to brush my hair and end up with dreadlocks. We have enough money, and we have enough love, to make that a possibility.

But, of course, it wouldn't work. I don't really like being separated from my hair straighteners for too long, and Neale would bitch-slap me with a dead mackerel if I didn't exfoliate every day. Plus, it's not all about the money, is it? I wasn't chasing this dream of mine for so long just for the money. Even if I'd won the EuroMillions on one of those bonkers rollover weeks, I'd still be working.

Because it's about more than that. It's about the music. It's about singing, and performing, and building the only career I've ever wanted. It's about that dream I've always had, and about that work ethic I inherited from my parents.

Daniel can get away with building his superstar career from the sound-proofed comfort of the South Downs – but, sadly, Jessika can't. Jessika needs to be out in the world, posing for those photos even though she feels awful, going to those parties, and putting in the hours perfecting her craft. Jessika needs the spotlight, even though Jessy sometimes wishes she could hide away in a darkened room and scoff a box of Matchmakers instead.

And Jessika – I really must stop talking about myself in the third person – has just received what might be the opportunity of a lifetime.

Chapter 2

It pinged onto my iPhone X last Thursday, and at first I thought it was just something fun from Vogue or Neale or maybe something a bit mushy from Daniel, but when I looked at the email, it came from an unfamiliar email address, but had a very familiar name.

Cooper Black.

Cooper Black, former frontman with hit boy band E-Z Street. Cooper Black, whose denim-clad limbs and perfectly ripped abs have graced the walls of millions of teenaged girls. Cooper Black, who is about to launch his much-anticipated, and apparently much cooler, solo career.

Cooper Black, who is – for some reason – a huge fan of Jessika:

Hey, Jessika,

I'm a huge fan. Love your voice, your style, everything about you. I think we could make beautiful music together – don't you? I have a 'featuring' slot waiting for you on the new single, if you're interested. Let's talk.

There's a lot going on over here in the States, and I'd love for you to be involved.

And now he wants me to leave everything behind and go and work with him in the US.

Part of me is so excited I could kiss a camel, possibly with tongues. It is beyond awesome – not only has someone like Cooper Black even heard of me, but he wants to record with me, perform with me. It's a chance to take my music across the Atlantic, to open up a whole new world of possibilities. It's everything I've ever dreamed of.

But it's also thousands of miles and several time zones away from the rest of my life. I'd have to move away from Daniel, from Vogue, from my family. I'd have to make a choice that I'm not sure I'm ready to make.

I have no idea what to do, and don't have a clue who to talk to about it, either. My mum and dad would just want me to do what makes me happy. Daniel would be heartbroken. Vogue would possibly feel betrayed. Neale would be pipping at the thought of going, and planning his wardrobe accordingly. They'd all see only part of the big picture – and it's up to me to see the whole shebang.

It's way too complicated for me to figure out – how do I pursue my own ambitions without hurting the people I care about?

At times like this, the thought of dressing up as Elsa and singing to a bunch of screaming kids in a soggy garden seems like an appealing option. The rain never bothered me anyway.

Potentially life-changing emails from all-American pop idols aside, everything is going brilliantly.

*

When Vogue (known as Paulette to her friends – which includes me, but I must admit I struggle with calling her that) – and I stitched up Jack Duncan, we used our position as leverage to get away from the clutches of his record label, Starmaker.

It was still relatively early days, but it was going even better than we could possibly have imagined. Vogue had been wonderful enough – and generous enough – to let me feature on her last single with Starmaker, 'Midnight', and that had gone to the top of the charts and was still being played on radio stations around the world.

In addition, my first single since our takeover, which had been written for me by Daniel, was a great success, which was a pretty brilliant way to launch the new label. Vogue, I knew, would also be recording some new material at some point, but, for the time being, she was concentrating on getting everything set up, and on the refurbishment of our new headquarters.

For reasons best known to herself, she'd fallen in love with a former lap-dancing bar in Soho, and that was where I was working today.

When you first walk into the building, it still feels a bit dark and desperate, but there is a real charm to it, I have to say. It's mid-way through its refit, and the first area to get the star treatment was the main room in the building, which is now our reception. There is still a stage kitted out with a pole in the middle of it and I have a sneaking suspicion that late at night, when she's on her own, Vogue lets out a few frustrations by swinging around on it. There's a lot of dark red velvet and gold paint, and the whole place is always filled with artistically arranged floral bouquets. Lilies, roses, everything incredibly fresh and fragrant – even when it's just us, we have the flowers. The building is a little weird, and a little edgy, but it works.

So far, as well as the reception area, we have two recording booths, with plans for two more. The basement isn't done yet, but, when it is, there'll be a full dance studio and rehearsal space. Neale has his own empire down there, stocked with cosmetics and beauty equipment and wardrobe, and he's like a kid in a toy shop with it all. I have occasionally caught him down there, sitting cross-legged on the floor, just looking around in awe, practically clapping his hands in glee.

The former dressing rooms have been partially converted into offices, for admin, for Patty, and for the extra staff we will eventually be taking on. I say 'we', but I actually mean Vogue. She does consult me when she's in two minds about somebody, but, on the whole, that's her realm, and I'm happy with that. I'm still taking baby steps in this industry, and concentrating on the music side of things is enough for me at the moment.

I arrived a little later than usual, as I'd made the journey in from Daniel's place in Sussex that morning, and made my way into reception. There wasn't any natural daylight in this area of the building when we first started – which is usual enough for a lap-dancing bar, I suppose – but, since then, the room has been opened up, spring sunlight pouring in and striping the red velvet booths and the exotic blooms.

Our receptionist, Yvonne, was already at her post, wearing one of those phone headsets that made her look like she was directing a troupe of dancers at a Madonna gig. Yvonne is only young, twenty-one in fact, but already has that 'Don't Mess With Me' face that I associate with my mother. She's half Chinese, and looks like she could be Lucy Liu's daughter – utterly gorgeous, in other words.

She gave me a nod and a wave as I walked in and scribbled my name on the book we use to make sure nobody ever gets left behind in a fire, and I grinned back. The place is always at least partly full of builders at the moment, wearing their steel-toed boots and crack-revealing jeans, the smell of sawdust and work competing with the fragrance of the flowers.

I gave them a little wave as I passed – they were on a tea break, for a change – and headed back towards the offices.

Pausing outside the door, I took a deep breath. I knew, from the clattering sound of talons hitting a keyboard and the echoes of Swedish death metal music, that Patty, our head of marketing, who we also stole from Jack's empire, was already there.

Weird thing about Patty – I'm still scared of her. She's no longer my boss in any way, shape or form, but I spent so long being terrorized by her that I still have a Pavlovian response to her presence. She's scrawny, rude and opinionated, but she's also brilliant at her job, which is why we brought her with us. She's amazing at handling the press in its many forms, a strategic mastermind at social media, and a genius at marketing the bejeezus out of anything she's asked to sell.

For months at Starmaker, she treated me like crap – but, as ever with these things, I definitely emerged from the experience feeling a lot stronger. She also used to mock me for my Liverpool accent, claiming she could never understand a word I said, which turned out to be ironic as she was a born-and-bred Geordie who'd simply learned how to speak posh.

When we offered her the position as head of marketing, we told her she had to start speaking like Cheryl Cole, but so far she'd refused. We also told her she had to start being more herself, rather than the shrill, cold battleaxe she'd turned herself into at Starmaker.

The only changes I'd noticed were her clothes, and her listening tastes. She'd abandoned the streamlined suits, designer frocks and skyscraper shoes in favour of skinny jeans and Doc Marten boots, and left to her own devices played very loud music made by bands with names like Bloodbath and Necrophobic. Neither of which made her any less scary.

I raised my hand to knock, but realized that a) she wouldn't hear me, and b) I didn't need to knock. This was my office too.

I walked in, a smile plastered over my face, and sat at my desk. It's weird, having a desk. At the end of the day I'm just a singer, but Vogue insisted I have my own space – or a bit of Patty's space, anyway. At least for the time being, until the other offices are finished.

The desk is decorated with framed pictures of my family and Daniel, and there's an Elsa from *Frozen* bobblehead that Ruby sent me for old times' sake.

Patty ignored me completely, but did at least turn the volume down on a charming song where someone was screaming lyrics about sacrificing a baby to the dark lord of the underworld. This, in Patty Land, is a major concession to societal norms.

'Your mother,' she said, finally acknowledging my existence, pointing a pen at me like it was a fully-charged lightsaber, 'is getting more coverage than you at the moment.'

'Um . . . yeah. I saw that. There's no harm, is there?'

I hated myself for it, but there was a slightly pleading note in my voice. I really didn't want to have to call my mum and tell her to close down her Twitter account. I'd be in her bad books for weeks, and I'd only just got back in her good ones.

'Not so far. But I'll be monitoring it closely. What are you doing here anyway? Shouldn't you be getting a spray tan or gorging on a celery stick?'

I clamped my lips shut, and started the now-familiar 'Count to Ten' routine I've had to adopt when dealing with Patty. She's skinnier than Olive Oyl and has no right to comment on my appearance, but that's never stopped her.

I ignored her and booted up my laptop. I noticed an email from Daniel, and couldn't help grinning when I opened it to see a whole message filled with love heart emojis. That boy!

I closed it down, and opened up the other email. The bizarrely scary email. The one from Cooper Black, that's been sitting in my inbox for almost a week.

He'd also left his phone number at the bottom, and signed off with several kisses. Not quite Daniel heart emoji level, but enough to make me think. I mean, Cooper Black is not only a megastar, he's an absolute babe. Floppy blond hair, film-star handsome face, a stomach so tight you could bounce coins off it. And I may be happily loved-up, but I'm not dead yet – no straight woman alive could fail to be impressed by him.

'What's the buzz on Cooper Black?' I said to Patty, suddenly curious. I knew he was making his solo debut, that he'd been working on his own material with some incredibly cool songwriters and producers, and that everyone was expecting him to completely break out of his slightly old-school boy-band vibe into something more mature and hip.

'World domination,' snapped Patty, glaring at me. 'And also, no selfies of his mother selling condoms to the unwashed masses of Liverpool.'

'There was never a selfie of her selling condoms! And people in Liverpool are *not* unwashed, you Geordie cow!' I snapped back. I regretted it almost as soon as I saw the smug look on her face – she knows exactly which buttons to press with me, and enjoys few things in life more than a spot of Jessika-baiting.

She made a mooing noise in response, and turned the volume on her music right back up to ear-splitting levels.

A quick browse of the crazy world of the internet showed me that while she was wrong about my mother and the condoms (I did check, just to be sure), she was definitely right about Cooper Black. Literally every social media platform on the planet was talking about him, there were interviews all over the mainstream media websites, and he practically had his own shrines on TMZ and E! Online. World domination indeed – the man who thought we could make beautiful music together was the hottest name in showbiz.

It was flattering. So incredibly flattering. And exciting – I mean, which singer hasn't dreamed of conquering America? The stadium tours and the big cities and the millions of new potential fans? I know I have. Cooper Black could be my passport to a whole new level of success, and part of me was desperate to say yes. Or at least hear him out.

But the rest of me? I was terrified. I didn't want to leave Daniel. I told myself it would only be for a little while, and that nothing would change, but my heart broke at the thought of being separated from him. I was staying in London that night, and even the idea of one night away from his arms was hard to deal with, never mind weeks or possibly months.

We're very much in love, but we're also very much at the beginning – and things still feel fragile. I'm probably wrong to feel like that, and perhaps it's the aftershock of Jack's betrayal that's left me insecure, but I can't help it. Daniel's never given me any reason to be worried about our future together, but I still am. I'm also worried about leaving In Vogue at such a delicate point. How would it look to the world at large if the label's first and therefore most successful signing suddenly upped sticks and buggered off to the States? Would it make us look weak? Would it make Vogue vulnerable to gossip and speculation about what was going wrong?

How would Vogue feel about it all, as well as Daniel? She was my mentor. She was my colleague. More than that, she was my friend – she was loyal and strong and honest. All of which were personality traits I really valued, and probably wasn't displaying myself right now, by hiding the whole Cooper Black thing from her.

If I did the WWVD test and asked myself What Would Vogue Do, the answer was obvious: she'd talk it through. She'd bring it out in the open. She wouldn't pretend it had never happened, while secretly really wanting it to.

Maybe it was time for me to do the same. And also for me to be honest with myself – because while all my concerns about Daniel and my family and Vogue and my life back here were genuine, I also had to admit that if I said no to Cooper

Black – to this amazing opportunity – then perhaps I'd find myself silently resenting them for holding me back, even if they had no clue they'd done it. None of that was fair, was it? I had to sort this out.

I signed out of all my accounts – leaving Patty in a room with access to anything personal was like tying myself to a railway track and waiting for a train – and stood up.

'Where's Vogue?' I said.

She glanced up at me, frowning, and made a confused 'I can't hear you' gesture with her hands.

'I said, where's Vogue?' I yelled, as loud as I could. Obviously, she chose that exact moment to turn off the music, and my very un-ladylike screeching filled the office, and possibly the whole of Soho.

'No need to shout!' she said, giving me her velociraptor smile. 'You're not at Anfield now! And I don't know where Vogue is. I'm not her keeper.'

She immediately switched the death metal back on, and I grimaced as I left the room. Served me right for engaging with her in the first place. Honestly, she's a nightmare – at least to me. The transformation when she's with people who matter – in other words, the media – is incredible. She literally oozes charm, instead of bile.

I walked back out to reception, determined to at least talk about the whole Cooper Black thing with Vogue. If I kept hiding it, I'd possibly explode, and make a terrible mess all over our shiny new headquarters.

I approached Yvonne – who always knows where everybody is, at any given moment – and was about to ask her, when I saw that she was talking into her headset, and making apologetic 'I'm on the phone' motions with her fingers. It was obviously my day for communicating through the power of mime.

I waved to show her I understood, and then flicked through the guest book. The one I'd signed myself into only a few minutes earlier. Yvonne was strict about that – so if Vogue was in the building, she'd be signed in, and I'd go up to her office in the attic and track her down. It would also show if she had a visitor, so I'd know not to bother her.

I traced my finger down the list, amazed at how many people had already signed in. All the builders. Yvonne. Neale. Patty. Vogue.

And – I saw as I stared at it in horror – one more person. A person whose name I'd never expect to see there in a million years.

He'd arrived at 10 a.m. The purpose of his visit was 'meeting'. And his name was Jack Duncan.

I was so shocked I simply froze for a moment. I hadn't even realized I'd done it, until one of the builders shouted out to me: 'You all right, love? Look like you've seen a ghost!'

One of his mates replied: 'A ghost wearing nipple tassels, if this place is anything to go by!' and they all dissolved into howls of laughter.

I tried to join in, but that part of my brain wasn't working. I mean, I'd seen Jack since it all kicked off. It was a relatively small world that we all shared, and it was inevitable that I'd bump into him at parties and events. We always politely avoided each other – personally, I'd rather skin myself alive than spend any quality time with the man, and I suspected the feeling was mutual.

But to see that he was here, in what I regarded as my own safe territory, was messing with my head. A head that had been pretty messed up already, to be honest.

After the shock wore off, the anger started in. I much preferred that – it gave me the energy I needed to run up the three flights of stairs to Vogue's office.

Her space is located in the old eaves of the building, away from the hustle and bustle downstairs, and has a brilliant view of the busy London streets below. She'd not had it completely done yet, but the walls were stripped back to bare brick, and it was huge – three cramped old rooms converted into one big open-plan affair.

I paused outside her door, slightly out of puff from the speed with which I'd dashed up there, and tried to gather my thoughts. I could be massively overreacting, I told myself. Vogue was not only a singer, she was a businesswoman, trying to make a success of a label in a highly competitive industry. If she was meeting with Jack Duncan, she must be thinking that he could be useful. That she could use him in some way. It didn't necessarily mean anything at all – music people had meetings all the time; their whole days were filled with pointless cups of coffee and empty schmoozing.

All of these very reasonable thoughts were chased out of my mind by one sound: the sound of laughter. Vogue and Jack, giggling away with each other behind that frosted-glass door, as though it was the most natural thing in the world.

I knocked once, sharply, and pushed the door open without waiting for a reply. They were sitting together on Vogue's faux zebra-print couch, and they were sitting way closer than the average business meeting usually required.

Vogue's eyes opened so wide they were the size of UFOs, and Jack jumped to his feet, spilling coffee on his jeans as he did. It probably scalded his thighs – or at least I hoped so.

He looked good, I had to admit. Still the same stylish dark brown hair; the same chocolate-drop eyes. The same stylishly casual clothes that screamed money. Still the same gym-buff body, and, most importantly, still the same slightly arrogant expression on his face.

'Jessy!' he said, at least having the good grace to look a bit flustered.

'That's *Jessika* to you,' I said coldly, standing with my hands on my hips and staring him down. 'I'm only Jessy to my friends.'

There was an incredibly awkward pause then, and Jack scurried around gathering up papers and his phone and stuffing them into his leather manbag. Vogue was looking at me with pleading eyes, but stayed silent as he prepared to leave. I stayed stubbornly in the door frame for a moment, half tempted to wrestle him to the floor, until he shimmied past me and escaped.

'Erm . . . nice to see you again. I look forward to working with you,' he said, as he disappeared off down the staircase.

Working with me? I thought. What the hell did that mean? The only way I'd want to work with Jack Duncan again was if he had a sudden fall from grace and had a new career as a toilet cleaner. Even then, I'd need to wear rubber gloves every time I flushed the loo.

I was furious. And confused. And pissed off – I thought that Vogue had always been honest with me. Now I was starting to suspect the exact opposite.

I closed the door quietly behind him – refusing to give him the satisfaction of hearing an angry slam – and turned to face Vogue.

Vogue is black, gorgeous and generously proportioned. She's almost six feet tall and rocking Naomi Campbell meets Marilyn Monroe vibe. Usually, in the office, she's make-up free and dressed down – and still looks stunning. Today, I noticed, she was in full slap, wearing her green contacts, and dressed to kill in leather trousers and high-heeled boots. I was guessing that she hadn't chosen that outfit to impress the builders. Frankly, they were impressed by anybody with boobs.

Now, I can be – how do I phrase this politely? – a bit on the slow side occasionally. My family have told me that I'm too gullible. Too trusting. That I always see the good side of people, even when they don't have one. My brother Luke has a theory that I'd invite Jack the Ripper into the house for a cup of tea if he looked like he needed cheering up.

But even I had to face facts: there was something going on here, and it wasn't going to be something I liked.

'Come in, please,' said Vogue, gesturing to me to sit next to her. I could tell from her body language that she was tense and upset, which is unusual – she's mostly astonishingly laid-back.

I couldn't bring myself to sit on the couch where he'd been sitting, so instead pulled a chair round from behind her desk.

'What's going on?' I asked, tapping my toes on the wooden floor. I was obviously pretty tense and upset as well. It was like a virus – and Jack Duncan was Patient Zero. 'Why was he here? And why were you drooling over him?'

'I wasn't drooling!' she replied, although the slightly

sheepish look on her face told me she knew she had been. I just raised an eyebrow, and waited for her to carry on.

She took a deep breath, puffing it out so hard her cheeks expanded, and gazed over towards the window. It was as though she didn't even want to meet my eyes while she talked. This, I knew, was going to be bad.

'Babe, look. . .I've been meaning to talk to you about this for a while. I know I should have spoken to you earlier, but you know what it's like – we're both so busy we barely have time to breathe. Between my crazy schedule and yours, we just haven't seen each other. . .'

'We went for sushi last Friday,' I pointed out. 'We were together for two hours pretending we liked raw tuna and drinking wine.'

She held her head in her hands, and for a moment I thought she was crying. Obviously, if I'd heard a sniffle, my tough-girl act would have softened, but when she finally emerged, she just looked determined.

'I know. You're right. I'm just making excuses, aren't I? I need to be honest now.'

'That,' I replied, crossing my arms across my chest in what I realized was a classic defensive posture, 'would be nice. Now, what was he doing here?'

'I'm giving him a job,' she said simply. I opened my mouth to respond, but found that I had no words. Which was a good thing, as she immediately shushed me anyway.

'No, let me finish before you go off on one – I'm giving him a job because I need the help, and because he's good. You know he's good. He discovered me, he discovered you, as well as loads of the others at Starmaker. Whatever you might think about him – and I know none of it's good – he is one of the best when it comes to spotting new talent. And we need that. I need that. I'm rushed off my feet here, there's so much to do – all the stuff I'd never even expected. Did you know I need a HR policy? How much Health and Safety crap there is? That I have to have meetings with insurance companies, and lawyers, and accountants? There's just too much for one person right now!'

I bit my lip, and made myself think about what she was saying. She had been getting swamped, I knew, with the demands of setting up a new business. I suppose I'd been happily focusing on the creative side of things, and she'd been dealing with everything else. In all honesty, I'd not stopped to consider how stressful, and just plain boring, all of that probably was. But still. . .

'OK,' I replied. 'I get that. But you've never really complained. You've never asked for help. I could do more.'

'Honey, I know you mean well, but you're not really the HR policy type, are you? And I don't mean that as an insult, before you get your knickers in a twist! I just . . . I'm drowning, all right? And I know your single did well, and I'm sure your album will too, but we need more. If we're going to be taken seriously in this game, we need more – I need someone out there, scouting for us. I need someone to be my eyes and ears at gigs and events and bloody kids' parties – and Jack has a way of finding gold dust in the most unlikely of places. You *know* that! And without new signings, we're going to shrivel up and die – you're great, Jess, but you're not enough. Not long-term. Jack. . .well, Jack can help me with the long term. I know he can.'

I was momentarily silent, staring at her and wondering how she could have kept a secret like this from me. Then I reminded myself that I was keeping a secret of my own – one that suddenly didn't feel all that shameful.

'I'm just . . . shocked,' I said, eventually, watching as she messed with the rings on her fingers, turning them nervously round and round, over and over again. 'You've genuinely never hinted at anything like this. This place – well, it was supposed to be different, wasn't it? It was supposed to be better. We were supposed to treat people well, and be fair, and . . . not screw people! Either literally or ethically!'

'It will be better!' she replied, sounding frustrated. 'It is better! I've talked it all through with Jack, and he knows the score. He knows what we're trying to achieve, and that we won't take any bullshit. He's keen – really keen – to make a change. He's different now, honest. What happened. . .well, it affected him, it really did. It made him think about the way he was behaving, and the way he was living his life, and he wants to be different . . . he wants to be better as well. And I genuinely believe he deserves a second chance.'

It's hard to tell, with Vogue, when she's blushing. She's such a confident woman, I've rarely seen her embarrassed – angry, drunk, amused, euphoric, all of those things. But not often embarrassed. Right then, though, I could tell she was. She was flustered and nervous and obviously feeling desperately uncomfortable, no matter how hard that speech had tried to convince me otherwise. And I suspected I knew why.

'And what about you, Vogue? Paulette? What will Jack Duncan be doing for you? It's not just his professional talent that's getting a second chance with you, is it?'

She looked up at me, finally meeting my eyes, and trying very hard to look defiant. She didn't quite pull it off but it was a valiant effort.

'No,' she eventually said, biting a chunk out of her lip as she tried to continue. 'No, it's not. We're giving it another go. I know that's not what you expected to hear, and I know it's a tricky situation. . .'

'*Tricky*?' I said, my voice rising about three octaves. 'Tricky? You really think that's the right word? For you getting back together with the man who broke both our hearts? The man who fooled us both? The man who jumped from my bed to yours, entirely possibly on the same day? I think that's a bit more than tricky! And I think you're completely mad for even considering it.'

She nodded, because nothing I'd said could possibly have come as a surprise to her. This was why she'd avoided telling me for so long – because she knew exactly how I was going to react.

'I know you think that. And I don't blame you. But it's easy for you to say – you were only with him for a few months, and went straight from him to falling in love with Daniel. And I'm happy for you, I really am. It was different for me, and at the end of the day, babe, even though I know you've got my best interests at heart, that you want to protect me, it's my life. It's my life, and my decision, and if it's all a terrible mistake then it's mine to make. Do you get that?'

She was starting to sound a bit angry now – and Vogue angry is a sight to behold. I hoped that at least part of her was angry at herself, because she knew on some level that what I was saying was right. She just really, really didn't want to hear it.

I stood up, and brushed down my top as though there were crumbs on it, just to give me something to do with my hands. I was so upset, I could feel the tears starting to build in the back of my eyes. I always cry when I'm angry – it's a really annoying habit, because it makes me look weak and vulnerable when I'm actually feeling self-righteous and strong.

'I get that,' I said quietly, and turned to leave. 'And you're right, it's your life. But it's also my career – so I'd ask you to keep him away from me, all right?'

I didn't give her the chance to reply. I just did my best flounce out of the room, and finally gave in to the urge to slam the door.

*

I spent the next ten minutes in the ladies', crying my eyes out. The loos hadn't been renovated at all, and still vaguely smelled of sweat and perfume and baby oil from the women who used to use them.

I locked myself into one of the stalls, and just let it all out. By the time I'd finished, my eyes were red and swollen, and my hands were shaking with emotion. I wasn't sure which was worrying me most – the fact that Jack Duncan, and everything he represented, was slithering like a snake into our new Garden of Eden, or that my friend was making a huge mistake in her love life.

They were both pretty shitty situations, and making it all so much worse was the fact that she'd been hiding it from me. I didn't know how long this had been going on, but it already felt like Jack was making his mark – as soon as he'd arrived on the scene, the deception had started. Maybe some of that was down to me – Vogue was scared of telling me because she knew I'd blow my top. Maybe if I'd been less of an emotional melting pot and more of a calm listening ear, she'd have felt able to confide in me earlier. Maybe not. Who knows?

Either way, I felt devastated. Like the rug had been pulled from beneath my feet. Like the future was now a very uncertain road, to be crossed late at night after six pints of lager.

I splashed cold water on my face, and stared at myself in the cracked mirror. There were still bright red lipstick kisses all around the edges from its previous customers.

I looked like a pufferfish, but I didn't suppose that mattered. But I felt like a zombie, which mattered more.

After a few deep breaths, I decided I had to talk to Daniel. He was one of the most calm, steady and sensible people I knew. Maybe that's why we worked so well together – I could get overexcited at an episode of *Coronation Street*, but he was always on a level. He'd hear me out, and let me cry, and then say something so utterly sensible and sane and perfect that I'd feel better about the world immediately.

I didn't see the point in going back to Patty's lair, where I wouldn't be able to hear myself think for all the baby-sacrificing, so instead I found myself a quiet corner in the little courtyard garden outside.

It's not huge – not in this part of London – but big enough for a table and chairs, and a few boxes of flowers. The noise from the street is pretty minimal, and it's an unexpectedly calm spot.

Usually it's occupied by at least one builder on a fag break, but it was blessedly empty when I emerged into the sunlight, clutching my phone and sniffling.

Daniel answered on the first ring, which told me two things: that he'd finished his chores around the farm (collecting eggs from the chickens and feeding our Billy goat, who we'd named Gandalf because he looked so wise and intelligent); and that he hadn't yet started work (finding new and funky samples to use on a track by Vella, one of the new artists he was working with).

'Good morning, gorgeous,' he said immediately, and I couldn't help but smile. Honestly, the fact that he could make me smile even when I felt so awful was enough to warm my insides.

'I love you,' I replied. 'You know that, don't you?'

'I do. Because you bought me that T-shirt that has it printed all over the front: Jessy Hearts Daniel. I'm wearing it today. Gandalf was very taken with it. You OK? You sound a bit . . . damp. Have you been crying?'

'Erm. . .yeah.' He knows me too well.

'Did Patty throw a dart at your face?'

'No! I confiscated her darts after the last time!'

'OK. Have you been thinking about that scene in *The Lion King* where Simba realizes his dad isn't going to wake up?'

'No, but now I am, and it's not helping. It's Vogue, Daniel. She's back with Jack. And she's given him a bloody job – here! I just can't believe it . . . and I'm so angry . . . and I'm not just angry, I'm worried . . . about her, and about us, and about everything!'

The words rushed out of my mouth so fast they sounded a bit blurry even to me, so I completely understood when Daniel didn't respond immediately.

After a few seconds, he finally spoke. But all he said was one word: 'Ah.'

It's a short word, and possibly not even a word at all, more of a sound or an exclamation, but it told me a lot.

Because while Daniel knows me inside out, I also know him inside out – and an 'ah' like the one he'd just murmured isn't a simple thing. For a start, he didn't sound shocked. He didn't freak out, or swear, or drop the phone in surprise. He just said one quiet little 'ah'. This was not the reaction I would have expected from Daniel, who, while not the kind of bloke who has fights or causes scenes, despises Jack Duncan with a quiet passion. Partly for what he did to me, partly for the way he conducts himself in business.

That one little 'ah', and the silence that followed it, told me this: Daniel already knew. That the huge shock I'd just had wasn't as much of a shock to him. That it wasn't only Vogue who'd kept this revelation to herself.

'You already knew,' I said, feeling somehow betrayed. I didn't make it a question – I didn't need to – I made it a statement of fact.

'I didn't know she'd decided,' he replied, using the calm tone of voice he uses when he thinks I'm about to go ballistic. 'I'd heard she'd been in talks with him, but just gossip. Nothing concrete. They'd been seen together a few times having meetings, and I knew he was looking to leave Starmaker. This was all grapevine stuff – nothing certain – and you know most of the grapevine stuff turns out to be crap.'

'We both know you made that up to fuel your sick fantasies, but why, Daniel? Why didn't you tell me? I just bumped into him upstairs! I could have done with some . . . I don't know, warning?'

'Well,' he replied, and I could hear the sounds of the garden around him. He'd walked outside – probably barefoot, probably holding a mug of coffee – and I could hear the animals making animal noises in the background. I could picture him there, and usually that would immediately reassure me – but now . . . well, I felt a bit thrown, to be honest.

'Well. . .' he repeated, and again I could picture him – he was sitting down on the sawn-off tree stump and looking out at the hills, 'first of all, I'm really sorry you're feeling so awful. If I'd known anything for sure, I'd have told you. But it was just gossip, so I didn't want to upset you for no reason. I could have got you all freaked out for nothing. And part of me thought – still does – that it was Vogue's story to tell, you know?'

I felt the tears coming back again, and squished them so hard with my eyelids they just squirted out a tiny bit at the sides. I was now frustrated as well as angry and scared, and it was a pretty toxic combination.

'Well, she didn't tell me the story. Not until I literally walked in on them, cuddling up on the couch together . . .'

'Oh!' Daniel said, now sounding genuinely shocked. 'Really? She's taken him back in *that* way? After everything that's happened? You've got to be kidding!'

'No, I'm not kidding. And I felt the same way. Look, I've got to go, all right? I can see a bevvy of builders heading in my direction with flasks and packets of Benson & Hedges. . .'

'OK. Look, I'm sorry I didn't say anything, Jessy. Maybe I should have. Probably I should have. And I'm really sorry you're so upset. And I love you.'

I stood up, and looked around at the completely empty garden. There were no builders. No flasks. No Benson & Hedges. I just felt shaken up, a bit knocked for six as my dad would say, and needed an excuse to get off the phone.

The fact that I was finding excuses to end a conversation with Daniel – and that I was fibbing to him – wasn't really helping me feel any more steady or in control. It was like the world had turned upside down.

'Love you too,' I said, quickly. 'I'll call you later.'

Chapter 3

I made my way back inside the building, just in time to see Patty disappearing out of it. There was, surprisingly, no cloud of sulphur surrounding her, just a faint whiff of Dior Poison. I hung back so I could avoid bumping into her, and then went back to our office. I have no idea how Patty would react to me crying – possibly, she'd be unexpectedly kind; possibly, she'd eat me like a praying mantis on a wildlife documentary. It wasn't worth the risk so I hid.

It was now blessedly quiet in there, and I was able to sit and think for a moment. To try to stop blubbing. To sort through my thoughts. Vogue had lied to me – or at the very least deliberately kept something huge a secret. And Daniel had known . . . kind of. Being fair, I understood why he hadn't mentioned it – he didn't know for sure and didn't want to upset me. But being unfair, it added to the sense of betrayal I was feeling – like the big kids had been ganging up on me. Not very mature, I know, but that's feelings for you.

I needed to talk to someone outside this world, and be reminded that there were bigger things in life than me and my petty problems. Well, maybe I actually needed to talk to someone about my petty problems – and, as ever, I made like E.T. and phoned home.

My parents are brilliant people. They're hard-working and solid and they love the bones of me. I know they're always 100 per cent on Team Jessy – even if they're telling me things I don't want to hear. The fact that we came close to having a serious falling-out at the end of last year has made me even more aware of how much I owe them, and how much I need them. It's easy to lose your sense of gravity in this business – and they're like those big clumpy space boots that astronauts use to keep themselves grounded.

I used the landline to call them, and was greeted by a fake Italian accent: 'Welcome to Luigi's House of Pancakes and Pain! What may I do you for?'

'Luke, why aren't you in college?' I asked, immediately. He wants to be a sports physio, and is doing his A-levels at the moment. Loosely speaking.

'Study morning,' he replied.

'So you're sitting in your room playing "Call of Duty"?'

'Yup! Do you want Dad? Mum's round at Becky's, looking after Ollie. And can you get me tickets to the Dua Lipa tour? And can you arrange for me to meet her as well?'

'Yes, I want to speak to Dad, and no, I can't get you a date with Dua Lipa. Or maybe I can. I don't know. Leave it with me.'

'Cool. I'll get Dad. He's watching the Formula 1 highlights and cutting his toenails.'

He left me with that charming and achingly familiar image and, within a few seconds, Dad picked up the phone. He's a big man, my father, tall and bulky, all of it topped off with a shiny bare head and a face that is usually smiling. He's known

– mainly by himself – as the Bald Eagle, but is actually called Phil. He's a taxi driver, and has an endless supply of stories, which all start with the same words: 'I had this bloke/girl/alpaca in the back of my cab the other night. . .'

'All right, love?' he said immediately, the roaring sound of cars pointlessly driving round a track floating over the line from the telly in the background. I was struck by an urge to just get on the train and go home. To sit with my dad, and listen to his stories, and feel like everything was right with the world. I'm lucky to have that kind of refuge, that kind of security – and to know that if I wanted to, I could give all of this up, get a job in the local McDonald's, and go back to being their Jessy. They'd love me just as much.

'Yeah, all good, Dad. Just wanted to hear your voice.'

'Oh! Well, that usually means you're trying to find your way out of a shit storm – what's wrong? If it's girl stuff and you want your mum, she's round at our Becky's, adoring Prince Ollie.'

'How's he doing?' I asked, smiling at the thought of my chubby nephew.

'Brilliant. I swear to God he's put on about a stone in the last week. He'll be nicking my tins of Guinness before I know it. How's the world of show business treating you? Saw a picture of you in a copy of *Hello!* magazine that got left in the back of the cab the other night. Your mother was worried you weren't wearing enough clothes to keep your circulation going.'

'Ha! I never wore much more on nights out clubbing in Liverpool either, Dad – it's just that you never saw a picture of it in *Hello!* magazine. I'm fine, honest. It's. . .well, just work stuff. Busy, you know? And. . .well, I've had an offer to go and work in the States with someone and I'm not sure what to do about it.'

There was a pause and the sound of the racing cars died down as he used the remote control. I hadn't intended to talk to him about the America thing – to be honest, I hadn't had a clue what I wanted to talk to him about, but that was the first thing that came out of my mouth. It was better than whingeing on about Jack and Vogue and Daniel. Mum and Dad had a vague idea that something had gone wrong with Jack, but as they'd never known we were a couple – Jack insisted on keeping it a secret, for reasons that later became obvious – they'd also never known the full story.

That was fine by me. The last thing I needed was my dad turning up in his Army & Navy Stores camo trousers and trying to knock Jack's block off – much as the idea felt appealing right now.

'How long would you be gone for, then, love? It wouldn't be permanent, would it?' he asked.

'I don't know at this stage, I've only just been asked. Could be a weekend, could be a month. It's a great opportunity, but, you know. . .'

'I know. You'd have to leave Daniel, and us, and that's scary.'

As ever, he'd hit the nail right on the head. He might not have any university degrees to his name, but the Bald Eagle is as sharp as they come.

It *was* scary – on all kinds of levels. But right then, feeling the way I was about people I'd trusted, it was sounding a bit less scary, and a bit more like an escape hatch.

'Yeah. Scary. But that doesn't mean it's wrong, does it?'

'No,' he replied, quickly. 'Sometimes it means it's right. I was bloody terrified when your mother told me she was pregnant with Becky – and now I'm a doting grandad! I suppose you just have to trust your instincts, love. They've never let you down yet.'

He was, of course, wrong on that front. My instincts about Jack had definitely let me down. And, maybe, my instincts about Vogue. I couldn't quite put Daniel in that category, but I couldn't deny I was having a bit of a wobble about him either.

'What does Daniel think about it all?' he asked, when I didn't answer him – I was too distracted pondering how crap my instincts were.

'Well . . . I haven't told him yet.'

'That's where you start, then, isn't it? He knows you. He knows the business. He's a sensible lad, and he'll be honest with you.'

I knew my dad meant well, but it was possibly the worst thing to say right then. Because that was exactly the problem – this whole thing with Jack, with Daniel having his suspicions about it and keeping them to himself, was making me question exactly how honest our relationship was. Plus, on my side, I'd been hiding the Cooper Black thing from him.

I mean, what would our Billy goat Gandalf say about all of that? I think he'd have been disappointed in me for keeping secrets.

'You're right, Dad. I'll speak to him, talk it over.'

'Good girl. You do that. And whatever you decide, love, you know we're 100 per cent on your side, don't you? Always.'

'Always – I know. Love you, Dad!'

'Love you too, Jessy. And put more clothes on, all right? You'll catch your death.'

Obviously, I felt better after that. But not better enough to talk to Daniel, not just yet. Instead, I went down to the basement to find Neale, my stylist and friend. Neale also knows me, and he knows the business, and more to the point, I knew he'd have a secret stash of chocolate, which I desperately needed. Nothing cheers a girl up quite like a KitKat.

I walked into his domain to find him plastered in make-up, listening to R. Kelly being played extremely loud through his speakers.

Now, Neale is gay, but he's never tried this before – at least not so far as I know. I stared at his multicoloured cheeks and brightly painted eyelids and glitter-coated lips and was lost for words. It all looked very weird – especially as Neale is a short, slender man with close-cropped dark hair and trendy glasses. He looked like he was about to march in the Nerd Pride Parade.

'Just trying out some new samples!' he said quickly, turning the music lower and gesturing to all the cosmetics spread out on the dressing table. 'They all get sent to me for free – honestly, Jess, it's like a real-life fairy tale!'

OK, I thought, we all have our different versions of happiness, and this was clearly his. I flumped down onto one of the beanbags he had scattered around the still-not-renovated room, and looked at him imploringly.

'I need chocolate,' I said.

'Oh! It's one of those days, is it? Feeling a little delicate, are we?'

He rooted around in one of the drawers, and handed me a snack-sized Twix.

'This is rubbish,' I said, tearing the wrapper off and stuffing half of it into my mouth. 'There's only one finger – it goes against all the laws of Twix!'

'You'd hate me in the morning when you woke up with a zit on your nose. Anyway, wassup? It's not even lunch-time and you look like someone just decapitated an Andrex puppy in front of you. They didn't, did they?'

I held my fingers up to tell him to wait for a while – I was too busy eating, drooling, and generally making a chocolatey mess of myself to speak. He started removing some of the slap from his face while he waited for me to finish, and didn't even look disgusted as I chewed – true friendship.

'Well,' I said, eventually, wiping my face with a tissue I swiped out of his hand, 'no Andrex puppies have been harmed in the making of this morning, as far as I know. But I kind of feel like one myself. There are a few things to mention, so I'll make a list. First, Vogue has gone and offered Jack Duncan a job here.'

Neale paused, his hand frozen mid-wipe, his face now half rainbow and half clear.

'No way! Doing what?'

'Scouting. Managing. Shagging. Whatever it is he does. I know it's her business, and her call, but still. . .'

'It makes you feel a bit sick in your mouth?'

'Yes! Or maybe that's the Twix, I don't know. Secondly – and this has to stay between us until I know how she's playing it – she's also taken him back.'

'*Back* back?'

'*Back* back. I practically found them bonking in her office. . .'

This, of course, is a very big overstatement – it's also distracted Neale, who is now gazing off into the distance, probably imagining Jack Duncan naked. As I've said, he's drop-dead gorgeous – to look at, at least.

'OK. Well, that's up to her, I suppose. But I can see why you're worried. This is all new, and the whole point of In Vogue was to get away from people like Jack, wasn't it? Even if he is fit enough to win Best in Show at Crufts.'

'Exactly! And on top of all that, it turns out that Daniel knew about it. Well, kind of knew about it. . .'

Neale pulled another beanbag over and sat by my side. He gave me a quick hug, and then a quick talking-to: 'What do you mean by "kind of"? You mean he'd heard some *gossip*?'

'That's what he said. He said he didn't want to repeat it in case it came to nothing, and he didn't want to upset me.'

'Well, I can see why you needed chocolate, honey. Daniel loves you to pieces, and there's no way he'd do anything to hurt you – he was trying to protect you, even if it doesn't feel like that right now. You know he's your happy-ever-after, don't you? I can tell you're annoyed with him, but you should probably take it down a notch and not do a full-on diva about it. Just because you're in a couple doesn't mean you have to tell each other every thought that enters your head, does it?'

He was right, of course. And it wasn't like I'd been entirely honest either.

'No, it doesn't. And while we're on that subject, what do you know about Cooper Black?'

'*The* Cooper Black?'

'No, the knock-off Cooper Black I got from the market the day I got that Prada handbag for twenty quid. Of course *the* Cooper Black!'

'OK, OK, no need to snap your bra hook at me. . .Well, obviously, he's a mega-babe from another planet. Super-hot right now. And – well, I do know one of his friends, actually, since you asked so nicely.'

'One of his friends? One of his real friends?'

'No – one of his knock-off friends I got from the market! Yes, a real friend – JB. He used to be in the band with him. JB's lovely – can't sing for shit, mind, but he looks great and he can dance. That's how I met him.'

'Out dancing?'

'Yeah. At that club I took you to once. You remember?'

It was hard to forget – or at least hard to remember, which is the sign of a good night out. It had been the night after my first single launch, when I'd performed with Vogue to a packed crowd of writers, movers, shakers, and my entire family. It had been an incredibly stressful time, not helped by the fact that I had a row with my parents afterwards. I'd needed two things in life that evening: a Big Mac and a carefree night out, and Neale and his pals had kindly provided me with both.

It had been a great night, but it had also left me with one

of the worst hangovers in the entire history of hangovers. Tequila, you swine.

It was also, and this I did remember, a gay club – a place Neale told me was discreet, where lots of famous people went when they wanted to be safe from getting papped. JB being there didn't mean he was gay – I wasn't – but I could tell from the slightly dreamy expression on Neale's face that my friend at least hoped he was.

I tried to dredge up an image of JB from his days in the boy band, and finally matched it: he was the bad boy. Cooper Black was all blond handsomeness – the kind of boy you'd take home to meet your parents, sexy but wholesome – and JB was the wild child. Shaggy dark hair, a body to kill for, blue eyes and a wicked grin. In his own way, he'd been just as much of a heart-throb as Cooper.

'Is he . . . ?'

'A big flaming queen with sugar and sprinkles on top?' supplied Neale, laughing at me. 'Yes, he is – he doesn't lie about it, but he doesn't broadcast it either. So be very, very careful to keep your lovely Liverpool mouth shut about it, all right?'

'Don't worry, I learned my lesson the hard way!' I replied, patting him on the thigh to reassure him. I really had, as well – last year, I accidentally 'outed' Neale in the press. It had been a masterclass in when to stay silent.

'Now, I have to ask you why you want to know all this stuff. What's with you and Cooper Black? Are you crushing on him, you little minx?'

'No! Yes! Maybe – I mean, I'm only human! But . . . well . . . he's actually been in touch and asked me to feature on his new single. And maybe do more work with him. And I just don't know what to do about it – it's a brilliant idea, but it might mean leaving Daniel. And Vogue. And this place. You know?'

Neale nodded emphatically, making his glasses bobble on the edge of his nose.

'I can understand that – but, well, wow! If you take all the personal shit out of it, it's fantastic, isn't it? The next stop on the Jessika world domination tour! And a huge compliment. . .So, what are you going to do?'

'Well, this morning, I was thinking no. Then all this crap happened, and I'm thinking maybe yes. But, before I decide, I suppose I'd like to know a bit more about him – what kind of person he is. Whether he's likely to screw me over. Whether he's a. . .'

'Showbiz twat?'

'Exactly! Because with Jack Duncan back on the scene, I have enough showbiz twattery to handle already. Do you think maybe you could ask JB for me, kind of on the QT?'

'Darling, I can do better than that – it must be your lucky day! You know I'm your fairy godbrother, right? Funnily enough, JB is in town. Let's all go out, and you can ask him yourself.'

*

Let's just say that the night got messy. It started with tequila, Big Macs and dancing. And after a riotous journey around London's bars and nightspots it was ending, it seemed, with a very competitive game of strip darts.

JB was a larger-than-life character, all hair and piercings and tattoos and muscles. Now the band was history, any constraints he'd previously felt were well and truly gone, and he was living it up in London.

Only ten minutes into the game, he'd already stripped down to just his Calvin Klein boxers and one sock. Neale was doing better, and was merely topless, his sinewy torso pale above his skinny jeans. JB flopped down next to me as Neale prepared to take his turn, his bulky chest glistening with sweat from an earlier dance session dominated by old classics like 'Ride on Time', 'Pump Up the Jam' and 'No Limits'. He gave me a sideways grin as we watched Neale nail the double twelve he needed to win. JB stood up, saluted him, and very slowly stripped off his last sock, like he was doing some kind of teasing burlesque routine.

Neale fanned his face in a mock sincerity that I suspected was very much real. It was obviously the sexiest foot he'd ever seen in his entire life.

'So,' said JB, taking a big gulp of his Jack Daniel's and Coke, 'the thing to remember about Cooper Black is that he's solid. He's got this whole all-American jock thing going on, with the perfect hair and the shiny teeth and the wholesome boy-next-door smile, but underneath all that, he's a solid guy. That's an act – like my wild boy sex machine was an act.'

I glanced at him – sitting there in his knickers, tendrils of rough black hair curling onto broad shoulders – and suspected that was no act. He *was* a wild boy sex machine, just not in quite the way most of his fans thought he was.

'So . . . he's nice?' I asked, incapable of forming a more

incisive question due to the fact that most of the blood in my veins had been turned into tequila.

'Yeah, he's nice, but he's funny too. Real funny, the guy has a wicked sense of humour. And he's talented. I can't sing – I can dance a little and I look good – but Cooper? He's the whole package. He always wanted to write his own songs, get into better material, but the way the band was marketed held him back. Now he's going solo, he'll fly – and his new stuff is awesome. I've heard some of it, and you can believe the hype. If he's asking you to get involved, I'd say go for it. It's a hell of a chance. Plus, I can tell you two would hit it off.'

Neale sat down on the other side of me, squashing me between the two of them. His legs were vibrating like somebody had wound him up – a clockwork stylist.

'Plus, you know, think of the nights out!' Neale said. 'And the parties! And the outfits!'

If you'd asked me that morning, none of that would have sounded attractive. That morning, I was distressed at the thought of spending even one night away from Daniel and our life together. That morning, the idea of jetting off to the States was a worry, not an opportunity.

Now, though, I was beginning to see things slightly differently. Even setting aside everything that had happened with Jack and Vogue, which had really unsettled me, I'd also had a brilliant night out with these two. I couldn't remember the last time I'd had a complete drink-yourself-daft, get-home-with-the-milkman blow out like this.

When I had to, I attended showbiz parties and events – it was part of my job, and I did enjoy it a lot of the time. But it was work – there was pressure to look a certain way, behave a certain way, to not flash my gusset or vomit in a gutter. And behind it all, there was always part of me that just wanted to bin it all off and go home to Daniel, and my other life.

Tonight, though, hadn't been like that. It had just been fun, pure and simple. Being out with Neale, who I could trust with my life, and JB, who was all kinds of hilarious, was different. It was even, I had to admit to myself, more fun than being with Daniel.

I love my Daniel to bits, don't get me wrong, but he's not a party animal. He's a stay-at-home creature. That's the way he's always been, and he isn't going to change. I wouldn't want him to change – but maybe, if I'm entirely honest, I did also kind of miss this sort of thing. The daftness of it all. The spontaneity of it. The sheer unadulterated pleasure of a crazy night out with real friends – especially ones who weren't, at any stage, ever, going to try to stick their hand up my top.

Usually, on my nights away from Daniel, I'm sad. I sit in my flat, after whatever event I've been to, and I miss him like crazy. We spend hours talking on the phone or on Skype, and I never feel totally happy until we're together again. Tonight hadn't been like that – in fact I'd barely thought about him, or even looked at my phone.

Partly because I was just having so much fun, and partly because when I did think about him, there was a tiny little 'ick' feeling making itself present. I wasn't used to that – we barely even argued, me and Daniel, we were usually so happy and settled together. But no matter how many times I told myself he hadn't done anything wrong by not mentioning the

Jack thing to me, the tiny little 'ick' was still there, tinging my thought processes.

The only thing to do in a situation like that, I've found, is to get so drunk you don't have any thought processes at all – and this had been the perfect way of doing that. Plus, you know, I had managed to get the scoop on Cooper Black, and his levels of showbiz twattery – which were, it seemed, superbly low for a man who'd essentially grown up in the spotlight of the music industry, adored and moulded since he was fifteen.

Still, even acknowledging the 'ick' had made me feel a bit uncomfortable – and also reminded me that it was almost 5 a.m., and that I hadn't called Daniel like I'd said I would. That was bad. He didn't deserve the silent treatment. I needed to get back to my flat and grab a few hours' sleep before I phoned him and tried to set this right.

I drained the last of my tequila, and turned to Neale. 'I'm going to get off now,' I said.

'Oh Lord, me too! He's only got his knickers left!'

I followed his gaze to the darts board, and saw JB fail to score yet again as his dart thudded to the ground. He turned towards us, and gave Neale the kind of lazy grin that promised every sin known to man, and then some. I couldn't help but laugh, and gave my friend a quick cuddle. I had no idea what was going to happen with those two, but I was definitely the spare wheel tonight.

I gathered my belongings – bag, phone, the inflatable hammer we'd somehow acquired during our evening's adventures – and stood up to leave.

Despite his distracted state, Neale still managed to grab

my hand, and issued a strict warning about making sure I got straight into a cab, and didn't talk to strangers on the way home.

'Thanks,' I said, leaning down to kiss the velveteen fuzz of his cropped hair. 'See you tomorrow.'

By the time I got back to my flat, I was about 50 per cent sober. The cabbie had been chatty, and reminded me so much of my dad I almost had a drunk-girl weep as we bounced over London potholes and braked to avoid hen parties crossing the road in zigzags. I signed his receipt pad for his daughter, and posed for the obligatory selfie, aware that I had now become the star in one of those familiar 'back of my cab. . .' stories that I'd grown up hearing. I was just glad I hadn't puked out of the window, or tripped over the kerb as I got out in front of my building.

When I was signed to Starmaker, I had a big place with views over the city, all paid for by the record label. It was plush and luxurious but completely lacking in soul or anything that made it feel like home. These days, I rented a much smaller but also much nicer place in West London. There was still a doorman – I needed the security, and my dad had insisted – but it's all a lot less fake and grand.

I fumbled with the key a bit as I let myself in – I was still about 50 per cent drunk after all – and also struggled to get my inflatable hammer through the door. It took a while for the logistical part of my brain, which is never to the forefront to be honest, to realize I had to turn it lengthways rather than widthways, to squash it through.

The first thing that hit me when I closed the door behind me was the smell. It smelled of toast, which immediately made my mouth water. Then I noticed the fact that the lights were off in the living room, and I always leave them on – some kind of hangover from the days when I lived in a much less desirable part of a city, and always wanted to give the impression there was someone home.

I dropped my bag, and hefted my inflatable hammer, taking up a street fighter pose. Or as much of a street fighter pose as you can manage in six-inch heels after eight hours of drinking. I kind of knew the hammer wasn't actually much help – it wasn't Thor's, after all – but it did make me feel a bit better as I tiptoed through the darkened living room, and into the kitchen.

Yep, I was right – someone had been making toast in here. That calmed me down – it seemed very unlikely that a burglar had crept in and popped a couple of slices of wholemeal under the grill while he cased the joint. What calmed me down even more was the fact that the butter was still out – which meant it was probably Daniel.

Much as he is nigh on perfect, he does still suffer from some male traits – like leaving everything scattered over the kitchen counter whenever he's used it.

I popped the pack back in the fridge – I was my mother's daughter after all – and crept back through to the living room to check my phone. Sure enough, there were seven missed calls, from both his landline at the farmhouse, and from his mobile.

I was instantly flooded with guilt and regret. I'd been a mean girl, retreating into my shell just because things hadn't been perfect. It was silly and immature and not the way I wanted to behave. I was suddenly so glad he was here, and slipped off my stupidly high sandals and walked into the bedroom.

He was just a lump under the duvet, but as soon as I entered the room, he shuffled around and sat up. His chest was bare and his blond hair was sticking out at all kinds of strange angles, and he looked totally edible. I froze for a second, feeling ashamed of myself, and also wondering if he was properly awake, because he was looking very confused.

'Nice hammer,' he said, squinting at me and wiping his blue eyes clear of sleep.

'Oh!' I said, throwing it to the floor. 'I'd forgotten I had it. . .'

He pulled the covers back, and patted the other side of the bed in invitation. I didn't need asking more than once, and immediately climbed in and snuggled up against him. We were both quiet for a few moments, settling into the familiar shape of each other's body, my head laid against his chest, his lips kissing the top of my hair. It felt so good – so natural, and safe, and right, to be back home in more ways than one.

'Good night?' he asked, his hands stroking my shoulder reassuringly. I realized that I needed the reassurance – that I had been worried about seeing him again. About whether we'd done any permanent damage, intentionally or not.

'Great night. I was out with Neale and . . . a friend of his. We played strip darts. Well, they did. I retained my dignity.'

'I'm glad to hear it. I've seen you play darts, I think that pub down the road from our college still has holes in the wall to prove it. You OK? I got worried when I didn't hear back from you, so I headed here. I needed to tell you in person how sorry I am, about the Jack thing. I know—'

'It doesn't matter,' I said, interrupting him, squeezing him tight. 'None of it matters. I'm just glad you're here. I didn't feel right without you.'

'It does matter, and I need to say it. You know I'd never intend to hurt you, but on top of you seeing Jack like you did, which must have been a shock, you were left feeling like I'd somehow let you down. And I had – even if I did what I thought at the time was the right thing. We shouldn't have secrets from each other. It's like keeping secrets from yourself, isn't it?'

I nodded, and held on to him even harder. He was right – and he hadn't been the only one keeping secrets, had he? I hadn't planned on raising the Cooper Black issue tonight – or possibly ever, depending on what I decided to do – but suddenly I felt like I should. I realized that keeping it from him had been eating away at me, and definitely contributing more to the 'ick' feeling than I'd given it credit for.

Daniel and I have something special, and hiding things was disrespectful to that. My mum and dad had survived decades, three kids, and a lifetime of hard work – and they'd done it together. If I wanted the same kind of relationship they had, I couldn't just ignore the difficult stuff and bury my head in the sand. Or even a bottle of tequila.

'You're right,' I said, 'and there's something else I need to tell you.'

I felt him tense slightly next to me, and realized how worrying that might sound to a boyfriend whose girl had gone AWOL for the night after an almost-fight.

'No, nothing like that, I'd never! It's a work thing, I suppose. I've had a proposal from Cooper Black.'

'Oh. That's a bit sudden. I can't blame him for loving you, Jessy, but have you ever even met the guy?'

'Not that kind of proposal, stupid!' I replied, poking him in the ribs. He knew that, obviously – he was just trying to lighten the mood. Make things easier for me. One of the many reasons I loved him so very much.

'He contacted me, and said he wants me to work with him. Do a feature slot on his new single. What do you think?'

Daniel was silent for a few moments – he's not the kind of person to respond without thinking, unlike me. He's far more measured and, I suspect, basically intelligent. I sometimes feel like I'm just a set of emotions on legs.

'Well, I think it's a great idea,' he said eventually. I looked up from my nest on his chest, and saw that he was staring off into the distance, chewing his lip, and looking serious. He was thinking through the implications, so I jumped right in – I'd been thinking about them for a lot longer than he had, after all, so I had a head start.

'I was worried about leaving you. And leaving Vogue. And leaving my family.'

He pondered it for a few more seconds, then said: 'Well, why would you need to leave us? If it's just a featuring, then you wouldn't even need to do it with him, in the States. He could just send over the track and we could record your part at In Vogue, or at home. You're finishing off your album anyway, so we'll be practically living in the studio for the next few weeks. It'd be easy. You could do it in your pyjamas.'

'You really think so?' I asked, hopefully, propping myself up on one arm so I could see his face properly. Daniel is a terrible liar, which is very much to his credit, and I knew I'd be able to tell if he was bluffing. Happily, he just had his 'figuring out the solution' face on, not his 'covering up bullshit' face.

'Yeah, of course. From what I've heard, he's going to be massive. I know the people he's been working with, and they're quality. This could be the biggest single of the year, and if you have the chance to be part of it, you should.'

'But what if it's more?' I asked, hearing all the tensions and underlying anxieties pour out in my voice. 'What if I have to go there to do promo, or launches, or a tour? What if it all grows and grows and turns into a giant octopus that eats all my free time and takes me away from you? It only feels like we've been together for five minutes, and we're just settling into life, and I don't want to leave you all alone with Gandalf!'

He stared at me, at my frowning expression and hurried words, and did what any sensible person would – burst out laughing.

He sat up, and took my face between his hands, stroking my skin in a way that wasn't just reassuring, but was starting to be quite distracting. Because, you know, my Daniel is also super-fit – and lying naked in my bed.

'Jessy,' he said, firmly, 'I love you. I've always loved you. And I have enough belief in this relationship that I'm not even remotely scared by Cooper Black, or you spending time away, or by a giant octopus. Besides, I have a lot of stuff coming up as well. Vella's asked me to do her whole album with her. She wants to come and stay at the studio, and get some musicians in, and lay the whole thing down live. That's another thing I've been meaning to talk to you about.'

I had, I realized, been acting like a total knob. I'd been worrying myself sick about something that might never even happen, and even if it did happen, not having the faith in me and Daniel to feel OK about it. And I'd been so caught up in my own worries that it never even occurred to me that this was a challenge for him as well – he had his own career to think about, a brilliant career. The whole world didn't revolve around me.

I'd been tearing myself up about a single I didn't even have to leave the house to record, and he'd been worried that I'd mind about Vella – one of those funky soul diva types – effectively moving into my territory.

'Will she stay in the barn with Gandalf?' I asked, smiling at the thought.

'I thought about that, but I think she'd be happier in the guest block, don't you? And she's cool. You'll like her. Maybe we can invite Cooper Black over for dinner, and set them up with each other. . .'

I pondered that for a moment. It would possibly be the most showbizzy blind date known to man, assuming they could both cope with a few days in the English countryside. Cooper was from New York, and Vella, as far as I remembered, was from Berlin, so they might be a bit thrown off by the mud and the chickens. Still. It was an amusing idea.

'Maybe,' I replied, letting my hand drift from his bare chest to another bare place, beneath the sheets. He responded in an immediate and very flattering manner. 'And maybe we should just stop thinking about Vella, and Cooper Black, and singles, and albums, and definitely Gandalf, and start thinking about ourselves.'

In one quick move, he had me lying flat on my back, and was undoing the buttons on my top.

'Or maybe we should just stop thinking altogether. . .' he whispered, kissing my neck in a way that had exactly that effect.

Chapter 4

After that night, life felt much calmer. Not any less busy, but more stable. I don't think I'd quite understood how unbalanced it had all been making me – I'd got so used to Daniel and me being solid and untouchable, anything that affected that solidity upset me on such a basic level.

And at the end of the day, once we'd both started talking about it openly, none of it was a problem – in fact all the demands we were facing were positive ones. A megastar wanted me to record a song with him. Another megastar wanted Daniel to produce her album. These were not serious problems – in fact they weren't problems at all. They just signified that our careers were blossoming, in a way that we'd both always dreamed of.

As relationship challenges went, they weren't bad ones to have – it's not like one of us was ill, or having an affair, or had fallen out of love with the other. We were just busy, and if we worked together, and were honest with each other, we'd find a way to manage. If I looked back at my parents' lives together, they'd managed to cope – I remembered times when I was younger when they literally never saw each other. Mum would do her shift at Asda, and Dad would ferry us round on the school run or our after-school clubs and activities, taking me to dance classes and Luke to martial arts classes and Becky to her friends' houses. Then when Mum got home, he'd often be straight out again, in his cab, the Bald Eagle prowling the streets of Liverpool. That eased off as we got older, and more independent, and presumably as they managed to pay off some of their financial burdens, but there was definitely a time in their marriage when they only saw each other for half an hour a day. They've never talked about it, or complained, but that must have been hard on them.

Even now, they have hefty schedules – not just with work, but with my elderly nan, and now with Becky and Prince Ollie to factor into the equation.

Daniel and I just needed to keep on loving each other, keep on communicating, and keep on keeping on. It would, I told myself, all be all right in the end.

We were also lucky in that a lot of our work could be done together. It's not like I was a pop star and he was a postman – he was a producer, and he understood my working life in a way that very few other people would. He understood the fake aspects, and he understood the great aspects, and he understood that I sometimes needed to disappear off for two days to do a series of radio interviews, or TV appearances, or guest slots at big concerts in Europe.

He also understood how much I loved it – he'd known me since I was a kid, and first started dreaming of all this. Not so much the fake aspects – I could live without those – but the music. The sheer joy of being able to make a living, a bloody good living, from doing something I loved. From singing and performing – those things still made me ecstatically happy. Even when I'd been struggling to make ends meet pretending to be various Disney princesses in an assortment of bad wigs, I'd never lost the joy of singing, and hoped I never would. As far as I could make out, it was the only gift God had given me, and I was grateful for it every single day.

There was something so pure, so simple, about singing. It could make me feel euphoric in a way that nothing else quite could. Having a boyfriend who understood all of that, and supported me in it, made me a very happy girl. Very lucky too – I'd met enough showbiz types by that stage to see how badly wrong it could all go in relationships. If one partner was famous and the other wasn't, it seemed inevitable that, at some point, jealousy and resentment could creep in. At the lost time, the lack of attention, the clash of lifestyles.

I didn't have that problem with Daniel, which was a blessing – especially as things weren't exactly going smoothly at In Vogue.

The building work was a living nightmare, Patty was still insanely vicious, and now, I had the added risk of bumping into Jack Duncan when I went into work. Vogue and I hadn't quite returned to an even keel, and I was worried that we never would.

She'd been OK with me doing the single with Cooper Black – in fact she'd been thrilled, as it could only be good for the label – but on a personal note, there was a tension there that we'd never had before.

I was worried about her on several levels. I just didn't trust Jack not to screw her over at some point. Either in business, or in her personal life. I'd tried to tell her that but she'd just shut me down with a full-on diva strop, and I wouldn't risk it again. She made it clear that it was none of my business, and I didn't have any choice but to accept that. It made me sad – we'd always been so close, and now there was a distance there that neither of us seemed able to breach. From her point of view, I suppose she felt like she couldn't talk to me about her life, because her life involved Jack, and I still struggled not to spit every time I heard his name.

So between the Jack Factor and the noise of the builders and the fear that Patty might one day actually sacrifice me to Satan on an altar made of dead kittens, I felt tense every time I came into the In Vogue headquarters. I didn't feel as invested in it as I had at the beginning, when it seemed like Vogue and I were working together to build something special. Now it felt like it was Vogue's, and possibly Jack's, but definitely not mine.

It had been over a month since Jack had taken up his role at In Vogue, and our paths had crossed three times. On each occasion, there had been tension – a combination of smugness and fear on his part. Smugness because he'd managed to creep back into our lives in a way I could never have imagined possible, and fear because he knew me well enough to realize I was only ever one funny look away from causing him some physical harm.

The last time I'd bumped into him, he'd tried to ask me out for a coffee. I think, if I force myself to be absolutely fair about it, that he did it in the spirit of wanting to make things easier for us all.

'Look, Jess,' he'd said, wearing the super-sincere expression

I'd come to hate, 'I know you're not happy about this new state of affairs, but it is what it is. And I promise you, I don't intend to cause any problems at all for you, or Vogue. I have everyone's best interests at heart. Let's go out for a coffee together, for old times' sake, and see if we can't find a way to work through this.'

He probably hadn't considered the fact that when we first started seeing each other – back in the olden days, when I was naive enough to think a man like him could love me, or in fact love anyone but himself – we always used to go for coffees. It was part of his seduction technique: taking me first to posh coffee places, then to posh restaurants, and posh bars, in his posh car, before finally making it back to his predictably posh bedroom. With anyone else, I could have seen a coffee as just a coffee, but with Jack? It was, in my mind, linked to a chain of disastrous and hurtful events.

'I can't come for a coffee with you, Jack,' I'd said. 'Because I can't stand being in the same room as you. Vogue might be happy to give you a second chance, but I suppose I'm just not as good a person as she is. Try to remember that, won't you?'

He'd backed off gracefully, and I'd retreated to my unofficial office in the ladies' loo, where I'd cried some angry tears and kicked the bin a few times.

I was, in response to all of this, coming in to In Vogue a whole lot less. It had gone from being a place of hope and refuge to one fraught with obstacles and distress. I realize this is childish – lots of people have a hard time in their workplace. Lots of people have to face difficult situations and stress and lots of people probably do angry crying in the ladies'. The difference for me, I suppose, is that I didn't have to – which is both really lucky, and also lets me off the hook from having to face up to those difficult situations.

Yep, I was being a wuss, but who wouldn't be, if they had the chance? The truth of the matter was that although the studios at In Vogue were brilliant, they weren't actually as good as the one Daniel had at home.

I was also at a stage where I could get away with it – the songs for my album were all written, all rehearsed and mostly recorded. They only needed a few finishing touches, some more mixing, a sprinkling of fairy dust – and all of that could just as easily be done at the farmhouse as in London. Plus, as Daniel had pointed out, I could do it in my pyjamas, which is always a winner. So that's what I'd done, and with a lot less angry crying.

The album was due out in a few weeks' time, and there had been a flurry of activity around it – Patty had sorted out interviews with the world and his wife, I'd been in enough magazines to wallpaper my old bedroom, and frankly, I was sick of seeing myself pop up on social media. The radio play was building, and all the signs were good – which was a relief.

I mean, I know I can sing, and I knew the songs were good. Great, even. But in my business, none of that is ever a guarantee – and both In Vogue and I had a lot riding on this album. And, of course, on the single – the one with Cooper Black.

I had, as soon as I'd talked it over with Daniel and Vogue, got in touch with him and said yes. My people talked to his people and, within a day, we had the single through, minus the vocals he wanted me to add.

It was a great track, and I could see why everyone was so excited about his new direction. It had a kind of cool hip-hop vibe to it, but with a raw bluesy sound to the lead voice that I thought was going to surprise everyone. In the boy band, the singing had been what you'd expect of its type – lots of harmonies and saccharine lyrics and the occasional R&B groove. This was very different, way edgier, more grown-up – and downright sexy.

I was the female counterpoint to the vocal storyboard; breaking poor Cooper's heart then looking on in regret as he goes on to 'Fly So High' (the name of the song). We'd agreed to film different segments for a video – me in London, him in New York – moodily walking round famous city landmarks while spontaneously bursting into song, dancing with strangers, and reaching out for each other's fingertips through rainstorms in both cities. Kind of silly to film, but the end result was amazing. It actually looked and sounded like we'd stretched out and found each other across thousands of miles – whereas in the real world, we'd never even met.

We had talked, though. A lot. Maybe a bit more than I'd expected. He was funny and charming and kind of wicked, and we could chatter for hours about music, what we loved and what we hated, what we wanted to do in our careers, how much we still had left to achieve, and how we were going to get there.

I wasn't naive enough to think that featuring on Cooper Black's new single wouldn't be a huge boost to my career – I knew it would – but I also hoped that we were becoming friends. JB had been right – he was nice, to say the least. He'd even talked to Daniel, and complimented him on his work as well. One big happy family.

I had no idea what was going to happen with the album, or the single – as ever, all I could do was work hard, and live in hope.

*

A few weeks later, I woke up buzzing with excitement. It was a *very* big day. Not only was it the day that both my album and the single with Cooper Black were released, but it was also my birthday.

At home in Liverpool, my mum and dad always celebrated our birthdays by buying those big inflatable helium balloons with numbers on them. And usually with a 'face cake' – the ones you get from the supermarket where they magically make an old photo appear on the icing, and you actually get to eat yourself. The older we got, the younger the photos were – for my last one, it was me as a baby, totally bald and covered in chocolate ice cream. Not my best look.

This time last year, I'd been at home, looking forward to nothing more exciting than endless Disney princess parties, a non-existent love life, and pondering my continued failure as both a singer and a human being. That had all changed when I met Jack Duncan at a rainy garden party in Cheshire, and for that at least I had to be grateful to him.

This year, the world was a very different place. Most importantly, I was waking up in the warm embrace of the most wonderful man in the world – my Daniel.

'Happy birthday, gorgeous,' he said, kissing me so well that I was suddenly far less sleepy. I wrapped my arms around his neck and pulled him in closer, deciding that the very best way to start my birthday was with some bedroom action.

Ever obliging, he quickly did the one-legged hop round the room removing his clothes, before joining me in a very vigorous celebration. This was most definitely already a better birthday than the year before.

When we finally made it downstairs some time later, I was thrilled to see two pink helium balloons bouncing around the kitchen, the 2 and the 4 getting twisted the wrong way round, as though I was actually turning 42. There was also a face cake on the table, bearing a picture of me as a toddler wearing a Santa hat and covered in Nutella.

'Mum and Dad?' I asked, poking my finger into the cake and scooping up a glob of chocolate cream and icing.

'Yep, they got them sent down at the weekend, and I was hiding them in the pantry. I was fairly sure that was a place you'd never go.'

He was right, of course – my cooking skills extend to ordering takeaways and burning toast. One of my many weak spots.

'So, do you want to know?' he asked, raising his eyebrows at me. He was wearing a pair of snug, battered old Levi's and an equally snug white T-shirt, and was looking spectacularly gorgeous. His feet were bare as well, which I always love for some reason.

'Know what?' I said, licking the frosting from around my lips.

'About the album. And the single. And whether there's life on Mars.'

'Hmmm, I suppose. Except about the life on Mars bit. That's just scary. I'm nervous?'

Petrified, actually. This was probably the most important moment in my career so far, and I was crippled with anxiety about it.

Daniel grinned at me, and I suddenly knew it was all going to be OK. That he would never, ever play me for a fool, and give me a grin like that if the news was bad.

'Number one with the album,' he said, simply. '*And* the single. You, Jessika, are on top of the charts – on both sides of the Atlantic. And it couldn't have happened to a nicer person. Well done, sweetheart. You did it.'

I was momentarily stunned, and even wondered if he was making it up. If the news was actually awful, and I'd sold zero copies of both, and everyone hated me, and I was going to have to go back to doing kids' parties again. Because it couldn't be real, could it? That I was number one with both?

I stared at him, slowly chewing a now overly sweet mouthful of face cake, and couldn't find the proper words to respond.

Laughing, he picked up his phone, and flicked to the relevant screen. I quickly saw it was a news headline, accompanied by a picture of me. Luckily, not one featuring a Santahat and Nutella.

BRIT STAR JESSIKA SCORES DOUBLE WIN, said the headline, followed underneath in smaller lettering with: 'Overnight pop sensation goes from Liverpool hopeful to global success'. I scanned the rest of the story, and read quotes from me that I'd never even given – it looked like Patty had been hard at work, reminding us all why we tolerate her. She'd got it just right – making me sound grateful and humble and jubilant in all the right places. There was also a quote from Vogue, saying she had 'never had any doubts' about her protégé's rise to fame; and one from Cooper Black, adding something lovely about how my vocals had helped turn the single from 'good' to 'great'.

Naturally enough, there was also a selection of photos from the past few months – me at my debut gig; at the first single launch; with 'music supremo' Jack Duncan at a party; with 'reclusive superstar producer Wellsy' at a restaurant; me in my Cinderella outfit from days gone by; and, finally, one of my mum and dad and Luke and Becky, standing outside our house in their Team Jessy T-shirts. Bless them all.

I was stunned. Not so stunned that I stopped eating cake, but completely gobsmacked – just as Patty had said in my quotes. If I'd ever used the word in front of her, she'd have mocked me mercilessly, but it was a very accurate description of the way I was feeling.

Really, could a birthday get any better? Hot sex with a man I loved, two number ones, and a gigantic sponge? I didn't think it could.

Daniel stepped in to give me a hug, and I squeezed him back, leaving chocolatey smears on his T-shirt. He didn't seem to mind – he was obviously thrilled for me.

'Come on, princess,' he said, when he finally let me go. 'You need to get dressed and get into In Vogue.'

'Do I have to?' I asked, sounding like a spoilt little girl

even to my own ears. 'Can't we just stay in today, and . . . snuggle?'

'Well, much as I'd normally like a whole day of snuggling with you, Jessy, I've got stuff to do, and so have you. Vogue called earlier – she's taking you out for lunch. It's her celebration too, and it's about time you two sorted yourselves out, don't you think? She's your friend, and you need to move on. She might have awful taste in men, but she's still your mate, and you don't let your mates down. Ever. Plus, we have our dinner in town tonight, remember?'

I nodded. Of course I remembered. Daniel had booked us a table at our favourite restaurant, and had told me to dress up, and I'd noticed his posh suit hanging up on the wardrobe door last night. For a man who usually preferred the quiet life and viewed dressing up as putting on a clean pair of Timberlands, he was going to a lot of effort – all for me. I needed to man up, and enjoy my day. I had every reason to be on top of the world, and if I could sort stuff out with Vogue, it would be even better.

*

'Sushi totally sucks, doesn't it?' I said, pushing the food around on my plate. It had been described as something fabulous involving seventeen different types of seasoning that I couldn't even pronounce, but, at the end of the day, it was really just some raw tuna and rice. At least to my uneducated taste buds.

'Yeah, kind of,' replied Vogue, 'but we must persevere. It's good for us. And the wine is excellent.'

She wasn't wrong there, and I lifted my glass in acknowledgement. I took a sip, and realized I was feeling slightly queasy – probably a combination of all the excitement, cake for breakfast, raw fish, and the tension.

The tension part was definitely getting easier to deal with. I'd arrived at our lap-dancing HQ to find the pole in the middle of reception decorated with balloons, and all the builders holding up a giant home-made banner that said, 'Number One!' Yvonne the receptionist was getting hammered on the phone, and pointed to a massive amount of flowers as I walked in. There were bouquets and plants and small trees in pots, as well as baskets of fruit and bottles of Champagne, and they were all for me.

Some were for my birthday, but most were congratulating me on the number-one spots. OK, so they might have been from people I'd never even met, but it was still really cool. Neale had emerged from his basement lair to cover me in kisses, and Patty had cracked half a smile as she whisked me away to do some 'phoners' – interviews with magazines and radio DJs over the phone. I was better at that stuff than I used to be, and had it all boxed off within a couple of hours. When it was all done, she shooed me out of the office, warning me I needed to be on breakfast telly the next day, so 'don't go all Scouse psycho and get totally rat-arsed tonight'. Ever the charmer.

I'd made time to chat to my mum and dad as well – I've learned my lesson on that front, and know I have to always put them right up there on my list of priorities. They even put Prince Ollie on the phone, but he didn't seem very impressed

– he just made a gurgling noise that sounded a bit like a fart, then threw the phone on the floor. Everyone's a critic.

And now, after an almost overwhelmingly exciting morning, I was sitting in the posh sushi place with Vogue, trying to be open-minded and pleasant. Daniel, of course, was right – Vogue was my mate, and I couldn't stay angry with her. It wasn't fair on either of us. Whatever happened with Jack was beyond my control, and I had no right to judge her for the way she lived her life. Even if I personally found it about as appealing as my lunch. Maybe Jack had changed; maybe he'd turn out to be her Daniel, and they'd live happily ever after.

I gagged slightly at the thought – or maybe it was the tuna, who knew?

'Look, babe,' said Vogue, reaching out and holding my hand on the tabletop, 'I know things haven't been good between us, and it's been tearing me apart. I should have discussed the Jack thing with you. Or at least warned you. I was just . . . well, I was a bit scared about how you'd react, you know? So I chickened out. And for that I can only apologize. I just don't want us to carry on like this. Everything's going right for us, but I can't enjoy it if I think you're hating on me.'

I squeezed her hand back, and smiled at her.

'I could never hate you, Vogue,' I said, and meant it. 'I was just shocked, that's all. It's your life – you were right when you said that. It's not my place to boss you around, I know that, but I was worried about you. I don't want you to get hurt.'

'I know, kiddo. I know. Neither do I. And hopefully, I won't. But if things do go tits up, I need to know you're there for me.'

'Of course I am,' I replied. 'Always. I'll be there with a

bottle of wine, a tub of Ben & Jerry's and a blowtorch for his balls if he ever messes you around. I'm sorry it's been so rough between us – we need to let it go. Concentrate on what matters.'

'Like the fact that you're number one in the UK and the US?' she said, grinning.

'Well,' I said, raising my glass again, 'I think that is something to celebrate, don't you? And not just for me. I couldn't have done it without you, Vogue. Here's to us, and to sisters doing it for themselves!'

'That,' she said, chuckling, 'is definitely something worth toasting. Cheers!'

We clinked our glasses, drank some more booze, and ate some more awful seafood. The world suddenly felt like a much calmer place.

*

'You look a-may-zing!' said Neale, later that day, as he stood back and inspected his work.

His work was, of course, me – and getting me ready for my romantic birthday night out with Daniel. Neale and I worked very much as a team these days – I knew exactly when he was about to unleash a toxic bomb of hairspray, and exactly when he was about to attack my boobs with a roll of tape. I also knew when to rein him in – usually when I saw him approaching me wielding a pair of scissors or a set of eyeshadows that shared a colour palette with a deranged clown.

Tonight, I'd been very clear: I wanted classy, understated,

and ladylike. I didn't need to look like a pop star ready to be papped, I needed to look like a grown-up woman having dinner with her grown-up man. Also, I didn't want to have hair like cardboard, or an outfit that made the ability to breathe an optional extra. I was going on a date with my boyfriend, not a showbiz party full of cocaine-snorting prima donnas.

I was also, truth be told, not feeling brilliant. I wasn't sure if it was just the end result of a busy and amazing day, or some dodgy sushi, but there were some deeply unpleasant rumblings going on in my tummy that I hoped wouldn't make an appearance while I was out with Daniel. I mean, we basically live together – we're well past the being embarrassed by the odd bedroom fart stage – but still, it's not romantic, is it?

Neale made a 'ta-da!' noise, and moved away to one side, so I could see myself in the mirror. Or, at the very least, so I could see this new version of myself in the mirror. I wasn't sure it was actually me at all, I looked so sophisticated.

He had, as usual, done an amazing job. He'd put me in a little black dress by Marc Jacobs, strapless and fitted, that looked like it belonged on a red carpet, not the basement of a former lap-dancing bar. It was paired with high-heeled black stilettos that were tall enough to impress but sensible enough to be able to walk to the toilet in, and a quick spray tan top-up to keep my bare legs nice and brown.

My blonde hair was swept up, but held in place only with pins and a light sheen of hairspray, so it didn't feel like solid wood. There were loose tendrils trailing around my neck, and he'd given me some gorgeous dangling onyx earrings for my birthday. My make-up was, as requested, grown-up – the kind that makes you look fabulous without any signs of actually being there.

'What do you think? Classy enough for you? You better not be eating a Big Mac in that outfit, lady!' he said, sounding as excited as I felt.

'Wow, Neale, just wow! Quick, take a picture of me on my phone, before I spill something all over myself! My nan sent me her usual £20 gift card for my birthday, and she'll think this is what I spent it on!'

'Well,' said Neale, snapping away as I posed and pouted, 'you can get some lovely frocks in Primark, but not quite this lovely . . . There, done. I hope you have a fabulous night, darling – you deserve it. And there's a text from Cooper Black on your phone, by the way.'

He handed me the phone back, and I opened the message. He'd been in touch several times during the day, thrilled and delighted about the way the single was performing, and I assumed this was more of the same.

I wasn't entirely right – this time, it was something even more exciting. And much bigger. And altogether more frightening.

'Jess!' it said – he'd soon realized I'm not Jessika to my friends – 'great news! How would you like to join me on tour? The gigs are all sold out, but we can add extra dates if you can make it. Say yes – the States are waiting for you!'

There were some kisses, and some emojis of champagne bottles, and a link to a website that showed all the places he was due to be appearing. Where *we* were due to be appearing, if I said yes. Amazing places – stadiums and football arenas and massive concert halls, in New York and Chicago and LA and Miami and everywhere in between. . .

It was an amazing opportunity. It was a terrifying opportunity. It was something a classy, sophisticated, grown-up woman like myself should be relishing.

My stomach let out a huge growl, and I felt a new wave of nausea roll over me.

Chapter 5

I suppose, with hindsight, that Daniel was nervous as well. I mean, he was totally outside his comfort zone – dressed up in a tailored suit, with shiny lace-up shoes instead of boots, smelling of gorgeous cologne, his hair freshly barbered. He was even wearing a tie, although it was plain black and he'd already tugged it down a little by the time I met him at the restaurant.

It was a small, old-fashioned Italian place that we both loved. It was really romantic – cosy, dimly lit and intimate, with a string quartet that played in the background. Tonight, a fire was lit – the first day this year that really felt autumnal. It served delicious food, which I usually enjoyed, but tonight, I didn't feel like eating.

Daniel held my chair out for me at the table, laughing when I looked worried. If he'd grown up with Luke as a brother, he'd be wary as well. It was one of my darling brother's favourite tricks, moving the chair away at the last minute so you ended up falling on your arse to the sound of the entire family chuckling away at your expense. Obviously Daniel would never do such a thing, but old habits die hard.

'You look absolutely amazing, Jessy,' he said, once we

were settled. He was gazing at me so intently, and sounded so sincere, that it actually made me blush. That, I thought, was probably a good thing – we weren't so old and settled that he couldn't still have that effect on me.

'So do you,' I replied, 'I don't think I've ever seen you look so smart. Your mum and dad wouldn't recognize you.'

As I spoke, I noticed that my tummy was growling again, and I hoped it was because I was feeling anxious. The whole going on tour with Cooper Black thing had knocked me for six.

I hadn't replied to Cooper yet, because I needed to think about it. This wasn't as simple as the single – I couldn't go on tour with him from the comfort of the farmhouse, and I definitely couldn't do it in my pyjamas. It would mean leaving Daniel, and being away from him for a significant amount of time.

I wanted to do it, I really did. I realized that I'd already started picturing it – playing to the kind of crowds I could only have dreamed of not long ago. Seeing a whole new country, experiencing a whole new culture. Singing live with a proper band. Sharing the stage with the world's biggest singing sensation. It was like a fantasy – the kind of thing that the teenage me had imagined while I was crooning into a hairbrush in my bedroom in Liverpool.

But what about Daniel? What about this gorgeous, kind, clever man sitting in front of me, tugging away at his tie and fumbling with the menu? What about this man who could still send my stomach into spirals with one lazy grin?

Not that my stomach needed any help on that front

tonight. It was already doing cartwheels with no provocation whatsoever.

I managed to chat to Daniel through the first course, but I couldn't actually tell you what we chatted about. I was distracted, and in some discomfort, and already guiltily hoping that we could leave soon. I probably told him about going for lunch with Vogue, and the gifts at the office, and the interviews I'd done. Or maybe I just sang the theme tune to *The Fresh Prince of Bel-Air* in Polish, who knows? In all honesty, he seemed just as distracted.

He was constantly fiddling with his clothes – his tie, his shirt collar, his cufflinks. Or he was running his fingers through his hair until it was all tufted up. Or asking me if I was OK, if the wine was nice, if I was warm enough. He's usually pretty laid-back, but the sense of occasion must have got to him. That, coupled with my own concerns and the fact that I felt queasier than I did after I rode the Big One three times in a row on my sister's eighteenth birthday, was making me wish we'd just stayed at home instead.

He was fiddling around in his pockets when I finally cracked and said it. He was mid-sentence, but I wasn't concentrating – the pain in my stomach was getting worse, and my vision was starting to blur a little as well. I felt hot and clammy and suspected that if it got any worse, my grown-up make-up would start dripping off my face and I'd end up looking like the Joker.

'So, Jessy, I wanted to ask you—' he said, looking even more uncomfortable than I did.

'Shall we just go home?' I blurted out, interrupting him

mid-flow. I sensed movement behind me, and glanced round just in time to see the violin player from the string quartet freeze like he was playing musical statues.

I whipped my head back around to see Daniel shaking his in a 'not now' gesture, and the guy disappeared off to the next table. I was glad – I really didn't have it in me to pretend to be interested in classical music just then.

'Sorry,' I said, reaching out and holding Daniel's hand. 'This is all really lovely and romantic. It's just that I'm feeling a bit. . .'

'A bit what?' he asked, guzzling down half a glass of wine in one swig, which was very unlike him.

'A bit sick, actually. And like I'd rather be in bed than here, to be honest. Would you mind? If we left, I mean?'

He gazed off into space for a few moments, and seemed to be trying to figure out what to say next. He wasn't quite himself tonight, and I started to worry that somehow he knew already – that Cooper Black had also told him about the tour plans, and he was upset about it. Upset that I hadn't told him straight away.

Before I could pursue that particular line of crazy any further, his face broke out into a smile, and I told myself I was imagining it. As ever, I was being a bit of a drama queen.

''Course not. I'll pay the bill, and then. . .Well, there's one more surprise for you, if you're up to it?'

He sounded so hopeful – so desperate – that I plastered a big fake grin on my own face, and replied: 'I am!'

While he sorted the bill out, I found two Rennies in my bag and checked my reflection in my compact mirror. Even though I felt hot and sweaty, I looked ghostly pale, and there were dark marks starting to show beneath my eyes despite the make-up. If I'd been at home, I'd have doused myself with cold water, but Neale would never forgive me if I did that while wearing a full face and a Marc Jacobs.

'Come on, Jess,' I muttered to myself, 'pull yourself together. Just get through the night. Keep calm and carry on.'

My reflection didn't reply, apart from my stomach groaning at me that it didn't like this plan at all, and that it didn't feel much like keeping calm and carrying on either.

Daniel returned to the table, our coats over his arm, and gently placed mine over my shoulders as I stood unsteadily. As we left, I heard the head waiter quietly wish him good luck – presumably I looked so bad by this stage that even random waiting staff were worried for my health.

We emerged into the street, where the air was blessedly cool, to be confronted by a horse and carriage. It was beautiful – a gorgeous, glossy black creature all dressed up with shiny buckles and feathers and smooth black leather. The carriage itself was like something out of a fairy tale, driven by a man in full old-fashioned gear, complete with a top hat and gloves. It was quite surreal, seeing it there, in the middle of a London street – like something from a different age had slipped through the space-time continuum and appeared among the cars and buses. It felt for a moment like my life had turned into an episode of *Doctor Who*.

'Your carriage awaits,' said Daniel, smiling. Shocked by this romantic gesture, I slipped off my high heels and climbed up, settling down into the squishy back seat as gracefully as I could.

I was trying to be enthusiastic as we trotted off along the street, but it wasn't easy. He'd obviously gone to huge amounts of trouble to try to make this night extra special for me, but all I could really think about was how nauseous I felt.

The carriage was pulled around the streets of London, heading past incredibly beautiful places like Westminster Abbey and Big Ben, all lit up and pretty as a postcard. Daniel had his arm around my shoulders, and it should have been utterly magical. It really should have.

But, by this stage, I was struggling to speak, and was in so much pain I was clutching my stomach with my hands beneath the tartan blanket the driver had given us. Daniel was chattering away, pointing out the sights, and I tried to go 'ooh' and 'aah' at what I thought were appropriate moments, but it was torture. With every prancing step, every cobble the wheels trundled over, my tummy was shaken up and down and round and round until I felt like I was being tossed and turned in a giant washing machine.

We finally drew to a halt at the edge of Hyde Park. Daniel and I had enjoyed a lovely time here as tourists last summer, walking around Speakers' Corner and through into Kensington Gardens, strolling to Buckingham Palace. Back then, the park had been filled with families having picnics and office workers lounging in the sun, during their lunch break. But tonight it just looked incredibly romantic. Street lights glittering in the night sky, trees dark and mysterious, like a secret place trapped in time.

Lovely as it was, I was mainly glad that the carriage had stopped because it gave me a minute to gulp in air, and try to control the saliva that was churning around in my mouth. These were not good signs, and I had the awful feeling that I was about to do something very un-romantic, all over my Marc Jacobs dress.

Daniel didn't seem to have noticed how ghastly I looked, which was probably a good thing. Reaching under the covers, he took one of my shaking hands in his. He was gazing at me in the moonlight, and I so wished I felt well enough to appreciate what a gorgeous moment this was.

'Jessy,' he said, sounding all serious and borderline worried. 'I wanted to ask you—'

'Hold on!' I said, pulling my hand away from his, leaning over the side of the beautiful carriage, and puking my guts up. It went on for what felt like hours, and my last thought, before I passed out, was, *I hope I didn't get any splashback on the poor horse*. . .

*

When I woke up, the first thing that hit me was the unmistakable smell of disinfectant that meant I was lying in a hospital room. I was in a bed, with a drip in my arm, wearing a scratchy floral green gown. A quick wriggle around told me that yes, it was also one of those gowns that leaves your bum hanging out in the open.

The lighting was dim neon, from one strip light in the ceiling, and the blinds were closed. I could see dark night sky around the edges, so knew it was still late, but had no idea what time it actually was, or where I was, or even who I was, I was feeling so rough.

My mouth was dry as sandpaper, and my hair was tumbling out of its pins, crusted onto the side of my face by what I instantly knew was puke. The smell, it seemed, was coming from me. How glamorous.

I inched myself upright, careful not to tug at the needle taped to my skin, and saw that I wasn't alone. Daniel was there, curled up into an uncomfortable-looking ball on a plastic chair, his coat thrown over him like a blanket, his fancy shoes discarded on the floor. I suspected my own clothes – including the poor, mistreated Marc Jacobs dress – were in the big plastic bag sitting in a heap next to the bed.

As soon as I started moving, Daniel woke up, stretching his long arms skywards and yawning. His hair was sticking out at strange angles, and he looked terrible – but wonderful as well. Wonderful because he was here with me, and instead of going back to the flat, had clearly spent an unpleasant few hours by my side so I didn't wake up in this place alone.

He smiled at me, and leaned forward to hold my hand.

'Hello, babe. How are you feeling?' he asked.

'Erm. . .pretty crappy, and a bit confused. Where are we? What happened? How long have we been here? The last thing I remember was. . .Oh my God! Was I sick on the lovely horse?'

I was utterly mortified, and felt tears of embarrassment sting my eyes.

'I'm so sorry, Daniel! You had this lovely romantic night out planned, and I ruined it all. . .'

'Don't be daft,' he said, squeezing my fingers. He'd either not noticed the state of them, or just didn't care. 'You couldn't help it. And you didn't hit the horse, honest. We've been here for about six hours, it's almost five now. The doctor said you were suffering from a nasty bout of food poisoning. Nothing serious, and they've got you on that drip to rehydrate you, but it wasn't your fault. He said you must have been feeling bad for hours – why didn't you say something?'

'I had been feeling terrible, to be honest, but. . .Well, you'd made such an effort. And it was my birthday. And I didn't want to spoil things for you. For us. I just kept hoping it would pass. . .'

'Well, I don't think A&E were quite prepared for seeing the UK's number one singer roll up to the entrance in the back of a horse-drawn carriage, that's for sure!'

I groaned, and buried my face in my hands. Oh God, how absolutely awful – and you could guarantee that somebody would have managed to get a shot of it on their phones. I knew it was food poisoning, and so did he, but the papers would have me down as being drunk, or worse.

'Don't worry, they got you into a private room straight away. You have brilliant health insurance, I discovered. Plus, I called your mum and dad and told them you were fine, just in case something got out and they were worried. Well, they're still worried, but only in a normal parental way. Give them a bell later to reassure them. And please don't freak out – these things happen.'

'Only to me!' I bleated, the exhaustion and the tummy ache and the stress all getting the better of me. 'I don't know how you put up with me! You'd organized such a lovely night as well!'

Daniel scooched out of his plastic chair and knelt down by

the side of my bed. I swear I could almost hear his kneecaps popping. He took hold of my hands, pulling them away from my face.

I was in full-on ugly crying mode now. 'Don't look at me!' I said, sobbing and snotting all over the place. 'I look awful, and I smell like the back alley of a pub at midnight!'

He stroked my cheeks, clearing away the tears, and managed to pull one particularly rigid clump of hair away from my skin. He was, bizarrely, grinning at me, instead of running for the nearest exit.

'You,' he said, kissing my forehead gently, 'have never looked more beautiful. This is what life is about, Jessy – being here for each other during the hard times as well as the good. Do you really think I love you just for the way you look?'

'No, I don't, but. . .Well, it helps, doesn't it? You'd have to be some kind of saint to find this attractive!'

He laughed, and leaned back to get a better look at me.

'Well, in that case, I must be a saint, which nobody has ever accused me of before. Look, I set up this lovely night for a reason. Haven't you been wondering why I didn't give you your birthday present this morning?'

I managed to pause in my weeping, and he passed me a tissue from a box on the bedside cabinet. I blew my nose, making a stonking great snorting noise that undoubtedly only added to my sheer foxiness.

'I hadn't, actually, no. It's been a bit of a day. I suppose I wasn't thinking straight. Have you got a present for me? Because I'd kill for a packet of baby wipes. . .'

'Sorry, I don't have those on me right now. But I do have

something else. Something I was planning on giving you at dinner, but that didn't quite work out. Then I thought I'd give it to you during our carriage ride, but. . .Well, here we are. Not in the most ideal of circumstances, but at least I'm in the right position. . .'

He rooted around in his pocket, and for a moment I had no idea what was going on. Until he pulled out a box – a small, black, square box. The type of box that can send any woman's heart rate into the stratosphere – and most definitely mine. I stared at him, and the box, and back to him. Was I imagining this?

'Jessika Malone,' he said, now on just one of his knees, 'will you do me the great honour of being my wife?'

For the second time in a day, I was well and truly gob-smacked. Completely floored – with gratitude, with awe, but mainly with love. This gorgeous man was here, by my side, at one of the lowest points of my life, asking me to marry him.

'You're still crying . . . that's not the response I was hoping for. . .' he muttered, looking suddenly crestfallen.

'Yes! Yes, yes, yes! Of course I will! I love you so much!' I shouted, throwing my arms around him as best I could under the circumstances. 'And I'm still crying because I'm so happy, that's all. . .'

He hugged me back, before finally clambering up and perching on the side of the bed. The look on his face told me how relieved he was – probably as much as being able to get off his knees as my answer. He handed me the small box and, with trembling fingers, I opened it up.

The ring was beautiful. A single diamond, huge and round,

on a simple gold band. It was elegant, and dazzling, and totally perfect. He managed to slip it onto my finger, and we spent the next few moments just gazing at it in wonder. It wasn't just a piece of beautiful jewellery – it signified something so special it took my breath away. It signified our whole future together, as man and wife. Our partnership – me and Daniel against the world. Just like it had been, in years gone by, and just like I always wanted it to be.

As I pondered that, I realized that before we went any further, I had to tell him about Cooper Black, and the American tour. My stomach turned over as I thought about it – either he wouldn't mind, and I'd go, or he would mind, and I'd stay. If I stayed, I knew I wasn't a big enough person not to resent him for it at some point or another.

But however the rest of the conversation went, I knew it had to be done – there was no way I could start off our engagement with an untruth hanging over our heads. It wasn't fair on either of us.

'Daniel,' I said, holding on to his hand, 'I'm so happy. I don't think I've ever wanted anything as much as I want this – to be married to you. But before we start making plans, I have to tell you something.'

'OK,' he replied. 'This sounds serious. Go for it. I don't think anything could bring me down right now.'

I took a deep breath, and told him: 'Cooper Black has asked me to go on tour with him. Mainly stadiums, across the whole of the States. I'll be away for at least a month.'

He was silent as he listened, just nodding to show that he'd heard. Then he squeezed my hand, and replied: 'And I'm assuming you want to do it?'

'I do,' I said, honestly. 'I really do. But if you don't want me to go, I'll understand. You're more important to me than my career, you really are.'

He gave me a little smile, and kissed me. Brave man, given the state of me.

'I know that. And because I know that, I'm absolutely fine about you going. I've said this before, and I mean it – we can survive anything. It's only a month. It'll be a brilliant opportunity. I can try and schedule the Vella album for the same time so I'm not mooning around the farm crying on Gandalf's shoulder, and I can visit you – I believe there are these little inventions called aeroplanes these days that have made international travel so much easier. . .'

'And then when I'm back, we can start planning. It'll be the best wedding ever.'

'Definitely. You can drive up to the church in your dad's taxi, and your mum can get us a cheap load of Prosecco with her staff discount at Asda, and my parents can do the catering. . . It'll be brilliant. Even if it was just me and you it'd be brilliant.'

'Because it's us,' I said, finally able to stop the tears. I felt so relieved – so euphoric – that I could even forget the fact that I was in a hospital bed wearing an arse-less gown.

'Yes. Because it's us,' he confirmed, kissing me again.

The kiss was getting slightly more serious when I first heard the noise outside in the corridor. The scuffling of feet on lino, and chatter of a group of people who sounded like they needed coffee, and some low-level arguing in familiar accents. I heard a nurse objecting, and someone objecting right back, and felt a big grin break out over my face as I started to realize who it was. The comment 'I didn't drive all night just to sit in a bloody waiting room, love' sealed the deal.

I looked at Daniel, and he was grinning too.

'The Bald Eagle has landed,' I said, sitting up properly and hiding my drip arm under the blanket. I didn't want them to freak out the minute they came in the room.

Within seconds, they were through the door – my dad first, wearing his favourite over-washed Rainbow T-shirt, followed by Mum, in her posh trackies, then Becky and Luke. Predictably enough, I burst into tears again the minute I saw them.

My dad rushed over and snuggled me up in the best dad-hug ever, and my mum was fast on his heels, sitting on the side of the bed, and fussing with my sheets and pillows and tidying my water jug and generally making everything feel so much better. She magically produced a pack of baby wipes from her bag, and started dabbing at my face.

Becky and Luke hovered nearby. They'd obviously set off the minute Daniel called them to say I was in hospital, and I had no idea why I was surprised – of course they did. I had the best family in the whole world, and now the best fiancé. I felt so unbelievably lucky – and none of it had anything to do with number one records or stadium tours. It was all to do with them, and how much I was loved.

'Gave us a bit of a fright there, love!' said my dad, eyeing me up and doing a parental check for damage. 'How are you feeling?'

''Cause you look like shite,' added Luke, who'd slumped

down in one of the plastic chairs as soon as he could, his ever-present phone in his hands.

'And you smell like something even worse,' chimed in Becky, giving me a big grin to show she didn't mean it.

'I'm all right, honest. Food poisoning.'

'Are you really OK?' Mum asked, tucking the blankets around my legs so I was almost mummified, in more ways than one. 'We were so worried about you!'

'I'm more than OK,' I said, meeting Daniel's eyes and waiting for the small nod that signified he was happy for me to tell them. 'I'm great, actually.'

They all looked at each other, momentarily confused and obviously wondering if I was on some heavy hallucinogens, until I pulled my left arm free of the covers.

I held my hand up and waved my fingers around, the diamond glinting under the neon strip lighting.

'We're getting married!'

Chapter 6

Landing in Miami a few weeks later, the first thing that hit me was the heat. As soon as Neale and I emerged from the air conditioned airport, woozy from jet lag and a bit too much champagne, I felt it: energy-sucking, skin-warming, borderline humid heat.

The second thing that hit me was a confetti cannon going off in my face, and the sound of a brass band playing 'Coming to America', the song from that old film with Eddie Murphy in it.

At first I thought I was having some kind of fatigue-and-booze induced hallucination, but as soon as I wiped the confetti from my eyes, I saw it – an actual band. They all looked young, and were wearing the kind of costumes I'd only ever seen in films and TV shows, like cheerleaders but with a military touch. Majorettes? They were all young, probably sixteen or seventeen, and had come into a V formation in front of us, their boots tapping on the ground and their perky hats bobbing on their heads. There was a drummer in lead, a huge drum hanging round his neck, keeping time for the rest of them.

Actual real cheerleaders – in frilly red and white outfits – emerged from the crowd, all big smiles and ponytails, dancing and cartwheeling in front of us.

I was frozen solid, staring at it all in disbelief, unable to react with anything other than an expression that probably had 'WTF?' written all over it.

Luckily for us, Neale was way more responsive, and as one of the cheerleader girls was flung high into the blue sky and did a double somersault mid-air, landing right at our feet, he burst into enthusiastic applause, jumping up and down and giggling.

'Oh, brilliant!' he shrieked, clapping his small hands together. 'I feel like I'm in a *High School Musical* film! All we need now is a topless Zac Efron and my life will be complete. . .'

We didn't get Zac Efron, which was a cause for sadness for both of us, but we did get Cooper Black – in the flesh. Despite our many chats on the phone and Skype, we'd never actually met in person.

He, I realized, was the one who'd been firing the confetti cannon; in fact he was still cradling it, like some kind of assault rifle, as he walked towards us. He was taller than I'd expected – my showbiz experiences had taught me that celebs are always shorter than you think in real life – and dressed in torn jeans and a slouchy T-shirt that showed off a big chunk of his chest. His hair was blond and artfully floppy, his muscular arms tanned. He had the kind of 'designer sloppy' look that I knew cost a fortune to achieve, and it suited him.

'Hey, guys!' he said, dropping his assault weapon to the tarmac. 'Welcome to Florida!'

He wrapped me up in a huge hug and I squeezed him back. OK, so I was knackered, and confused, and way too hot in my skinny jeans and high heels, but I had to admit, it was a heck of a greeting. When he eventually pulled away, he gave Neale the same treatment, which I really liked. I learned long ago to judge people not by the way they behave towards the rich and famous, but the way they behave towards the people around them. I'm famous – Neale's not – but Cooper Black was here welcoming us both. That was a nice touch, and made me feel even more warmly towards him.

Neale, predictably enough, was holding on for dear life, giving me a cheeky wink over Cooper's broad shoulders. My friend operates a 'take it where you can get it' approach to physical contact.

'Wow,' I said, once the hug festival was over, gesturing to the brass band and the cheerleaders and the giant banner that said 'The US of A welcomes Jessika!'. 'Quite a reception.'

'Yeah, well,' replied Cooper, grinning at me lazily, 'I like to keep things low-key, you know? That's my style – laid-back!'

'If this is laid-back, I'm terrified to see you stepping it up a level. But, well, thank you. I look like crap, and don't feel much better, but this was special.'

'You look just fine to me, babe,' he said, doing a fake sleazy examination of me with his glance. At least I thought it was fake. I narrowed my eyes at him, and raised one eyebrow in reproof, waving my ring finger around.

'I know, I know!' he said, backing off and holding his hands up in a surrendering gesture. 'You're taken! Huge congratulations on your engagement, Jess. I'm thrilled for you. And just a little bit heartbroken...'

I gave him a quick clip around the head – this always worked when my mum did it to us for 'clowning around', so

I thought it was worth a shot. Cooper Black was hot – hotter than the Florida climate – and I didn't want any misunderstandings to get in the way of what could be a fabulous working relationship.

'Hey,' he said, laughing, 'watch the hair! It took me hours to get it messed up in exactly the right way! Come on, there's a car waiting for us – I thought I'd take you on a quick tour, and then we can head back to the hotel. My guys will take your luggage for you. You just concentrate on relaxing, and getting ready to have the most fun humanly possible with your clothes on. . .'

'Spoilsport!' said Neale, trotting after him like an overly eager puppy. 'Cooper, do you by any chance know Zac Efron?'

I laughed, hoisted my flight bag more firmly onto my shoulder, and followed. As I did, I found myself twisting my beautiful engagement ring round and round on my finger. We most definitely weren't in Kansas any more, Toto, and I had to keep reminding myself of what really mattered in the world. I had the feeling I was heading right into the eye of the storm, and needed to keep a tight grip on reality.

*

I managed to stay awake throughout the rest of the day, which was a minor miracle given how tired I was.

Cooper had taken us on an amazing drive in an open-topped jeep, me in the front and Neale in the back, like our overexcited child, ooh-ing and aah-ing at everything from the views to signs for roadside diners, completely bewitched by our new surroundings. And I could understand why – it was all pretty amazing.

We covered the Art Deco district of Miami, and part of the strange road that links the mainland to the Florida Keys, where we saw flashy resorts and tiny shacks selling fresh seafood and people fishing and every type of car known to man, from super-stylish Ferraris and Lamborghinis through to clapped-out trucks that looked like they were made entirely of rust and bumper stickers.

We all stopped off at a picnic-style café for Key Lime Pie and drinks, so close to the ocean it felt like you could reach out and touch it with your fingertips. The sky was a dazzling blue, the promenade dotted with palm trees, and it was blissfully hot. You wouldn't think that winter was fast approaching here. Once I started adjusting to it – shades on, factor 50 applied, sandals swapped for flip-flops – it was gorgeous, making my skin tingle and glow in the way that only some quality time in the sunshine can do for you. I could probably have fallen asleep there and then, stretched out on the grass, and woken up with a bright red face and a sweaty bra situation, but Cooper kept us on the move.

The hotel we were all booked into was in South Beach, with amazing views out over the ocean. After we'd been settled into our rooms – Neale and I had suites next door to each other – we met up again at the restaurant outside for an early dinner.

I have to say, tired as I was, this was people-watching heaven – unlike anything I'd ever experienced. We were on the main drag, a long strip of glitzy shops and bars and clubs and galleries, and the whole place was buzzing. Everywhere

I looked, there were young, glamorous people, chatting and eating and drinking and flirting the night away.

The accents, the clothes, the whole thing, was just so alien – light years away from London, never mind Liverpool. I suppose, ultimately, people are people – they were socializing in the same way they do at home. But the fact that they looked so different and sounded so different and the weather was so different just made it feel . . . well, different!

Although it was relatively early, the music was already playing, there was dancing in the streets, and several people on roller skates were whizzing by, wearing hardly any clothes. I shook my head several times to try to clear it – it might be pre-party central in Miami, but in my body, and back home, it was late, and pretty much bedtime.

I wondered what Daniel would be up to just then, and pictured him listening to music or watching TV or maybe doing a bit of work.

It instantly made me miss him, so I clamped down on it, and concentrated on enjoying myself instead. We hadn't managed to speak since I left, just exchange messages, and I knew the messed-up timeline was going to take some getting used to.

He was five hours ahead of us, and I couldn't keep calling him in the middle of the night – one of the very few things that could get Daniel in a nark was interrupted sleep. It makes him grouchy. It had been my choice to come and do this, and I couldn't turn into a giant wuss now I was here, and start phone stalking him just because I was a bit out of my comfort zone. Maybe I just needed to work harder on expanding my comfort zone instead.

Plus, I thought, sipping my mojito – probably the best I'd ever had – and looking out at the beach and the waves, it wasn't that bad, was it? Some people would kill for this. I was here, in Miami, with one of my best friends, staying in a luxury hotel, surrounded by beauty of all different kinds. And tomorrow, once I was hopefully feeling less like a zombie, I'd be playing my first ever gig to an American audience.

I felt nervous, but excited. Cooper had sent me all of the songs in advance, and I'd rehearsed the crap out of them. They were great – pop songs, yes, but with a cool R&B beat and lots of sexy harmonies. I'd played them to Vogue, and she'd been impressed – which isn't easy. She was already making approaches to Cooper's record label, I knew, to look at ways we could collaborate on future material and releases.

He'd also sent me videos of the few dance routines he'd included – he was trying to move away from the ultra-choreographed and into something more natural – and I had those nailed too. I was as prepared as I could be for someone who was about to start a tour with a person they'd never met before, in a country they'd never visited.

Tomorrow, it would get even more real – we would be spending the day soundchecking and doing live rehearsals in the stadium, as well as having final fittings for costume, and squeezing in some media appearances and interviews. No matter how much I'd rehearsed the songs, or nailed the dance routines, tomorrow would be important, because that's when we'd put it all together in the flesh. The staging, the sets, the lighting, all of the complex logistics that go on behind the scenes to put on a big concert, were already sorted – I just had to slot into what was probably already a well-oiled machine. I just hoped I managed it.

Cooper's assistant, Felicia, I could already see, was going to be a godsend. She seemed to be always on hand, ready to tell us what we should be doing, wearing, and possibly thinking, and for that I was grateful. I probably would have come down to dinner in my pyjamas and a face mask if she hadn't called by my room and chivvied me along.

Felicia was a tiny but very loud Cuban lady who reminded me a lot of my mother. Not in age – she was probably younger than me – but in her attitude. She was forever on the go, buzzing around, checking messages and schedules, jotting down notes and clearing tables and ordering drinks and generally presiding over our entire existence like a benign dictator. She had one of those brilliant Noo Yoik accents, and whenever she spoke, you had no choice but to listen.

Cooper had a tendency to call her 'mom', and a tendency not to notice that this annoyed her – I spotted her gritting her teeth several times when he said it. He was clearly very fond of her, but she did have a habit of reminding him to go to the loo at regular intervals, as though he wasn't quite capable of knowing when he needed to do that himself, so I could see where he was coming from.

The way Felicia looked at him, though. . .well, that was less than maternal. I'd say, if we were in a school playground, that she'd be the girl who was really rude and bossy to him because she was secretly harbouring a crush. And who could blame her? The man was gorgeous. So was she, in a leggings and Converse and Nirvana T-shirt kind of way – make-up free, glossy dark hair in a plain plait down her back, super-pretty but not an ounce of glamour about her. The kind of girl who could get a make-over in a teen flick and walk into prom looking like a supermodel instead of a nerd, you know?

Either way, I appreciated having her around. Our group was decidedly testosterone heavy, filled with hunky waxed dancers and burly sound guys and technicians who looked like Vikings and bikers. This, I'd noticed, was often the way – no matter how cool or modern the sound, how current the act performing, the roadies and guys who made the whole thing work at gigs pretty much always looked like Vikings and bikers.

Then, of course, there was Cooper Black himself, who definitely looked like he could be descended from an ancient Norse god. There were some female backing singers, I was told, but they weren't arriving until tomorrow. So, for now, the only ones of us rocking ovaries were Felicia and me – although Neale was also turning into a small puddle of excitement at the whole thing.

Cooper was attentive during the whole evening, his arm slung over the back of my chair, entertaining me with stories about his time with the boy band, and JB's many wild escapades that somehow miraculously escaped becoming tabloid fodder. He was a good companion – witty and warm and possessed of one of those really dry, sarcastic senses of humour that I always liked. I think it reminded me of home, and growing up with my family in Liverpool, where people were literally taking the piss out of you from the day you were born. In a nice way.

He'd grown up in Brooklyn, he told me, with a mum who

was a kindergarten teacher, and a dad who drove a cab, just like mine. He was the first and only child of theirs to display any show business tendencies, and he put his early inspiration down to those stories that I'd also been raised with – the 'back of my cab' stories.

Apparently his dad had picked up everyone from Bob Dylan to Paula Abdul at some point or another, and would always come home with autographs and funny tales and occasionally free concert tickets. My dad's stories weren't quite so impressive – he was still dining off the time he had Richard and Judy in the back of his cab – but essentially they were all the same stories, just with different names and faces.

Maybe it was that solid upbringing – he had three older sisters as well – that had kept him so level-headed, but he really didn't come across as anything like you might have expected. He had his first hit when he was seventeen, and had been in a band since he was fifteen, but somehow he was still grounded, and funny, and kind, and all-round normal. Apart from needing Felicia to tell him when to wee, that is – but I knew first hand how your life could change when you were famous.

There was a brief spell for me when the world spiralled out of control – living in a flat I didn't pay for, eating food I didn't shop for and wearing clothes I didn't buy.

Once people have invested time and money in you, once you become a commodity, they want to protect their investment – which often results in the commodity in question living in an insane bubble where nobody ever expects them to do anything other than perform like a trained seal, juggling balls on demand, and where nobody ever says no to them. And if nobody ever says no to you, or disagrees with anything you say, no matter how ridiculous it is, you eventually fall into the trap of believing your own hype, and that you're never wrong.

That's not good for anyone, long-term, and it was a credit to Cooper Black – and his family – that he'd managed to survive it with any sense of self intact.

'So,' he said, after the fourth round of mojitos, 'how are you feeling now? Ready to party? Things don't really hot up around here until midnight. . .'

I glanced at the people around us, listened to the already bonkers noise levels, and could only imagine what it was going to be like later. I wanted to see it, but my eyes were already sore from fatigue, and I could feel my energy levels dipping. Sometimes not even the world's best mojito can do the trick.

'Probably not tonight,' I replied, honestly. 'I've really enjoyed myself, and it's been great meeting everyone, but I'm completely exhausted. I'll probably call it a day before long, and go catch up on some beauty sleep. I'm so tired I could probably nod off with my head in the salad bowl, to be honest.'

'That would be awesome,' he replied, grinning at me. 'If the pictures ended up online, we'd have to claim it was a whole revolutionary kind of spa treatment.'

'Yeah. You could arrange the cucumbers over my eyes and say it was for extra zest.'

'The Miami Make-Over. I can see it now. There could be a book. A fitness video. The whole shebang.'

'It's definitely an idea, and after a few more of these mojitos, I might be up for it, who knows? So what usually happens then, on nights like this? Do you all party like it's 1999, or are you sensible?'

'Well,' he said, gazing off into the distance and giving it some thought, 'it really depends on what mood I'm in. And who I'm with. JB's coming out to join us soon, and things will most definitely take more of a walk on the wild side then. But tonight? I'll maybe stay up a while, then Felicia will send me to bed. Big day tomorrow, for all of us. My first full solo concert tour.'

I gulped down a huge mouthful of mojito, and felt a wave of fear tickling my stomach. Big day indeed – and I so hoped it was all going to work out.

'You OK?' he asked, looking concerned. 'You look like you just swallowed a toad.'

'Yeah. No. Not sure. I just don't want to let you down.'

He gave me a big hug, and kept my head squashed into his chest. It was comfortable there, and probably easier to fall asleep on than a lettuce leaf.

'Don't be crazy! Of course you won't! You'll make it so much better – it's gonna be a huge adventure, for both of us!'

A huge adventure, I thought, looking around me. Well, it had certainly been pretty exciting so far. And so what if I was feeling knackered?

Tomorrow, I decided, as I saw Neale get up and start vigorously salsa dancing, is another day. And I'll face it better after a few hours' sleep.

Chapter 7

Well, as the old song says, what a difference a day makes. . .

Just twenty-four hours after I took that last sip of mojito and staggered back to my hotel suite, drained and sleepy and tipsy, I was on top of the world.

Or, to be more accurate, standing in front of it – or at least what felt like a big chunk of it. The concert was over, the crowd was screaming and Cooper was grinning, holding my arm up in the air like we'd just won a boxing match. I was drenched in sweat and thought I might be on the verge of losing my voice. The lights were dazzling, and my heart still pounding from that last finale – an encore version of the single, 'Fly So High', but with a stronger dance beat and an intense routine to go with it. I couldn't have been more exhausted if I'd spent three hours solid doing Zumba classes at the gym.

Despite that, it was still one of the very best moments of my entire life. I'd done it. I'd performed in front of thousands of people, without a single mistake – no wrong steps, no accidental trips, no wardrobe malfunctions. Cooper seemed delighted, the audience were still screaming, and I couldn't get the stupid grin off my face. I'd really done it. I was elated, energized, euphoric – and had never been more in the mood for an after-show party in my life!

It felt kind of surreal, to be honest, as we finally left the stage, clambering down the stairs, ears ringing from the noise levels, emerging from the spotlight into a far less glamorous backstage area. Felicia greeted us with a massive grin on her face as she pretended not to want to hug a sweaty Cooper. Someone passed me water, and I glugged it down, unable to stop smiling. A man wearing a Beyoncé T-shirt walked past with a huge Pit Bull Terrier on a lead, and Neale ran up the corridor dressed head to toe in leopard print. Like I said, surreal.

Surreal, though, was fast becoming my new normal. Nothing about the last two days had felt even remotely like anything else I'd ever done before. Yesterday had started with a long-haul flight, peaked with a marching band and cheerleaders, and ended with mojitos and the sweet rhythm of salsa.

This day had started early, and passed in a whirlwind of hard work, sweat, quickly snatched chicken salads, hastily gulped bottles of water, and enforced charm for media interviews.

We'd been along to the local radio station for their breakfast show at what felt to me like stupid o'clock, and that had been an absolute blast. I love doing radio – mainly because it doesn't matter what I look like while I'm talking. No such thing as a bad hair day in radioland.

After that, we'd done a few phoners in the car on the way back, chatting to journalists from various newspapers, magazines and websites about the tour, and our work together. There was, I noticed, always a question or two about my relationship with Cooper and whether it was strictly professional. I was used to being asked about Daniel, but throwing Cooper into the mix seemed to have piqued their interest further. It was understandable: he was gorgeous and famously single.

Cooper fielded these type of questions the best, doing a mock heart-broken voice and breaking the news that I was a 'taken lady'. That always got a few laughs, and seemed to satisfy the interviewers – though I knew from experience, and from working with Patty, that it was entirely possible one or more of them might decide to take it seriously and run with a 'Jessika broke my heart' line. We both knew that could happen, and we both knew it was nonsense, and that if we ignored it long enough, it would go away.

I was fairly sure that Daniel knew that as well. We'd had a long talk about this kind of thing before I left, laying down some ground rules about only believing what we saw and heard ourselves, and not living our lives second hand, being influenced by tabloid gossip that had little base in reality. That kind of thing was always entertaining when it was about other people – I'm as guilty as anyone of reading it! – but not so much fun when it's about you, and your fiancé is thousands of miles away.

After the interviews, Felicia had taken us straight to the stadium – a sports arena – to get on with preparing for our two-night run there. The place was already a hive of activity when we arrived; crawling with worker ants who were unpacking boxes and metal crates, setting up equipment and trailing what seemed like miles' worth of electrical cables around the stage.

The lighting was being rigged up to giant scaffolds and cleverly engineered hoists in the ceiling, and blasts of sound at different levels made me jump every few minutes. The scaffolding and stage were literally covered in Vikings and bikers: black T-shirts on, check flannel shirts flapping, climbing and crawling and hammering all over the place. Some had torches, others had tools, some were wielding giant rolls of black gaffer tape – it was amazing, like some kind of grunge-inspired, perfectly-choreographed ballet.

I'd played some big gigs before now, but usually just turned up and did my spot as part of an ensemble cast. I'd never been involved this closely in a stadium tour, and it was a complete eye-opener. I mean, we've all been to them – I saw Katy Perry on The Prismatic World Tour a few years ago in Liverpool, and it was unbelievable. There were pyramids and a jungle and fireworks and all kinds of madness – and now I was seeing how much work and preparation went into making that kind of magic happen.

I'd been introduced to about seven thousand people, many of whom seemed to be named Todd, and finally got to meet the backing singers – three black ladies in their forties who, I suspected, could sing the arse off any of the rest of us. They looked like they ate *X Factor* stars for breakfast, and even listening to them practise their a cappella harmonies was a humbling experience.

Before we got into costume for a dress rehearsal, we did a basic soundcheck, and I got to stand on that stage for the first time. OK, so I was still surrounded by hairy men with rock band logos on their chests, who all wanted me to get out of the way so they could tape something vital to the floor, but still, I was there. Standing on the biggest stage I'd ever seen, looking out at a stadium that held more than fifty thousand people. That, in fact, would be holding more than fifty thousand people that night – because all of the Cooper Black gigs were sell-outs.

That afternoon, the seats were empty, and the standing room area at ground level was filled only with technicians and road staff – but it was, despite that, a very special moment. I even pulled out my phone and took a quick photo of the cavernous space, sending it to Daniel with the message: 'Nervous? Me?'

It was around a dinner time back home, and he'd responded straight away. There was a picture of the chickens, who I had insisted were named after flowers, fluttering around their coop. 'Buttercup and Violet say don't be silly, you'll be eggs-ellent.'

I groaned out loud at the terrible joke, and quickly sent him some hastily typed kisses in return. We'd managed one snatched conversation this morning – well, morning for me, mid-afternoon for him – when I was between interviews and he was taking a break from work. Even that had taken about five rounds of phone ping-pong before we managed to connect, and had been conducted in the back of a limo, where I was struggling to be heard over Felicia's barked commands and Cooper's drawling 'yes, Mom, no, Mom' comebacks.

I really hoped that Daniel would, like he'd said, come out and visit at some point during the tour, because I so wanted to share all of this with him. The place, the weather, the stadium, the whole madness – I'd love for him to see it all with me.

By the time we'd finished all our checks, tested all the PA

equipment and the AV equipment and probably some other equipment with different initials, done a run-through with the dancers, and completed a live rehearsal with the band and the backing singers, it was around five in the afternoon – and it already felt like I'd done a whole day's work. Which I kind of had, as we'd started with our breakfast interview at 6 a.m. I know pop stars and actors and the like earn a lot of money, but I don't think I realized until I was actually doing it exactly how hard they work, either.

There was time for a quick dinner, grabbed in the dressing rooms, before Neale finally got to work on his part of the performance – or 'creating the masterwork that is Jessika', as he humbly stated.

He'd been on a huge adrenaline rush, I could tell – partly because of the excitement of the whole trip, the stadium, the atmosphere here, but also because JB had been in touch to say he was joining us when we reached New York, on the next stop of the tour.

'Is there anything going on that I should know about?' I'd managed to ask, between him fiddling with my hair and disappearing into my cleavage.

'Nope! We're just friends.'

'Friends with benefits?' I'd asked, wafting away a cloud of hairspray, eyes clenched shut. 'Because you seem awfully excited about seeing just a friend. . .'

He tugged my hair into place – possibly a little bit harder than he needed to – and patted me on the cheek, like he was my grandma.

'Don't you worry your pretty little head about me, princess,' he said, frowning at me. He did this a lot, and I'd learned not to take it personally – he wasn't frowning at *me*, really, just at something he needed to fix, some tiny blemish or flaw that only he could see. He was a perfectionist on my behalf.

'I'm not worried,' I said, gritting my teeth as he started on the mascara – always my least favourite bit. OK, so technically, they weren't my eyelashes, but they were connected to them, and were also very close to my actual genuine eyeballs. I was always scared he was going to poke me with the brush, and I'd end up rushed to A&E, blinded in a terrible freak make-up accident. As ever, it didn't happen.

'Good. Because you need to be focusing all of your energies on tonight, my love. Align your chakras, open your third eye, feel the force – whatever it is you need to do, you'd better start doing it. I can, of course, make you look tremendous, but the rest is up to you. There are over fifty thousand people out there waiting to see this performance, and I'd say that at least a quarter of them will be rabid Cooper Black fans who hate you for stealing their man. Plus, it's being streamed live on Cooper's channel.'

I'd gulped, and tried not to cry – Neale would kill me if that mascara didn't get a chance to dry on first. I didn't actually know about the live streaming. And it hadn't even occurred to me that some of the fans out there would be hating on me.

Well, I'd decided, all I could do was try to win them over, and ignore them if they threw rotten tomatoes at me.

After the final primps and preens were done, and I was fully made-up, styled, and dressed in my relatively low-key stage costume of skintight black and neon Lycra, there was just about time to drink some more water, go to the loo, take a few deep breaths and check my phone. I don't know why I thought that was necessary, but I was glad I did – Daniel had messaged me to say he was 'doing an all-nighter' so he could stay up and watch the show. 'I'm with you in spirit,' he said, 'but my flesh is staying on the sofa with a tub of Pringles. Love you to the moon and back – you'll be brilliant xxx.'

There were also messages from my mum and dad, from Becky, and from Vogue – all wishing me luck, and telling me how much they believed in me. There was even one from Patty, saying my interview coverage 'wasn't too awful', which in Patty speak is a major compliment.

The messages – including Patty's, strangely – were just the last-minute confidence boost I'd needed, and by the time I emerged into the labyrinth of concrete walls and brightly lit corridors at the back of the stage, I was starting to feel like I'd got the eye of the tiger back again.

Felicia met me halfway along, mouthpiece and earpiece both in place, clipboard in one hand and a walkie-talkie in the other, telling me to move it along. Which was easier for her, as she was wearing combat pants and Doc Marten boots, as opposed to eight-inch heels and a Day-Glo catsuit.

I clopped along as best I could, until she gestured for me to stop. We paused, at the side of the steps that would lead me onto the stage, and she gave me a brilliant smile, raising her hand so we could briefly high five. Her entire face changed when she smiled – it was a shame she didn't do it more often.

'You'll be great,' she said, as one of the tech guys made

final adjustments to my mic pack, 'don't worry. Now, five, four, three, two, one. . .'

Right on cue, over the din of the roaring crowd, I heard Cooper's voice: 'And now, ladies and gentlemen, all the way from the UK, a very special guest – put your hands together and make some noise for a very special friend of mine, the very talented Jessika!'

I'd frozen for a second, worried they'd all start booing. I heard nothing but cheers, and after one sharp shove in the back from Felicia, I was staggering up those stairs, just about correcting myself before I emerged on stage.

Standing there, waving at the audience, knowing I needed to switch on my showbiz persona pretty quickly, I had a miniature wobble. A tiny moment where I felt like a fraud – where I suffered what Vogue called Imposter Syndrome, where you worry that you're actually crap, and sooner or later the world will see you for what you really are, and expose you as a sham.

But I replayed those phone messages in my mind. Reminded myself that back home, my friends, my family – the love of my life – were all waiting, and watching, and cheering me on. And I looked up to see Cooper Black, the man these people had really come to see, giving me such a big, genuine, encouraging smile, that all my doubts melted away as quickly as they'd come.

'Hello, Miami!' I said, hearing my words echo around the arena, and feeling the adrenaline start to pump through my veins. It was showtime – and I was ready.

Chapter 8

The morning after, I was ready for nothing more challenging than managing to direct a chocolate croissant into my mouth. Even that was tricky – I kept missing, as I seemed to have the cognitive skills of a chimp at a tea party.

Neale was in my hotel room with me, wearing a Japanese-style kimono and fluffy baby-blue mules that looked like he'd stolen them from Betty Draper's wardrobe. He claimed they'd been left in his hotel room, but I wasn't convinced.

Like myself, he was suffering. Because, like myself, he'd got stupidly drunk the night before, and stayed out dancing until the sun came up. To be fair, it had come up spectacularly, stripes of gold and pastel dancing over the waves, painting the whole beach orange – absolutely glorious, and completely worth waiting for.

The after-show party had been in the hotel, and was a ridiculously glamorous affair. There were all sorts of people there I recognized – actors, singers, TV stars – and even more who I didn't recognize, but thought I probably should. You know, people who are so good-looking and so well-dressed that you just assume they're famous?

There had been a seafood buffet – which I personally

treated with some caution after my sushi incident – and the champagne was flowing all night, and the music was cool to start with and hot by the end. There was dancing, and singing, and possibly the creation of a few babies, if some of the guests' behaviour was any indication.

In the middle of the perfectly toned flesh and flawless teeth and long legs and designer clothing there were also two tables full of Vikings and bikers, who didn't look like they'd bothered changing their outfits at all, and who generally stuck with each other apart from occasionally joining in with a limbo dance challenge or a twerking session. Honestly, you've not lived until you've seen a sixteen-stone sound guy with a ginger beard and ratty dreadlocks do a twerk-off with a size zero supermodel.

Cooper had looked after me all night, making sure I always had a drink or was having fun, constantly checking in on me to see if I was OK. I was, of course, more than OK – the gig couldn't have gone better, and I was surfing on a huge performance high. There's an adrenaline rush from being on stage that nothing comes close to.

Some of the reviews had gone up online within an hour of the show finishing, and they were all great – genuinely blown away by Cooper's new material, by his new direction, and by my contribution to the spectacle.

'She may look a little like Showbiz Barbie,' said one – I tried not to be offended, and reminded myself that at the end of the day, I *was* blonde and I *did* have a perky pony-tail – 'but Jessika is the real deal when it comes to talent. The perfect complement to Cooper Black's cool new R&B

stylings, the Brit singer added even more star quality to an already stellar event.'

Lots of pictures were popping up as well – taken by fans on phones, by the press, by Cooper's own PR people, by staff from the stadium. Some were of the gig itself, some taken as we left the arena, some snapped of us as we arrived at the hotel – including one where Cooper had his arm draped over my shoulder, and I was gazing up at him, giggling at something he'd said, my hand flat against his chest.

I couldn't even remember what it was – he was a funny guy, and I laughed a lot when I was around him – but that picture did look . . . well, a little bit personal. The caption reflected that: 'In perfect harmony? Cooper Black and Jessika take their on-stage chemistry out to party at one of Miami's hippest hotels. . .'

I told myself I was being stupid to worry, and that there was no need – that Daniel would completely see through the bullshit; that he trusted me; that I would never give him a reason not to trust me and he knew that. I was busily convincing myself of this when a text landed from my brother Luke: *Looks like you're gonna eat his face off, sis*. Smiley face, winky, devil grin, pitchfork.

I'd called Daniel immediately after that – if Luke was thinking it, maybe he was thinking it. Even if he didn't want to. And, I thought, 2 a.m in Miami was 7 a.m in the UK, and he should be up and about by now. Except, of course, I reminded myself as his phone went straight to voicemail, that he'd been up until a few hours ago to watch the concert live – he'd even left me a message afterwards saying how brilliant it was; trying to sound enthusiastic, but clearly exhausted.

It was, I supposed, a bit much to expect him to be awake again already, all geared up and ready to deal with my paranoia when he had a life of his own to get on with. Vella was due to arrive the day after, and I needed to give him the space and rest to prepare for that – working on her album was a big deal for him, just like this tour was for me.

That decided, messages responded to, Luke well and truly sworn at, I simply got on with the business at hand – having a good time. I had, I thought, kind of deserved it, and if kicking ass on my first ever US stadium gig wasn't a good enough excuse to get drunk, I didn't know what was.

Neale had definitely agreed, and we'd done some serious dance-floor shimmying together – at one point I vaguely remembered him being hoisted onto the shoulders of Ginger Beard Twerking Viking, and carried around the room like a doll. He ended up draped across the top of a shiny black grand piano, where he started crooning like Michelle Pfeiffer in *The Fabulous Baker Boys*.

The backing singers had joined in, and at one point I seriously thought I might die laughing as he hammed it up in his leopard-print ensemble. He looked fabulous, but sang like a cat with a ruptured appendix.

Now, after way too much alcohol and way too little sleep, we were trying to eat our room-service breakfast, struggling to master as much hand–eye coordination as toddlers in high chairs covering themselves in puréed carrots. Our mothers would be so proud.

'Someone keeps moving my mouth,' I said, groaning and dropping the croissant to the plate, where I poked at it suspiciously with my finger.

'I know what you mean, sister,' he replied, pushing a slice of toast around with disgust, staring at it viciously. 'I think this toast is made from some kind of mutant bread. It has a life of its own. Still. . .Good night, wasn't it? Do you think it'll be like this every night?'

'Oh my God, I hope not. . .' I answered, sipping coffee and predictably enough, dribbling it down my chin. 'I've already been reduced to this after one party. Surely they can't keep this level of insanity going?'

'I don't know,' said Neale, gazing at himself in the mirror and adjusting his glasses on the edge of his nose, 'from what I've heard, the party doesn't even start until JB arrives.'

He blushed – ever so slightly – as he said that, and I had to laugh.

'Neale, you must remind me to challenge you to a game of high stakes poker some time. Every time you mention that man's name, you turn to jelly. Are you still trying to tell me there's nothing going on?'

He dusted imaginary crumbs off his kimono, crossed his fluffy mules, and pouted at me.

'I just have a crush, what can I say? I'm perfectly happy admiring his gorgeousness from a distance, so don't start getting any of your ideas and turning into Alicia Silverstone in *Clueless*. It is what it is. He's a superstar, I'm the make-up guy.'

I frowned at his words, not at all happy with that assessment.

'You're more than the make-up guy,' I said, firmly. 'You're the bedrock of In Vogue. My best friend. One of the coolest people I've ever met. And I think you're being a bit insulting to JB to assume that he thinks like that – he didn't come across as a diva to me. Why shouldn't he be interested? I've never seen anybody rock leopard print quite like you.'

'Well, you are right about that, honey – it's so me – but please, please, *please*, leave it alone, will you? Your interfering never ends well, does it?'

He had a point, and I couldn't think of a way to argue with him without proving it. So I resorted to plan B, and threw the evil croissant at his head instead. He easily ducked it, and it thwacked onto the carpet, where I half expected it to crawl away and hide under the bed, plotting its next step in world domination.

'Anyway, let's talk about you,' he added, giving me a wicked grin. 'You do know how some of those pictures of you and Cooper looked, don't you? Have you talked to Daniel?'

'I haven't talked to him, no. . . Well, not properly. This time difference is messing with my head. Or maybe it's the eighteen gallons of champagne, I don't know. But we've swapped messages and we talked about all of this before I left, and he knows how the business works. And, most importantly, we trust each other. He knows I would never, ever cheat on him, and I certainly wouldn't be stupid enough to do it in public. It's all fine.'

I might have sounded a little strained by the end of that speech – probably because I was feeling that way. I was missing Daniel, and feeling a bit cut adrift by being away from him – not just him, but the farmhouse, and In Vogue, and my family.

I was also, I had to acknowledge as I picked up the croissant – I didn't want to make a mess for the cleaning ladies – starting to enjoy myself a bit too much, despite all of that. Which was a strain all of its own.

Chapter 9

New York, New York. So good they named it twice. I couldn't argue with that – the whole place was amazing.

I'd never been to the city before, and as soon as we checked into our hotel in Midtown, I felt like I was in a film set. The yellow cabs, the honking horns, the skyscrapers, the pretzel vans, the hustle and bustle. Glittering snow settling on Fifth Avenue. It all felt so alien, and yet so familiar.

The second gig in Miami had gone just as well as the first, and we'd arrived at JFK on a high. For Cooper, this was a hometown run, and he was super-excited to be playing three sell-out nights in a row.

After we settled in to our new temporary home, in hotel rooms that were the size of my whole flat in London, he arrived with a minivan and driver, and announced that he was going to take me and Neale out on a tour of the city. After much squealing and clapping of hands – Neale – and much debate about how high our heels should be – both of us – we set off, armed with fully charged phones for copious amounts of photo-taking. Neither of us was cool enough to pretend we weren't tourists.

The first surprise of the day was our driver. It was JB, waiting for us outside the hotel, dressed in a full chauffeur's outfit complete with cap, which he doffed to us as we approached. His wild dark hair was curling around his shoulders, and his nose piercings and the trail of a tribal tattoo on his neck gave him the look of a pirate. I gave him a quick hug and a kiss, and tried not to laugh as Neale followed suit.

I really wasn't imagining it – JB definitely held on to him for a little bit longer than was necessary, and I thought Neale might actually explode, he went so red. I'd seen him around men he liked before, but I'd never seen quite this reaction – it was sweet. And funny. And there was no way I was going to be able to stop myself trying to set these two up. Even if it was just a fun holiday romance that only lasted as long as the tour, Neale deserved it. Just because I wasn't getting any, erm, romance, that didn't mean he couldn't.

I raised my eyebrows at him as he followed me onto the van, and sat down by my side, primly crossing his arms and legs.

'Don't say a word,' he said, fiddling with the air conditioning. It was hot – not Miami hot, but definitely on the sticky side.

'Surely I can say one word?' I answered, smirking at him.

'Maybe one. Just one. Choose wisely.'

'I can't limit it, I'm sorry. As soon as I saw JB in that outfit, I started thinking about Richard Gere in *An Officer and a Gentleman*, you know? In his uniform? The bit where he—'

'Marches into the factory and scoops her up in his arms and carries her out? I know, I know! Me too! Oh my God. . .this is all too much. . .I may swoon. . .'

I started laughing, and used a folded-up copy of a New York

city map to fan him with. He mopped his brow, and looked as flustered as a Jane Austen heroine after a close encounter with Mr Darcy's jodhpurs.

'You guys OK back there?' said Cooper, appearing in the seat in front of us. He was wearing a super-tight black T-shirt that left little to the imagination, and was looming above us like some kind of muscular urban warrior. Maybe it was contagious, I don't know, but a little bit of Neale's giddiness definitely made its way into my mood as well. I twisted my engagement ring around on my finger, and reminded myself again that my heart lay elsewhere. Even if, every now and then, my other body parts had a difference of opinion about that.

'Aye, aye, Captain,' I said, doing a mock salute and grinning at him. 'What's the plan?'

'Well, as the first gig isn't until tomorrow, we kind of have a few hours off. Obviously, you could have spent that time doing something boring, like relaxing in a luxury spa, or shopping on Fifth Avenue, or drinking cocktails, but I thought this would be more fun. This is my home city, and I want to show it off. Felicia's gone to see her family in Queens, and the crew are all busy getting the venue prepped, so my handsome chauffeur friend and I are going to show you around. I warn you, there may be alcohol involved.'

'I'd be shocked if there wasn't,' I replied. 'My liver is having to adapt very quickly to your lifestyle, Cooper.'

'You're a trooper, Jessy. Now, driver, onwards!'

For the next few hours, JB expertly navigated us around the city streets, as Neale and I oohed and aahed out of the windows, totally captivated by it. Cooper wisely judged the cultural frameworks we worked in, and tailored much of the tour to fit in with TV shows and movies. Because we're common like that.

He showed us the archway from *When Harry Met Sally*; the house where the *Friends* all lived in Greenwich Village; the spot where Holly Golightly gazed into the windows in *Breakfast at Tiffany's*, and the Flatiron Building that Spider-Man leapt all over with his superpowers. We saw the place where Carrie from *Sex and the City* used to live, and the hotel where Kevin got stuck for Christmas in *Home Alone* 2, and the Macy's where Buddy used to work in *Elf*. Most excitingly of all, we even visited the fire station that was used as the HQ for the Ghostbusters. I half expected to see them all in there, as I gazed through the window, JB and Neale re-enacting the 'don't cross the streams' scene behind me.

The tour then took us out to Brooklyn, where we had a picnic lunch in a park with stunning views of Manhattan. It was like something from a postcard – the iconic buildings lined up beside the river, shimmering in the sunshine like modern-day fairy-tale castles.

We curled up on the grass in blankets with champagne and a hamper full of treats, occasionally getting asked for autographs or photos by some of the younger people in the park, but generally being left in peace. I knew things would get extremely hectic the following day, when we started more rehearsals in what was to me a whole new venue, and this was a blissfully calm moment in our schedule.

I lay stretched out in the sunshine, Cooper by my side, enjoying the warmth of both the weather and the company.

Next to us, I could hear the low murmur of JB and Neale chatting, and Neale's frequent giggling. He sounded so happy, and it was lovely to hear.

'Those two seem to be hitting it off,' I said, closing my eyes and relaxing. It was easy to do that around Cooper – no matter how big and famous he was to the rest of the world, around the people he knew, he was always just himself: funny, and kind, and sweet.

'I know,' he replied, 'it's good to see. How about you? How are you doing? Are you missing home?'

'Well, it's not even been a week yet, I suppose, but, yeah. In some ways at least. I mean, I miss Daniel. And my family. But I'm having a brilliant time, and you're not so bad to be around.'

'Wow, thank you! "Not so bad", eh? I'll make sure I get that one put on my gravestone . . . "here lies Cooper Black. He wasn't so bad to be around". You're not entirely terrible yourself. Anyway, are you ready for the final stop on our tour?'

'Yep,' I said, sitting up and stretching my arms. 'It's either that or I fall asleep, right here.'

We all clambered to our feet, a little reluctantly, and made our way back to the van. Within minutes we were driving through the streets of Brooklyn, past yellow school buses and corner cafés and bookshops and cute little boutiques that I could see Neale was itching to get into.

'Imagine the treasures in there, my love,' he said, pointing out of the window at a store called Vonda's Vintage, where a mannequin was dolled up in full Seventies gear, with bell-bottomed jeans and a tie-dye halterneck top.

Not long after, JB parked the van outside a large house – on a corner, four-storeys high, what Cooper told us was called a 'brownstone'. There was a small courtyard garden, and JB beeped the horn as we pulled up.

The door to the house opened, and two middle-aged people stood there, smiling and waving. The man was on the short side, with a huge head of salt-and-pepper hair and an impressive beer belly, and the woman was tall, slim, and blonde. I immediately guessed who they were, and realized that Cooper most definitely got his looks from his mother's side of the family tree.

'Hey, Mom, Dad!' yelled Cooper, jumping out of the van and running over to give them a hug. 'Look who I found. . .'

Chapter 10

The concerts we played in New York were just amazing. I didn't think it was possible to top Miami, but I soon discovered that it was.

I suppose I was getting more confident as the shows went on, still nervous but no longer feeling like I might be sick as I stood at the side of the stage, waiting for Cooper to introduce me. The fans in New York were even louder, treating Cooper like the home-grown hero he was, and the amount of media we did was insane.

We visited TV stations, did radio broadcasts, featured on live PAs from Times Square, held press conferences at the hotel, made appearances to support Cooper's favourite charities, and even managed a surprise visit to his old high school. I was very disappointed to find out it was just a normal high school, and not the kind of performing arts high school I'd hoped for, with everyone wearing leg warmers and having impromptu dance-offs in the streets.

The single was still holding its own in the charts, and back home, my album was also still in the Top Ten. This tour wasn't just a great learning experience for me, it was skyrocketing my profile. Patty was delighted, and was busily making the most of it at her end, going nuts on social media and asking me to send her selfies she could supply to the UK press as exclusives.

Vogue was thrilled, too, because all of this was good news for the label, and for the new talent she was looking for. Or, probably, Jack was looking for, but I didn't want to spoil my mood by thinking about that too much.

Neale was in his element, loving the style and the fashion and the glamour, and, of course, the fact that JB was staying with us for the next couple of weeks. He was still insisting the two of them were 'just friends', and to be fair, I'd never seen any physical contact beyond the usual hugs and kisses we all shared. But their chemistry was off the scale – seriously, seriously hot – and it seemed such a shame to waste it. Now I knew JB was sticking around, I resolved to cook up at least a few situations where they were 'accidentally' left alone together. Ideally in a hot tub with a bottle of fizz and a crate of oysters.

I'd spent a lovely night having a home-cooked dinner with Cooper and his family – his mum and dad and sisters, as well as Felicia, who they all obviously adored. He was so relaxed around them, and they were so quick to jump on him if he sounded even remotely puffed-up about himself that they reminded me of my own family. My own family, who I missed desperately, but knew were delighted for me. I really hoped that one day, my dad would get to meet Cooper's dad, who it turned out, by some weird twist of fate, was also a cab driver and the two of them could have a long, drunken conversation about celebrity taxi appearances.

Everything, in fact, was going brilliantly – apart from one

thing. Daniel and I just never seemed ever able to quite connect properly. I'd call him when it was early morning for me – by which I mean about 11 a.m., because late-night gigs do not blend seamlessly into crack-of-dawn wake-up calls – and late afternoon for him, hoping to talk properly, but often he was working. I could tell he was distracted, much as he tried not to give it away, and could hear the music and chatter in the background.

By the time he'd finished for the day, usually around 9 p.m. his time, and was able to relax and call me, I was usually in the middle of soundchecks, rehearsals, or doing an interview. And from about 7.30 p.m. my time, I was either on stage or getting ready to be on stage – and much as I wanted to speak to my beautiful boy back home, I couldn't exactly pause mid-dance routine, whip out my phone, and get all lovey-dovey, could I?

It didn't seem to matter too much with other people in the UK – I was happy enough communicating with Vogue via text and email; and my family were content as long as they knew I was safe and well. The occasional smiley face and picture of my party outfit was enough to convince them of that, and in return they sent me photos of Prince Ollie and updates on their lives, how things were going in Asda and which new shops had opened in Liverpool ONE.

But with Daniel, it was tougher – I loved him so much, and missed him so much, that whenever I let myself think too hard about it, I started crying. For the last few months we'd lived together, never going more than a night apart, and always on the end of the phone.

We'd made a big commitment to each other by getting

engaged – the biggest two people can make without their reproductive systems being involved – and now it felt like we could barely find time to talk.

I didn't blame him; I didn't blame me. It wasn't a situation that either of us had deliberately caused – it was just the way our careers were taking us for the time being. I knew it wouldn't last for ever, and before long I'd be back in his arms again. And, more importantly, back in the same time zone. My tour would be finished, and Vella and her band would have left the farmhouse, and we could go back to being Jessy and Danny for a while, instead of both focusing on being Jessika and Wellsy.

Maybe, I told myself after sending what felt like my fiftieth 'love you' message of the day, we'd even get away on holiday, perhaps for Christmas as it was coming up. We'd never had a holiday together – we'd both always been too busy. But after this, after we'd both worked so hard and been so focused, we would definitely deserve one.

I'd been pondering this on our final night in New York, and wondering idly as Neale did my face for the last of our gigs, where we could go. Somewhere hot and relaxed, and totally switched off from the rest of the world. Somewhere that didn't even have Wi-Fi. A tropical island where we could pretend to be castaways, but with someone else to cook our tea, or maybe one of those remote mountain chalets surrounded by goats and wildflower meadows, or even just somewhere closer to home, like the coast of Ireland, or a log cabin in the Highlands, or a yurt in Wales . . . anywhere. Anywhere, as long as it was just us, together.

I glanced at the clock on the dressing room wall, and saw that it was just after 7 p.m., which made it around midnight back home. He might still be up, I thought, grabbing my phone and ignoring Neale's bleating protests.

I hit the dial button, and waited through the clicks and purrs of the international lines connecting, tapping my fingers nervously on my Lycra-clad knee. I just wanted to hear his voice, no matter how briefly – just a minute, just long enough to say, 'Hey, baby, order us some holiday brochures, will ya?' Because maybe, I thought, having that to look forward to would help get us through the rest of this month apart.

The phone rang and rang, and I was just about to give up and disconnect when it was answered.

'Hi! Daniel's phone!' said an accented female voice, followed by a giggle. I could hear loud music in the background, and the sound of people partying. I frowned, and added the time difference up again – yep, it was midnight there. Which, I reminded myself, was a perfectly acceptable hour for showbiz people to still be up and partying. Except, of course, that I never counted Daniel as a showbiz person – he's the sensible one, tucked up in bed ready to do his chores in the morning.

'Umm, who is this?' I asked, feeling twitchy. I'd have assumed I'd somehow got the wrong number, but she had said it was Daniel's phone – which did leave one more question: 'And where's Daniel?'

'It's Vella, and Daniel's just done a late-night run to that little service station place, you know? We ran out of booze, disaster!'

The 'little service station place' was a good twenty-mile

drive from the farmhouse, so their need for booze must have been quite extreme. Especially as there'd been enough to stock a small pop-up bar the last time I checked.

'Oh. Right. Vella. Tell him . . . tell him Jessy called, will you?'

'Sure thing, Jessy!' she said, and immediately ended the call. I had no idea if she would – she already sounded like she'd had enough to drink. Obviously couldn't take her ale, I thought bitchily, which in Liverpool was one of the biggest insults you could throw at someone.

I was still staring at the phone, feeling so much worse than I had ten minutes ago, when Neale tapped me on the head with a very spiky hairbrush. I cringed, and snapped myself back into the real world.

'Earth to Jess, Earth to Jess! It's showtime in less than twenty minutes, and unless you want to go on stage looking like a bag lady, I need to finish your face!'

'Oh! Of course, I'm sorry,' I muttered, screwing my eyes up to squeeze back the tears. All this time, I'd been wondering how Daniel felt when he saw pictures of me and Cooper together. How he felt when he read false stories about our 'close relationship'. If any of it made him worry or doubt me. I suppose I'd imagined him at home, pining, tortured by my absence and my new-found friendship with one of the planet's hottest heart-throbs.

What I hadn't imagined, of course, was that he'd actually be at home partying with one of the planet's hottest divas. Or how completely shitty that would make me feel.

*

We had another day off in New York, which I spent cheering myself up by going on huge shopping sprees with Neale. We shopped until we literally almost dropped, and I anticipated a lot more luggage on my flight home at the end of the tour. I bought clothes and make-up and souvenirs, including a really cute 'I Heart NY' outfit for Prince Ollie. I wanted to get something for Daniel, but he was a hard man to buy for – so I settled for a fake NYPD T-shirt.

I'd spoken to him the day after my lovely chat with Vella, who I now hated with the kind of illogical passion that only a jealous girl can hate with, and everything had felt a bit off. Neither of us said that, but we both knew it. I was tense, and he was tired, and we were both too busy. The whole thing was making me edgy and nervous, and I needed to get a grip. I'd been so focused on whether Daniel trusted me or not, I'd forgotten to ask myself a very important question: did I trust him?

I wanted the answer to be a resounding yes, but I'm only human. I was away from my man, and hurting, and being chipped away at by doubts that I knew he probably didn't deserve.

All of this was running through my mind as we headed to Boston, where we were booked for two more sell-out concerts. As it wasn't too far away from New York, we were heading there in a tour bus – a long, sleek thing that had Cooper's face plastered all over the side of it.

Inside, it was less of a bus, and more of a hotel on wheels. There were seating areas, and little bunks for naps, and every toy and gadget you could wish for – Xboxes and PlayStations and DVD players, even a tiny galley kitchen filled with drinks and snacks. And, it pretty much goes without saying, a huge fridge stocked with beers and spirits and soft drinks. This whole tour seemed to run on alcohol, and I wasn't immune – it was only 11 a.m. and I was already hitting the vodka. But at least it was with cranberry juice, so I told myself it was healthy.

I was sitting at a table with Neale and JB, who were flirting and giggling their way through a game of blackjack. They were, at least, keeping their clothes on, unlike that game of darts we had what felt like light years ago. Back in the land that time forgot, when I felt like I had a vague sense of control over my life.

I was trying to concentrate on reading, but in fact kept getting distracted – by their fun and games; by the vodka; and mainly by my own incessant Googling. I knew what she looked like already, but by the time I finished, I knew everything about Vella. Or at least everything the internet could tell me. She was twenty-four; born in Germany to Caribbean parents. Started off in the hip hop scene, and moved into dance music – she had one of those huge, powerful voices they used on the choruses of club tracks, the kind that made you feel euphoric or frenzied, depending on the beat.

Her first solo album had come out last year and been a huge hit. Her second was currently being masterminded by my very own 'reclusive genius', Wellsy. Vella was also – and this was hard to ignore – drop-dead gorgeous. Small and curvy and very, very sexy.

I closed down my phone in a huff, knowing I was only making matters worse, and decided to go and sulk on my own somewhere. I wasn't exactly good company, and besides, I wanted to give JB and Neale as much time on their own as possible, in the hope that one of them would finally find the balls to push their relationship in the direction it so clearly should be heading towards.

I left my phone on the table – I needed a digital detox – and headed to an unoccupied seat. There was plenty of room on here, as a chunk of the crew were following on a bus of their own. When I looked around, I saw the backing singers, together as usual, and the dancers – all of them perfect specimens of humanity. Up near the front, I saw Cooper's tousled blond head, and next to him Felicia's – she was moving around a lot, looking quite animated, and I suspected she was outlining his schedule to him, telling him what he should do and when. Every now and then, he nodded in response, and I could imagine him saying 'yes, Mom' in that sarcastic tone he uses on her.

Poor Felicia, I thought. Anyone with a pair of eyes – apart from Cooper himself – could see that she was into him. And yet he seemed to see her only as a sister figure, a friend – it was like it barely registered with him that she was even female, never mind an attractive female. It must be torture, being around him so much, constantly dealing with his casual and unintentional rejection.

I stared out of the window, resting my head on the glass, and watched the endless stretches of road fly by. Miami had been brilliant. New York even more so. And I was sure Boston would be amazing as well – but travelling between them like this just reminded me that real life is dull and mundane wherever you are. Being stuck on a bus is being stuck on a bus, whether you're heading from NY to Boston or from Liverpool to Rhyl.

I might possibly have dosed off for a while – in fact I definitely did – and only woke up again when I felt someone taking my vodka glass from my hand. I immediately grabbed it back in a death grip – you can take the girl out of Liverpool and all that – and looked up to see that Cooper was sitting beside me.

'Easy, Tiger!' he said, laughing, holding his hands up in a gesture of surrender. 'You were about to spill that all over your thighs. . .'

'Well, we wouldn't want that, would we?' I replied, necking the remains of the glass in one. 'There, problem solved. Except now I need a refill.'

'I'll get you one – as soon as you tell me what's wrong. You've been messed up, and that's not just the vodka. What's going on with you, Jessy? Is there anything I can do to help?'

Not, I thought, unless you can hire an international assassin to take out Vella, or give me a complete personality transplant. I was even sick of myself.

'No. I'm sorry, I don't mean to be a grumpy arse. I'm just . . . homesick, I suppose.'

I realized as soon as I said it that it was true. That I wasn't just missing Daniel. That I was missing everything – my mum and dad, and Vogue, and my flat, and the farm animals, and even the crappy British weather. I'd been away for ten days now, but it felt like a lifetime – it wasn't just the physical distance that was taking its toll, it was the cultural difference.

I was loving the States – the people, the food, the lifestyle, it was all fabulous. But, well, it just wasn't home, was it?

I've always been a bit like this. It's pathetic. Even on outrageously drunken fortnights in Ibiza with my old friend Ruby, I'd get to about day eight and wish I could leave. Often that was because Ruby had ditched me for some DJ she'd just met and disappeared off into a light-stick romance, but it was also because at heart, I'm a homebody. I can pretend to be a glamorous international jet-set traveller, but, deep down, I'm not. And right then, I'd have given anything to be back in Liverpool, ideally in the living room with my dad, watching *Homes Under the Hammer* and eating crisp butties.

'I get that,' replied Cooper, thoughtfully. 'I spent years of my life on tour, and although it's a blast, there's no place like home, is there? All you can do is stay grounded, remind yourself who you are and where you come from, and hold tight to the people who make you you. In my case, that's my folks – and, I suppose, Felicia. I've known her for ever, she's from the same place as me, she just gets it. You're out here in a foreign country, all on your own. That can be tough.'

'I sound like a complete whinger, don't I?' I said, feeling tears welling up in my eyes. 'This is all brilliant. The tour's brilliant. I'm having an amazing time – I don't mean to complain so much. I think part of it is the time difference. Me and Daniel, well. . .'

'You keep missing each other?' he supplied, smiling gently at me. 'Communicating via text? Having snatched conversations when you're both surrounded by other people? Trying to pretend everything's OK when you're actually exhausted and stressed?'

'Yes!' I said, amazed. 'Exactly that! How did you know? Am I that obvious?'

'No, not at all. Like I said, I've spent years of my life on tour. And for at least some of that, I was in a relationship, and it was hard. Trying to maintain your commitment to someone long distance. Trying to be understanding, and make yourself understood. Holding it all together when it feels like it's falling apart. It's too easy for the cracks to creep in when you're so far away from each other – tensions that would mean nothing if you were together build up until they feel huge and, before you know it, the barrier between you feels too big. I've been there, and I didn't handle it well.'

'What happened?' I asked, genuinely curious. 'With the girl?'

'Nothing good. I was too young anyway, and she was a civilian – she was at college, studying to be a teacher, and she just didn't understand all of this crazy shit. At least with Daniel, you've got a man who does, because it's kind of his world too.'

I nodded. He was right. If Daniel was a fireman, or a bus driver, or a dog groomer, there's no way any of this could work – but he was a music producer. And while that made him busy, at least it should give us a fighting chance of trying to work this out.

'I know,' I replied. 'I need to try harder – relax about it, put some faith in our relationship. Trust him more.'

'Trust him?' Cooper said, frowning at me. 'Why wouldn't you trust him? There's no way a man would cheat on you – you're the bomb! Plus, he doesn't strike me as that kind of guy.'

'Me neither. But how well do we ever really know anyone?'

'Fair point. And I've never even met the dude. But I know you, and I trust your judgement.'

I laughed out loud at that one; a laugh that definitely sounded on the bitter side. When I look back on my love life – in fact my life in general – 'good judgement' isn't something that immediately springs to mind as a notable personality trait. Before I left Liverpool, I'd been two-timed by an amorous window cleaner called Evan. And when I was in London, I fell for Jack Duncan – a man who not only two-timed me, but did it with one of my closest friends, right under my nose. My judgement was about as reliable as Del Boy Trotter.

Still, I told myself, Daniel was different. Daniel was not one of those men. Daniel was Daniel.

'Look,' said Cooper, giving me a quick cuddle, 'I'm gonna go and get you a fresh drink. And then, why don't we try and plan a visit for him? I know it's hectic – he's busy, you're busy. But you're going to have to make time for each other – for your relationship – if it's going to have a chance. Let's get Boston out of the way, and then get him over here. We have three days off then before Chicago. If he can't make it then, invite him to opening night in the Windy City – I'm sure he'll love it. What do you say?'

I thought it over. Maybe he was right. Maybe I was giving in to despair when there was a solution right there, waiting to be grasped. Daniel had said that he'd come out and visit, but I hadn't pushed the subject. I told myself it was because I knew he was busy and didn't want to pressurize him, but truth be told, I also didn't want to pressurize myself. This whole tour – this whole whirlwind – was insane, and I was struggling to keep my feet on the ground.

Maybe it was time to fight, and channel all that unfair anger I was feeling about Vella into some positive action. I'd invite Daniel out to meet us on tour. He'd say yes. We'd be together again, and have delicious make-up sex, and everything would be right in the world.

Now, all I needed was that vodka, and I might even be able to manage the phone call.

*

By the time I did get to speak to Daniel, it was in less than ideal circumstances. We'd arrived in Boston, and checked into our hotel, and I was so tired and drunk that I spent the first afternoon sleeping while everyone else went out to see the sights.

I was annoyed with myself about that – here I was, in one of the most historic and beautiful cities on the East Coast, and I was locked in my hotel room dribbling on the pillow and sleeping in my clothes. Not classy.

Still, I'd needed it – the rest, the recovery, the solitude. I dreamed about Vella, of course, walking down the aisle in a purple wig, with Daniel as the groom and Jack Duncan as the best man. I, for some reason, wasn't a human being but a pug, kept on a lead and wearing a diamond-studded collar. Dreams are weird, right?

By the time I came back to consciousness, I was slightly hungover, and hungry. I glanced at my phone and saw that it was after 8 p.m. – I'd lost the whole day. I also saw that I'd missed several calls from Cooper, even more from Neale, and precisely none from Daniel. He was probably busy with his wedding plans, I thought, fingering my engagement ring and trying to get my head straight.

I listened to my messages as I pottered around my hotel suite, carefully avoiding mirrors until I'd had some time to repair myself. I could live without the shock of the Pug Bride of Frankenstein staring back at me.

Everyone, it seemed, had gone to dinner – without me. That, of course, was fair enough. Just because I was having some kind of mid-twenties life crisis, it didn't mean that everyone else had to go hungry. But still. . .I suppose I was feeling wobbly. Like I was walking on shifting sands, trying to stay upright when the waves came crashing in. So even though it was fair, I still felt a bit sulky and rejected.

The last message was from Neale, and he'd only left it twenty minutes earlier. Possibly the sound of it landing was what had woken me up, and rescued me from that hideous dream. It said that he was heading to the rooftop hot tub, and I should come and join him. It also said that he'd left me a 'little treat' outside my room.

I pulled open the door, glad there was nobody outside to witness my less-than-glamorous appearance, and saw a tray on the floor. On it was a small bottle of red wine, and one of those big silver dome affairs you see in films, over the top of a plate.

I picked the tray up and carried it back inside, sniffing as I went to see if I could figure out what it was. Of course, in films, it would be lobster or steak Béarnaise or venison, or something else suitably fancy. This being my life, though, when I put it down on the table and pulled off the lid, I saw a chicken and mushroom flavour Pot Noodle and a bag of Wotsits.

Perhaps, if I was a proper pop star and international traveller, I'd have been disappointed, but in fact it just made me sigh with pure happiness. Some of my very best culinary memories involved chicken and mushroom flavour Pot Noodles, and what kind of a human being didn't love Wotsits? One of my favourite things to do, as a child – who am I kidding, as a grown-up too – was to eat so many Wotsits that my fingers turned orange. Simple pleasures and all that.

I put the kettle on to boil while I took a quick shower, and then took the precaution of eating my gourmet feast while still in my bathrobe. In my vast experience of such things, I've found that it is physically impossible to eat a Pot Noodle without getting at least some of it on your clothes.

Feeling much better after my nutritious snack, I got ready to join Neale on the roof. I wasn't sure exactly what was up there, but a quick look at the leather-backed hotel guide on the desk told me there was a hot tub for twelve, a small heated pool (weather permitting), and a 'sun deck'. As it was now after nine, I supposed it would be more of a moon deck.

I decided to put my swimmers on beneath my robe, and pop my feet into a pair of those free slippers you get in posh hotels, where the sole feels like it's made of cardboard. My suite was on the top floor of the hotel anyway, so it was just a matter of jumping in the lift. I didn't need to be ready for a photo shoot, so I didn't bother with make-up. I did, however, use a baby wipe to get rid of the Pot Noodle juice on my chin – they may be low, but I do have some standards.

Within a few minutes I was emerging into the warm night air, pausing as I came through the door to simply stand, stunned by the breathtaking view. As lit-up cityscapes went, Boston definitely had a good thing going on.

I had no idea what I'd expected – Cooper, maybe, some of the dancers; definitely some kind of low-level party at least. Instead, the whole place was empty – apart from me, Neale and JB.

The two of them were in the hot tub, bubbles cascading around them, both holding champagne glasses and looking relaxed. I suddenly realized, with absolute horror, that I was the third wheel. The gooseberry. The embarrassing extra. I considered simply turning around and making a run for it, going back to my room and watching Pay-Per-View on the telly, but I was too late – I'd been spotted.

'Jessy!' shouted Neale, waving at me so hard his champagne started to slosh out of the glass. 'Jump right in – the water's lovely!'

I waved back, put my key card down on one of the tables next to my bag, and went to join them. He was right, I thought, as I climbed into the tub: the water really was lovely.

'Hey, Jess,' said JB, giving me a lazy salute, and passing me the champagne bottle. 'We only have two glasses, but you seem like the kind of girl who doesn't mind her booze straight from the source.'

'You're not wrong there,' I replied, taking a quick swig. I needed it – I was feeling pretty uncomfortable. Not because they weren't being welcoming, they both seemed really happy to see me, but because I felt like I was intruding. They'd been here, in a hot tub, on a romantic rooftop, all alone – exactly like I'd hoped they would be, one day. Then I came and blundered in and spoilt it all.

'Where is everyone?' I asked. 'I expected this to be party central.'

'Oh, you know, out and about,' said Neale, squinting at me. He'd taken his glasses off for his soak, and I knew he was blind as a bat without them. 'Cooper has a cousin here, so he went for a visit. The dancers are looking for a club to show off in. The tech guys are down in the bar, scaring small children. We just thought we'd take tonight to relax.'

He blushed slightly as he said 'relax', which made me immediately sing Frankie Goes to Hollywood in my mind.

'Well, thanks for the dinner, anyway – I was starving when I woke up. You know me too well.'

'I do indeed. There was a shop in the market that sold all kinds of British food – PG Tips and Fry's Turkish Delight and Walkers crisps . . . amazing how much I've been missing all that crap!'

'I know what you mean,' I replied. 'And Wotsits hit the spot perfectly. So . . . what are you guys planning for the evening?'

They exchanged looks, and JB answered: 'I'm going to take Neale here on a tour of Boston's Irish bars. You've got to come with us. There'll be Guinness, and music, and drunk people jigging.'

'Sounds just like Liverpool,' I said, smiling at the thought. Liverpool has a strong Irish community – the Malones, as you might guess from the surname, are part of it – and some fabulous Irish pubs. I felt a little melancholy at the thought, and maybe going out on a leprechaun-based pub crawl would be just what I needed to cheer myself up. But, as I'd decided literally the minute I arrived on the rooftop, I wouldn't be there for long – those two were never going to get it together if I was always hanging round.

'Yes, come with us!' said Neale, splashing his short legs around in the water like an excited child. Bless him – I knew he had a crush on JB, but he was still willing to share. True friendship.

'I don't think so, guys,' I replied, sipping my champagne and stretching out in the bubbles. It's always a bit weird in hot tubs, isn't it – wondering where those jets are going to shoot next? It can get very personal. 'I'm completely wiped out, to be honest, and I'd just drag you down. You go without me, but take loads of photos, OK? Then I'll feel like I was almost there.'

'But minus the hangover,' added JB, raising his glass so we could toast that triumphant concept.

'Yep. Because I already have one of those. I accidentally seemed to drink most of a bottle of vodka on the tour bus. I think a session in front of the TV with room service might be more my level tonight.'

Neale put up a half-hearted fight, attempting to convince me to come out of pure loyalty, but I held firm, and within half an hour started fake yawning – well, it started off fake, but before long it was real. I genuinely was tired, and a bit emotionally wrung out, truth be told. I announced that I was going to go back to my room, wished them a great night, and climbed out of the tub. The champagne seemed to have topped up my booze levels, so I was slightly unsteady, but managed to avoid falling. That wouldn't have been a good headline: POP STAR FALLS TO DEATH IN DRUNKEN ROOFTOP PLUNGE.

I put my robe back on over my bikini, popped my feet into the slippers, and made a sharp exit with my bag. I noticed, as the lift doors closed in front of me, that Neale and JB had already forgotten I existed – which was exactly how I wanted it. If this all worked out, and those two got together, I could make like Cilla Black and buy a new hat for the wedding.

The thought made me smile, and I was smiling all the way until I reached my suite door – and realized that I'd very cleverly left my key card up on the roof. I could picture it now, glowing in the moonlight, in all its plastic loveliness.

Sadly, picturing it and having it were not the same things, and I found myself standing outside my door, soaking wet, wearing a pink polka-dot bikini and a hotel robe, locked out.

This left me in something of a dilemma. I could, of course, simply go down to reception and explain what had happened, and I was sure they'd sort me out. But that would involve being seen – and potentially photographed – by possibly hundreds of people. It was a big, swish hotel, and I was sure they weren't used to random Scousers wandering around in their skivvies, dripping water onto their Persian rugs.

I could go back up to the roof and get the key – that was probably the most straightforward thing to do – but I really didn't want to intrude on JB and Neale again. They'd made me feel welcome, but I could sense the sexual tension shimmering between them, and didn't want to be responsible for getting in its sexy, shimmery way.

I had my phone, so I could call down to reception, and ask for a member of staff to come up – but again, that felt way too embarrassing. It was taking the whole image of a blonde moment to the next level.

Instead, I decided to just wait it out. I was soggy but warm, I'd eaten a Pot Noodle so my body was fully stocked on essential vitamins and nutrients, and the hallway was quiet and cosy. There were only two suites up here on the top – mine and Cooper's. Cooper, I was sure, would be back before too long, and he'd nip down and get a key for me. Or I'd just leave it an hour or so, then go back up to the rooftop for my own – JB and Neale were bound to have gone by then, back to their rooms on the floor below me, kitting themselves up in shamrock T-shirts ready for their Irish-themed night out.

Looking back, none of this sounds that sensible, but you know how it is when you're a bit tired and a bit drunk? The strangest of things seem to make sense. Like walking home on your own and having no idea how you got there the next day, and even less idea where that plastic pink flamingo came from. Or giving the man behind the counter in the chippie your phone number, because he gave you an extra sausage for free. Or swapping your fake Jimmy Choos for another girl's pair of Converse, purely on whim. The list is practically endless: Daft Things I Have Done While Drunk. I should write a self-help book about it.

Anyway, as I slid against the door and fell silently to the

ground, bundled up in my robe, hair dripping down my back, it seemed to be a perfectly sensible decision.

Funnily enough, though, it didn't seem quite as sensible when I next became aware of the world around me. I must have dozed off, which wasn't surprising, and when I opened my eyes, my left cheek was glued to the carpet, and one of my slippers had come off.

I'd been woken by the insistent sound of a woman, saying: 'Madam, are you all right? Madam?'

The use of the word 'madam' started off politely, but after about the thirteenth repetition sounded more like she was saying 'get up off the floor, you drunken slattern'. Eventually, she started to accompany the word with the odd poke to the ribs, perhaps concerned that I was dead, and she'd have to do something serious like fetch the manager or call the cops.

'Ugggh,' I said, eloquently, pulling my face off the carpet and the pool of drool that had gathered around it. I rubbed my skin – it felt sore, and was undoubtedly a lovely shade of carpet-burn red – and managed to sit up. I did a quick dignity check, and although my score was extremely low, neither of my boobs had popped out, so that was something.

'OK,' I said, hoping that one word would make her go away. She was dressed in a maid's uniform, complete with apron, and was looking at me like she was still considering calling the cops.

'Sorry,' I added, apparently incapable of using more than one word at a time.

She nodded, and stood up straight, placing her hands on her hips. She was middle-aged, but trim and fit-looking, as though all her hoover-wrangling and feather duster workouts had turned her into Jane Fonda.

'Is this your room, madam?' she asked, indicating to the door. I nodded, and grunted: 'Lost key.'

I blinked my eyes rapidly a few times, in an attempt to clear the fog, and climbed to my feet.

'What time?' I asked, delighted to have upgraded myself to a two-word person.

She glanced at her chunky wristwatch, and frowned. 'Just after 6 a.m.,' she said. 'I've been cleaning the rooftop bar, and found this on the table – is it yours, madam?'

She picked up the key card from her cleaning trolley, and looked as though she was thinking twice before handing it over. I can't say that I blamed her – this was one of the super-sleek penthouse suites, and I probably didn't look like I belonged there.

'Yes. Mine. Jess Malone. With the Cooper Black tour.'

She still looked slightly doubtful, so I added: 'Honest.'

I managed to pick up my bag and get it open, pulling out my passport. I look OK on my passport photo – full face on, hair tidy, wearing actual clothes – and it seemed to do the trick. She handed over the key card, silently, and I felt her mum-like judgement hanging in the air between us.

'Thank you!' I gushed, not sure whether I should hug her or carry on apologizing. In the end, I just scooted around, opened the door, and practically fell through it.

I collapsed onto the bed, only now realizing how terrible I felt. I was damp, and chafed, and dehydrated, and also desperate for a wee. I'd been there, in a soggy heap on the carpeted hallway, for hours – Cooper clearly hadn't come back. Either that or he'd taken one look at me and decided I looked comfortable enough to step over.

I wanted to crawl under the duvet and get warmed up, but first, I needed to go to the toilet. I tried to roll off the bed and onto my feet, but instead somehow ended up in a heap on the floor. By the time I'd pulled myself upright again the room was spinning, my bladder was bursting, and my phone was ringing.

I grabbed my phone, and did that weird hop walk to the bathroom that you do when you're completely busting and don't want to leak. I must have looked like the 'before' section of a TENA Lady advert.

I slammed the door open and made it to the glorious throne just in time, as I pressed 'answer' on the call. Multi-tasking at its finest.

I hadn't looked at the caller name – I was distracted by biological functions – but immediately heard Daniel's voice on the other end. I sighed in relief, both at hearing him and at the biological functions.

'Jessy?' he said, his voice having that slightly distant echo I'd got used to hearing on the trans-Atlantic line. 'Are you OK? I've called a few times and there was no answer, and you weren't picking up your hotel room line either, and what's that noise?'

'Umm. . .' I replied, suddenly embarrassed, 'I'm just running a bath. Sorry, I was asleep. In the hallway . . . long story, happy ending. Look, can you come out and visit? I have two nights to play here in Boston, then some time off. Come and stay. We can fly to Disney World, or just hole up in a hotel room. I really need to see you. Please say you'll come.'

There was a pause at the other end, and I could hear music and chatter in the background. It faded, and I imagined him leaving the studio, maybe walking outside.

'How's Gandalf doing?' I asked, flooded with a severe case of homesickness as I pictured the scene. 'And the chickens? And . . . you?'

'We're all good, thank you, Jessy. But we're also busy . . . you know, with Vella. And the album.'

For a moment, my brain created a cartoon tableau where a rescue donkey and a coopful of hens were crowded into a recording studio, fiddling with dials and drinking Red Bull and wearing headsets. It was weird, like one of those pictures of dogs playing pool in smart waistcoats.

Once that had cleared, it started to register that Daniel was saying no. That he couldn't come and stay for my days off. That he was busy with Vella. I felt sick to the bone, and worried that I was actually going to throw up. I felt so off-balance – all at sea without my Daniel-shaped rubber ring to keep me safe. Because my Daniel-shaped rubber ring was 'busy'.

I was devastated, but tried to keep it out of my voice as I replied.

'Oh. All right. I understand,' I said, telling myself to get a grip. Daniel had his own life, his own career – he was successful and hard-working and ambitious, and his entire world didn't have to revolve around me. It made sense – but somehow, my brain couldn't quite convince my emotions that it was at all sensible.

We'd been apart for less than a fortnight, and already it felt like things were unravelling. Falling apart. It was like being trapped in a tunnel, and watching a train head towards you in slow motion, knowing it was going to squash you flat as a pancake but not sure how to stop it, or get out of the way. It was pathetic; I was pathetic. And honestly, what did it say about our relationship? That we couldn't even get through this smallest of challenges?

So far, everything between us had been blissful, but we'd never really been tested, had we? What did this mean for our future? How would we cope with more time apart, or busier schedules, or the demands of being married? How would we deal with having kids, and sleepless nights, and babies with colic?

OK, so I might have been getting a bit ahead of myself there, but that was the future we'd both said we wanted. And it was the future I'd counted on; assumed we'd be strong enough to build together. What if I was wrong, about everything?

I'd started crying by this stage, and was trying to hush it up so he didn't notice. I felt like enough of a loser without throwing blubbering into the mix.

'What about next week?' he said, just before I'd decided to make my excuses and hang up. 'Vella's off to Milan for a fashion show, and the band are taking a day off then. I was going to spend it working on the tracks we've recorded, but. . .but I can put that off. I can catch up later. I can. . .well, I'll sort it out. Because I really need to see you, too. I miss you so much. Where are you next week – Chicago?'

'Yes,' I said, snivelling a little and tugging a wodge of loo roll off the holder to blow my nose with. 'Chicago. You'll come then? You really mean it?'

'I really mean it. I'll get Pat from the village to come and look after the animals, and I'll carve out a night. It'll probably only be one, I'm afraid, but if you want me, I'm yours.'

'Yeah,' I replied, standing up and flushing the toilet. 'Of course I want you. Let's do that. I can't wait to see you.'

'Good. I'll sort out the details and let you know. And . . . was that a toilet flushing? I thought you were running a bath?'

'Um . . . yes. I was. I wasn't on the loo having a wee or anything, honest. That wouldn't be classy. . .'

'And you, Jessy Malone, have always been class personified. . .'

I was blushing, even though I was thousands of miles away, but by the time we ended the call, I also felt so much better. Daniel was coming, and we'd sort it all out. We'd find a way through this, and we'd be fine with colicky babies, and everything in the world would be right again.

Apart from my face, I thought, grimacing in the mirror at my one-sided carpet rash. I looked like I'd had a close encounter with a sheet of sandpaper – Neale was going to kill me.

*

During that first gig in Chicago, I suddenly understood that whole Abba song, 'Super Trouper'. I was singing and dancing and doing everything I'd been doing all through the whole tour, but that night, it felt different. It felt different because Daniel was there – and somewhere in the crowd there's you.

I hadn't seen him yet, which probably wasn't surprising

given the size of the audience – I suppose I'd been so excited, I thought I'd magically develop some kind of super-trouper superpower and be able to spot his head among the thousands of other heads in the stadium.

I couldn't – I obviously wasn't going to be joining The Avengers any time soon, damn it – but I knew he was there, and that was all that mattered. Every note I sang, every step I moved, felt different – because it was all for him.

We were supposed to have met at the airport earlier, but his flight was delayed and I had to stay at the stadium, anxiously checking and rechecking my phone until the Holy Grail of all text messages landed: he was here. He was clearing customs. He was having a full-cavity body search (joke). He was in a taxi. He was at the stadium.

He was here, somewhere in that swaying, shining, light-stick waving mob, and the very thought of it made my heart sing. I tried to concentrate on what I was doing – because what I was doing was important – but part of me couldn't wait for the gig to end, so I could be back with my man. Back in those arms I'd missed so much.

Cooper had sorted him out with backstage access passes, and we had a table booked at a restaurant that Felicia had recommended – on the ninety-fifth floor of the Hancock Tower. I didn't know Chicago well – let's face it, at all – but I already knew that it was beautiful, and I'd finally be able to share one of these amazing American experiences with Daniel. I'd enjoyed it all so far, but seeing it with him would make everything ten times better. At least. Possibly a million times better.

Usually, when I come off stage, I'm adrenalized but

exhausted, running on fumes and excitement. This time, though, I was pipping to get off and meet Daniel. I thought I might actually kiss him to death.

After the final encore track, and the last bows, and the last cheers, I scampered down the steps at the side of the stage, knowing I was sweaty and probably had a bit of a pong going on, but not caring. Sure enough, as soon as I emerged into the neon-lit concrete corridor that always seem to lie behind the glamour of a stadium, I saw him.

He was waiting at the end of the passage, leaning against a wall, his leather rucksack thrown over one shoulder, checking his phone. His blond hair was a little too long, and his T-shirt was creased, and one of his Timberland boots had come unlaced. He'd never looked more gorgeous.

I paused for a moment, and felt a lump in my throat as my feelings threatened to overwhelm me. It was a bit like the emotional version of when you first put a salt and vinegar crisp in your mouth, and your taste buds go into meltdown.

I knew I loved him. I knew I'd missed him. I knew I was excited to see him, but none of that knowledge quite prepared me for the rush of love I experienced when I saw him again.

I ran down the corridor, as fast as I could in my spiky-heeled boots, and literally threw myself at him. He looked up just in time to give me a big grin as he caught me, wrapping his arms around me and hoisting me up so my legs were clutched around his waist. We bobbed around like this for a few moments, bouncing off the walls, laughing and kissing and generally celebrating the moment.

Eventually, he put me down, and I slid to my feet. I could

see that he was distracted, and looked over my shoulder to see Cooper approaching us.

He grabbed hold of Daniel in a big man-hug, which made Daniel look only a teensy bit uncomfortable. He's not really a man-hug kind of guy.

'Hey, Daniel!' he said, now shaking his hand vigorously. He was still wearing his deliberately torn T-shirt and leather trousers, covered in a sheen of sweat from our exertions on stage. 'It's so good to finally meet you in person – what did you think of your girl, then? She did you proud, didn't she?'

'Yeah,' replied Daniel, giving me a sweet sideways smile, 'she always does. Great show, Cooper – I love the new material.'

'Thanks, man, that means a lot coming from you. Anyway, I'll leave you two lovebirds to it. There'll be a bit of a party going on back at the hotel later – come and join us if you have the energy.'

He gave us a cheeky wink that actually made me blush as I realized what he meant. He assumed we'd be going straight back to the room to bang for Britain. And actually, I thought, slipping my hand into Daniel's and gripping his fingers, now I thought about it, that sounded like an excellent idea.

I was about to suggest it as Cooper waved and retreated towards the dressing rooms, but Felicia chose that exact moment to make an appearance, carrying her clipboard, earpiece and mouthpiece in place as usual – I was starting to think she'd had herself genetically modified so they were always there.

'Hey, guys!' she said, scribbling on her pad, eyes fixed downwards. I wasn't sure if she was talking to us, or into her mouthpiece, and Daniel looked similarly confused.

She looked up, frowning. Oh. She *was* talking to us.

'Hey, Felicia! This is Daniel!' I said quickly, trying to make up for what might have appeared like a bout of rudeness, pointing at him unnecessarily.

'I guessed that from the way you were molesting him,' she replied, in her sarcastic New York drawl. 'Great to meet you, Daniel. OK, the table's all booked, and a car's coming for you in twenty minutes – is that enough time for you to get changed, Jessy?'

I nodded, my dreams of a bonk-fest dashed. Felicia had organized this for us, so I couldn't say no, and besides, it would be fun. Daniel was probably starving, and I certainly was, and it would be a chance for us to spend some time together seeing the city.

'Meet you outside?' I said to him, staring into his eyes and trying to tell him how much I loved him with a look.

He squeezed my fingers, and said: 'I'll be waiting. Give my love to Neale – hopefully I'll get a chance to see him before I leave tomorrow.'

As soon as he said that, I felt my mood dip. Tomorrow. He'd be leaving again, practically as soon as he got here.

'Don't look like that,' he said, lowering his head to kiss me. 'We still have tonight.'

He was right, I thought – it was silly to spoil the time we did have by fretting about the time we didn't have. His delayed flight had cut into our schedule, but we still had a lovely meal to look forward to, and a whole night together in the hotel. I could go with him to the airport tomorrow, as well. It wasn't much, but it was a shedload better than nothing – and for now, it would simply have to be enough.

I nodded, tiptoed up to kiss him again, and then wandered down towards the dressing rooms. I looked back as I went, and saw that he was already back on his phone, running his fingers through his hair and looking tired. Bless him.

I showered and got changed in record time, dressed in comfortable skinny jeans and a sexy top that showed a bit of boobage, completed it with some strappy sandals, and was ready to go. My hair was still on the damp side, but I was sure he'd forgive me.

Daniel was quiet on the ride through the city, but at least he was here, next to me, holding my hand. We both looked out of the windows of the sleek limo Felicia had kindly booked for us, enjoying the views of the river and the skyscrapers and the parks we passed.

By the time we were in our seats at the restaurant, though, he was still quiet. That was OK, I told myself – we were a couple. We were engaged. We could ride out a bit of quiet time, especially when it was accompanied by these absolutely gorgeous views of the city. We were so high up it felt a bit like we were eating pasta in heaven, sipping our wine and gazing down at the lit-up cityscape below.

'It's gorgeous, isn't it?' I said, gesturing outside. 'I never knew cities could be so beautiful until I came to the States.'

'Yeah, it's amazing. This must have been quite an experience for you, seeing all these cities, visiting all these places you've only ever seen on the TV?'

'Oh God, yes! That's exactly it! Especially New York. . .'

I wittered on for a while, telling him about New York, and Miami, and Boston, and all the adventures we'd had in those places. There was a lot to tell, and as the words spilled from my mouth, I realized that I'd been feeling so lonely without him. That without him to share it all with, it hadn't been anywhere near as amazing as it could have been with him at my side.

I also realized, as I finished my second glass of wine, that although he was listening, and nodding in all the right places, he seemed distant. A little disconnected. As though perhaps his head was elsewhere.

I clamped down on an immediate surge of anxiety – was he thinking about Vella? Was he wishing he was with her? Was I boring him rigid? Had he come here to end things because he'd fallen madly in love with a German soul singer?

Or was I being completely bonkers? That, all things considered, seemed the most likely option. I reminded myself of how tired I'd been that first night in Miami. How the jet lag had caught up with me, and stopped me partying – almost stopped me functioning, in fact. He'd had a long, exhausting day, after what was probably a long and exhausting work schedule.

He'd come all this way for me – just for one night. If he was a little bit less than enthralled by my conversation, surely I could forgive him?

'Hey,' I said, finally, as one of his blinks seemed to stretch into what might have turned into a snooze, 'so tell me about how things have been going at home. How's Vella's album coming along?'

His eyes snapped open, and I saw him trying to refocus.

'Oh, great. The songs are brilliant, but not so brilliant I couldn't make them better, if you know what I mean? There was room for me to work on them, and she's . . . well, she's very open. To ideas. Willing to try new things. So that's all good. It's been busy, that's all. Having people staying there is a lot more time-consuming than I expected. There are parties. In the farmhouse. I'm used to watching *Homeland* and going to bed, but those guys. . . Well, their definition of "bedtime" is a lot different than mine. I don't know how they do it.'

Probably with the assistance of copious amounts of drugs, I suspected, but didn't say it out loud. Daniel wasn't naive – he'd grown up in Liverpool, and worked in the music industry all of his adult life. The fact that he was clean-living didn't blind him to the fact that everybody else wasn't – but presumably, they'd been respectful enough not to turn the farmhouse into a crack den, or snort cocaine from rolled-up tenners on the pine kitchen table.

Vella, I told myself, was probably a cranked-up drug-whore who would look fifty by the time she was thirty. Especially when all her teeth fell out. It's amazing how bitchy I can be, without even trying.

'I can imagine,' I said, pushing the last bit of food around on my plate. 'You must be wiped out. I can't tell you how much I appreciate you coming to see me.'

I was expecting, perhaps, a certain response to that. Maybe something along the lines of 'How could I not? I can't live without you.' Or at the very least, 'You're welcome.'

Instead, he just nodded, did another long blink, and jumped slightly as his phone pinged. It had been doing that throughout the night, although to be fair, he always ignored it – it might have pushed me over the edge if he'd been constantly checking the bloody thing.

The waiter approached to clear our plates, and asked if we wanted to see the dessert menu. And while I am not the kind of girl who ever willingly says no to a nice pudding, I could tell from Daniel's slightly pained expression that he really didn't want to stay. He was visibly wilting now, his body completely unadjusted to the new time zone, and to its travels.

'No, thank you,' I replied, smiling and reaching for Daniel's hand. 'Just the bill, if that's all right.'

Daniel looked immediately relieved, and added: 'I can't believe you said no to pudding.'

'I know,' I said, gathering my bag and coat together. 'If ever you needed it, there's proof of how much I love you.'

I'd told the limo driver to have the rest of the night off, and we got a cab back to the hotel. I wondered, briefly, if the taxi driver recognized me, and if I'd end up as one of his 'back of my cab' stories. I gave him a big tip anyway – big tips had funded my singing lessons as a kid back in Liverpool, so I always paid it forward.

We went straight up to my suite, bypassing the party that I could see booming away in the hotel lobby. Don't get me wrong, those parties are a lot of fun, but I most definitely had different priorities that particular night. There would be other parties, but my next evening with Daniel could be weeks away.

He sat down heavily on the bed as soon as we got into the room, and I gave him a long, simmering kiss as he sat there.

'That was nice,' he said, when I finally pulled away. 'I've missed that. Gandalf tries, but he's no match. Look, Jessy, I'm sorry I'm so tired.'

'That's OK, I understand. But you're not too tired, I hope?'

I replied, heading towards the en-suite bathroom. I had weeks' worth of sexual tension stored up and ready to go, and had even bought a sexy new outfit to wear for the occasion.

'Of course not – I'm a bloke,' he answered, grinning at me and kicking off his boots.

I muttered a little 'yay!', and trotted off into the bathroom, feeling as giddy as Bambi. I quickly brushed my teeth, and stripped off my clothes, dumping them in a heap on the floor. I had my fancy underwear all ready – black lace bra and knickers, suspenders, lace-topped stockings, the full works. Once I was dressed – or undressed – I spritzed on some perfume, and checked myself out in the mirror. I looked good, so good that I gave myself a quick thumbs-up, before opening the door. Tonight, I thought, was going to be a hell of a night. . .

I emerged into a now-darkened room – he'd switched all the lamps off, presumably to make it more romantic. Only the light from the bathroom spilled out, casting a pale orange glow around me. Around the bed. Around my Daniel.

Who was, I saw, already under the duvet. Fast asleep. And snoring.

*

As locations went, it didn't get much better. I was sitting on the outdoor terrace of our hotel in San Francisco, enjoying mid-morning sunshine and gazing out over the Golden Gate Bridge.

But as moods went, it couldn't really get much worse.

'Come on, Jess, give me a smile,' said Cooper, peering at

me over his coffee cup. It was our first morning here, and we were taking a late breakfast outside. Three more sell-out nights started this evening, but for once, I just couldn't feel excited about it.

I looked at Cooper, and gave him a huge and dazzling and obviously fake smile. The kind people do when it's announced that they've not won an Oscar, and have to look happy for the winner while they secretly want to stab them.

'Ouch!' he said, backing away as though I'd threatened him with physical violence. 'I've changed my mind. Don't smile at me again, it might actually kill me.'

He looked so horror-struck that it actually made me smile for real, which was a minor miracle. I'd been on something of a downward spiral ever since Daniel's visit, and I kept telling myself that I really needed to get a grip.

Nothing bad had happened, after all. In fact, nothing much at all had happened – and perhaps that's what was bothering me. I'd been disappointed when I came out of the bathroom dressed as a sex kitten only to find him in a coma, but I understood. I may have shed a few tears – as much in frustration as anything else – but I understood. The poor man was wiped out.

So I'd taken off the fancy underwear, cleaned the make-up from my face, and tiptoed back into the room. I slipped under the covers with him, and wrapped myself around him as closely as I could without waking him up. Not that there seemed to be much risk of that – he was out for the count. I lay awake for what felt like hours, but was probably minutes, feeling weird – I was next to him, physically, my head on his chest and my hand touching his shoulder, but somehow it still felt as though he was in a different continent. We hadn't quite had time to reconnect.

When I woke up the next morning, I felt optimistic again – which might partly have been due to the fact that Daniel was already awake, and clearly feeling a lot more lively than he had the night before. We'd made love, and it was sweet and gentle and precious, but over way too fast. Not the sex part – there wasn't any problem there – but the aftermath. The snuggle time. The lying in each other's arms, talking nonsense and giggling. The stuff you take for granted when you live together, or even in the same country.

'God, I needed that,' he'd said, rolling onto his back, laughing. 'It's been way too long.'

'I know,' I'd replied, nestling into him, hooking my leg over his stomach. 'I thought we might have forgotten what to do.'

'Nah. It's like riding a bike.'

'Ha!' I said, slapping him on the chest. 'Some women might take offence at that, you know!'

'I was counting on you not being most women,' he replied, twisting round to pick up his phone from the bedside cabinet. He looked at the time – just after 10 a.m. – and pulled a face.

'I've got to be at the airport for noon,' he said, quietly, as though saying it quietly helped.

'Oh! I thought . . . I thought you'd be going later in the day. I'd hoped we could have lunch, or see the sights, or have more sex, or . . . something . . . '

'I'm sorry, babe,' he'd said, kissing the top of my head. 'But I really need to get back. I know it's not perfect, and I wish I could stay longer, but I've got so much to do.'

Inside, disappointment flooded through my body like an ice bath, but on the outside, I managed to hold it together. Just about.

'That's OK, I understand. And thanks for coming.'

I looked up at him to see if I'd pulled my mature act off, but I could see that his head was already somewhere else. Again, I got that sensation of us being physically close but emotionally distant – it was as though a barrier had built up between us that neither of us was willing to discuss. And even if we were, there was no point doing it now – it would only result in us parting on a sour note, and feeling even worse.

In the end, I'd waved him off at the airport, looking on as he walked away, phone glued to his ear already. It was as though he'd never even been.

His visit was supposed to have made things better between us, but instead I felt awful. Watching him trail off into the distance, I don't think I'd ever felt so lonely. I desperately wanted to chase after him, or talk to my mum, or go out for a drink with Vogue. None of which I could do, because I had to be back at the stadium and ready for rehearsals for that night's gig.

Now, several days later, we'd settled back into that deeply unsatisfactory pattern of living in different time zones with missed calls and friendly texts. It wasn't really surprising that I was feeling a little on the blue side – but none of that was Cooper's fault, I reminded myself.

I was young, healthy and here – in the California sunshine – and I should be making the most of it.

'I'm sorry, Cooper,' I said, twisting the end off a croissant, viciously. 'I'm a pain in the arse at the moment, I know. Just ignore me.'

'As if I could!' he replied, pouring me another coffee. He was dressed in denim shorts and no top, which, under any other circumstances I'd have found distracting, but I was too sad to even lech.

'What's wrong, sweetie? Is it Daniel? Things not any better?'

'Not really, no . . . I'm not sure his visit did much other than point out the fact that things aren't brilliant. I assumed we'd just slip back into being . . . ourselves, you know? And to some extent we did. But he felt . . . different, somehow.'

'Are you sure it's just him who's different, Jessy? How do you feel about things?'

He leaned back in his chair, sunglasses propped up on his blond hair, and looked at me intensely. I suppose he might have a point, and maybe, if I was entirely honest with myself, part of the problem lay at my door. I'd been so caught up in my own life, in the tour and partying, that I'd lost track of Daniel's. I only ever thought of Vella in relation to my jealousy issues, not as his work, and had been seeing his career as a hindrance to our relationship – when in reality, mine was the one causing the problems.

'I don't know, it's all so messed up. Everything between us has always been so relaxed, so genuine. I mean, we've known each other since we were babies! I think being with him and things feeling strained was worse than not being with him at all. It's made me unsettled, and made me feel weak. Like I don't have any control over anything.'

I stuffed half a croissant into my mouth to stop myself saying anything more. Nobody likes a whinger.

'I get that. But I think you're overreacting. You two have a relationship you've built over decades, and it'll take more than a month of things going wrong to destroy that. You need to have a little faith.'

Hmmm. Again, I knew he was probably right, but just then, it didn't feel like it. And I got the feeling that talking about it wasn't going to help. I needed to keep busy, stay focused, take my mind off everything. I chewed down the croissant, gulped in some extra coffee, and stood up. The view, I thought, glancing over the terrace again, really was astonishing.

'I will. But for now, maybe I'll go shopping. If all else fails, credit cards prevail.'

'Cute – did you make that up?'

'No, it's one of Neale's. Talking of which, I think I'll go and find him. Last night, I invited him and JB out to dinner, and then cancelled at the last minute, just so they'd have some time on their own. They're driving me nuts – they're so obviously right for each other, but neither of them seems to have the guts to make it happen. So I ended up in my room eating room service on my own, while they were hopefully enjoying a romantic dinner for two.'

'Well,' replied Cooper, popping his shades back on and propping his bare feet up on the table, 'I've known JB for a long time, and to be honest, when he wants something, he usually just goes out and gets it. . .'

'Hopefully,' I said, picking up my bag and preparing to leave, 'that's exactly what happened. Anyway, I'm off – and just to warn you, I can see Felicia on her way over. . .'

'Oh God,' he drawled, 'how close is she? Do you think I

could get away with hiding under the table and hoping she doesn't see me?'

'No. And don't be such a twat – you'd be lost without her.'

I walked away, saying a quick hello to Felicia as I passed her, and headed back into the hotel. Neale and I had adjoining rooms in this one, and we tended to leave the connecting door unlocked in case of emergencies – usually the kind that involved crisps, make-up or gossip.

My own room was uncharacteristically tidy, as I'd by now mastered the art of limited unpacking, my ever-growing stash of tatty American souvenirs in one corner. I anticipated adding a couple of Golden Gate snow globes to my haul before this run was out.

It was mid-morning, so even if Neale had been up late – fingers crossed – I decided he would probably be up and about by now. And if he wasn't, I'd wake him up using my patented Chucking a Pillow at His Head technique. Those snow globes wouldn't buy themselves.

I tried the door, and found the handle unlocked, pushing it open as I shouted: 'Rise and shine, sweet cheeks! Time for some retail therapy!'

Unfortunately for my retinas, there was absolutely no need for me to tell Neale to rise and shine. He was most definitely already risen, and was being assisted in his efforts to shine by a naked JB. I paused in the doorway, unable to move, totally horror-struck. Both of them stared at me, all three of us frozen still in shock, a tableau of bare flesh and confused expressions.

JB broke the impasse by bursting out laughing, and Neale scurried frantically to cover himself up with the sheets.

It was too late for that. I'd just seen parts of Neale that I'd never wanted to see in my entire life, and I thought my face would burn off, I was so red.

I muttered several incoherent words of apology, and made a hasty exit, almost falling over in my hurry to retreat back into the safety of my room, where there was no naked men, and I could die of embarrassment in peace.

Well, I thought, collapsing down onto the bed and fanning myself with my hands, at least they'd got their act together. I just wished I hadn't seen them in the middle of the act – I felt deeply traumatized. Served me right for not knocking, I supposed.

A few minutes later, Neale came shuffling through the door, dressed in his kimono, JB railing behind him. JB had managed to pull on his jeans, but hadn't bothered with a top. That wouldn't normally bother me at all, but now I'd seen the rest of him, any exposed flesh at all gave me flashbacks.

He was grinning from ear to ear, and obviously seeing the funny side of the whole thing. And I supposed it was kind of funny – maybe one day, like a hundred years from now, I'd even be able to laugh at it myself.

'Jessy!' said Neale, flapping away as he perched on the edge of my bed. I had my hands over my face by this stage, completely mortified. 'I'm so sorry! You poor thing, are you OK?'

'No,' I muttered from beneath my fingers. 'I think I have PTSD. I may need to see a counsellor.'

I heard the door to my mini-fridge opening, and the sound of JB cracking open a can of something. It reminded me that I probably needed a vodka. Soon.

'It can't be that bad,' said Neale, stroking my hair soothingly. 'You've seen naked men before.'

'Not two of them. At the same time. Doing sex. And never you! Never you, Neale. Oh my God, I will never be able to unsee that.'

'Come on, babe,' said JB, still sounding amused, 'some people would pay good money to see that kind of thing. . .'

'Not me! I'd pay good money not to see it!'

I finally dragged my hands away from my eyes, but could still feel a ferocious blush covering the whole of my face and neck, like prickly heat. I sat upright, and took a deep breath.

'OK. . .' I said, puffing air in and out between words. 'Aaaand breathe. . .So, first of all, I'm sorry, I shouldn't have just walked in. And second of all – hurrah! It's about bloody time!'

Neale and JB exchanged a look. It was one of *those* looks – one that said, *Shall you tell her or should I?*

'Actually, Jessy,' said Neale, popping his glasses back up his nose, 'this isn't exactly a new development.'

'What do you mean?' I asked, frowning at him.

'Well, we've kind of been together for a while now.'

'What do you mean by a while? Was it that night in the hot tub in Boston? I'd feel so much better if it was. Then it would have been worth the carpet rash.'

'Nothing would be worth that carpet rash, child! I can't believe how long it took me to cover that up, but no. It kind of started in London. The night we played strip darts.'

'Yep. I scored a bullseye,' drawled JB.

He was leaning against the wall, still semi-naked, looking relaxed and sipping a Coke. I stared at him. And then I stared at Neale. And then I felt like a huge, gigantic idiot. All this time, I'd been plotting and scheming to try to get them together, and they already were. No wonder they always seemed so relaxed in each other's company – the reason they'd seemed like the perfect couple was that they already were!

'Oh!' I said, feeling flustered and excited at the same time. 'Well, that's amazing! I mean, I feel a bit silly though – and not just because I walked in on you. But because I've been trying to fix you up, when you were already together. Why didn't you just tell me, and save me the effort?'

'Well, not to put too fine a point on it, my lovely, but you'd have been planning a wedding and signing us up for adoption agencies within minutes.'

I opened my mouth to argue with that, but then remembered that I had actually toyed with the idea of buying a new hat for their nuptials, before I even knew they were a couple. So maybe – just maybe – he had a point there.

'And it was just the beginning for us,' he continued, when he realized I was choosing to gape like a goldfish instead of replying. 'Neither of us knew what was going to happen, or where it was going to lead, or how long it was going to last. Or even if it would be anything more than a bit of harmless naked fun.

'It's turned out to be . . . well, much more than that. Although the naked part is fun. Anyway, I was going to talk to you about it, honestly. I'd planned to tell you when we were in Chicago, but then Daniel came, and you didn't seem quite yourself after that. I've been worried about you – when you cancelled dinner last night, I thought you were too depressed to be seen in public, and were locked away on your own, eating your body weight in chocolate.'

I guiltily remembered that there actually had been quite a lot of chocolate involved in last night's room service bonanza, but decided that didn't need to be mentioned. It was American chocolate, so it didn't even count.

'No,' I replied. 'I was all right, honest – I only cancelled so I could give you two a night on your own. I thought I was helping you on your way to . . . well, whatever you call that thing I saw in your bedroom a few moments ago.'

'Well, that was very sweet of you, but, as you saw, we don't really need any help on that front. Now, before we all had our nervous breakdowns about being caught with our pants down, as it were, did I hear you mention retail therapy? Because if that's what you need, then I'm very much your man.'

I glanced at JB, and watched as he crumpled up the Coke can and threw it at the bin, which was right on the other side of the room. Naturally enough, it went straight in – he was that kind of dude – and he gave a little fist pump with a heavily tattooed arm to show his happiness.

'But don't you two have stuff to do . . . couple stuff? I don't want to get in the way,' I replied. And I didn't – whatever kind of doubts I was having about my relationship with Daniel, and however desperate I was to buy snow globes, the last thing I wanted to do was intrude. Despite his earlier embarrassment, I'd never seen my friend so happy, and I'd hate myself if I dragged him down.

JB laughed, and walked over to ruffle my hair, like I was a little girl.

'Don't be crazy, Jess. You're part of the gang, all right? You could never be in the way. Now, why don't you two get yourselves out there and do some serious damage to the stores of San Fran? I'm perfectly happy to go to the gym, get drunk, and watch *The Real Housewives of Beverly Hills*. That Lisa Vanderpump is my all-time idol.'

He ambled towards the connecting door, pausing only long enough to give Neale a humdinger of a kiss on the way.

'I'll see you later, all right? Then we can pick right up where we just left off,' he said, before leaving. Neale stared after him, blushing as much as I had earlier. They might have been together a while now, but he was clearly still in the grip of first love. I couldn't help but smile at my loved-up, kimono-wearing pal – it was all so sweet.

Neale turned back to look at me, biting his lip.

'So,' he said, after I raised my eyebrows at him, 'I suppose you're going to want to know every last detail, aren't you?'

*

I did find out every last detail. Well, the censored version at least – I covered my ears and sang the chorus from Katy Perry's 'This Is How We Do' very loud every time it got too personal. I mean, I was interested, but there were limits, you know? I settled for understanding that Neale was over the moon – 100 per cent happy; totally ecstatic; thrilled beyond belief.

For the first time ever, in fact, Neale was in love, with a man who loved him back. They also, I couldn't help but hear

– before Katy kicked in and drowned out the details – had a tremendous sex life.

I was genuinely delighted for them, and our whole shopping morning was punctuated by me randomly hugging him and squealing like an overexcited schoolgirl. My own love life might be limping along at the moment, but at least one of us had good reason to be wearing a smug smile – and it really couldn't have happened to a nicer guy. Neale had helped me through so many dark times I'd lost count – he'd listened to my whining, he'd given me great advice, he'd held my hair back when I was sick in the loo, and he'd put my make-up on the next day to help me look sensational again.

He was the complete package, and I couldn't have been happier for him. We celebrated with several rounds of coffee, cake and, once it felt like a civilized time to crack open a bottle, some champagne. I think he was relieved to have the cat out of the bag, and reverted to his usual light-hearted, gossipy self, with occasional spells where he just stared off into the distance, and I knew he was in some kind of loved-up trance, wondering how he ever got so lucky.

I understood that loved-up trance. I'd been in that state a lot myself, with Daniel. OK, so right now wasn't one of those times, but I'd been there – I knew how it felt. That amazing rush of love and affection and lust, the way every minute spent away from that other person felt like a minute wasted. The way you simply couldn't wait to be with them again, and found yourself pining after only a few hours apart.

After lunch, and shopping, and a whole lot of giggling, I deposited Neale back at the hotel before I went off to find

Felicia and Cooper for our soundcheck. As soon as the suite door closed behind me, I heard the two of them laughing, and it made me smile. They seemed so utterly relaxed around each other – just so very right together.

I made sure, this time, that I locked the connecting door, and paused for a moment before I went back out into the real world. I looked at my phone, and saw a message from Daniel.

'Rainy day here,' it said. 'Hope it's better with you xxx.'

Something about that – despite the kisses – made my heart sink a little bit further. I mean, I knew the excitement and giddiness of the first flush of love didn't last for ever. I knew that every couple – even Neale and JB – would eventually settle down into something calmer, something more balanced. You couldn't maintain the insanity of infatuation for too long, or you'd simply burst with the frenzy of it all.

That had been starting to happen a little, I supposed, with me and Daniel. We had our domestic life together – the farm, the animals, cooking and watching TV, snuggling up on the couch, the familiar rhythms and rituals of daily living. And I'd been happy with that – I loved it, in fact. We both had careers that were technically on the glamorous end of the social spectrum, and it was actually a blessed relief to come home to a normal life together.

I'd been more than ready for that – for some boring domesticity; for nothing more exciting than burning the toast at breakfast and wondering how many eggs the chickens would lay that day. I'd been ready to settle down – which was a good thing, considering the fact that we'd got engaged.

But now here I was, on the other side of the world, feeling

like I'd completely lost touch with him. That our lives had somehow skidded off in opposite directions, and we'd lost that closeness. That intimacy. Now, it seemed, we were reduced to sending each other bland text messages about the bloody weather. How very English of us.

'Nice and sunny,' I typed back. 'Love you xxx.'

I knew, as I tapped out the words, that it was true – I did love him. Of course I did. But this time apart seemed to have changed both of us, or at least made us ask some questions about our life together. Questions I didn't think had been completely answered, and were left hanging over our heads like the rain clouds Daniel was talking about. They might get blown away, or they might suddenly burst and drench us both.

I shook the thought off, knowing it would lead nowhere good, and gathered my bag and grabbed a bottle of water from the mini-fridge. I was still hearing the screeches of laughter floating through from the room next door as I headed down to the foyer.

I'd kept busy during the morning by going shopping with Neale, and now I had work to do. It was probably for the best. Apart from anything else, I'd die of embarrassment if I stayed upstairs any longer, listening to Neale and JB getting jiggy with it. I was thrilled about his new-found happiness, but, if I'm entirely honest, it was also making me even more sad about my new-found lack of it.

I emerged from the lifts – or elevators, as I'd never remember to call them – into the lobby. It was bright and airy, all fresh flowers and white marble, and I tried to take a moment to look around and take it all in. This tour was so hectic, our schedule so jam-packed, that I'd started to take it all for granted – the amazing hotels, the brilliant cities, the awe-inspiring concerts. I suppose you get used to anything if you do it enough times, but I didn't want to reach that stage yet. I didn't want to be a cynical and battle-scarred showbiz professional – I still wanted to be able to look around me and think, *Wow – look at that!*

One of the first things I noticed, once I'd taken in the decor, was Felicia. She was standing with her back to me, wearing her usual uniform of skinny jeans, a rock T-shirt and black Converse. Her dark hair was flowing down her back in a thick plait, and she was totally still.

I followed her gaze, and was unsurprised when I saw Cooper, down at the other end of the room, leaning against a pillar and checking his phone. The light was spilling over him like a golden blanket, making his hair glow and his handsome face shine. He looked like a statue from some kind of legend – utterly dazzling and gorgeous.

I wandered over to her, and did that little throat-clearing thing you do when you don't want to startle someone. She jumped, and looked a bit guilty, like she'd been caught out doing something wrong.

'Why don't you just tell him?' I said, gesturing to Cooper.

She immediately blushed, and started to bite her lip. 'Tell him what?' she asked, quietly.

'Tell him how you feel.'

She stared at me, and I could see all the confusion swimming over her face – I suspected she was debating whether to blow me off, pretend not to know what I meant, or just ignore me.

All of the little techniques we use in life to protect ourselves from things that could potentially hurt us.

Instead, she just gave me a sad little smile, and replied: 'Because it would destroy everything.'

I nodded, and was about to say something more, but the moment had passed – she had her phone out, and was striding across the lobby with her 'sergeant major' face back in place. I felt so sorry for her. And for me. And for Cooper – I had no idea if he even suspected how Felicia felt about him, but if she never told him, he wouldn't even get the chance to decide how he felt in return. I understood her caution, but it was so sad – such a missed opportunity for possible happiness.

That, in fact, set the mood for the next few days. If I had to describe it in emoji form, my time in San Francisco would be sad face all the way. Even though the concerts were hugely successful, and the city was beautiful, and Neale and JB's news had boosted my spirits, I still couldn't quite shake the mood.

Despite the triumphant gigs and the whirl of media attention and the sheer adrenaline rush of performing, I felt off-key. A bit drained. Like a wonky table that needs a beer mat under its leg to stay straight.

Maybe, I thought, I'd always felt a bit like that. And maybe Daniel had been my beer mat. No wonder I felt unsteady without him.

On the last night of our San Francisco run, I ended up joining the rest of the gang at an after-show party in a restaurant near the hotel. I wasn't really in the mood for it, but was trying not to be a negative nelly, as my mum would have said.

Anyway, it was a good bash, and I was at least attempting

to enjoy myself. There was food and drink and probably, for some people at least, a few narcotics to keep them partying.

I was sticking to water, because the last thing I needed in my state of mind was a hangover the next morning. Anyway, I was still on something of a high from the gig, so for the time being, I was perfectly capable of partying without assistance. Or at least capable of watching other people party.

The dancers, as ever, were taking centre stage, letting loose and getting limber to the sound of the tracks the DJ was artfully selecting. Cooper was busy chatting away to the backing singers, and Felicia was tucked away in a quiet corner, keeping a watchful eye on things and staying alert to any problems. She was so good at her job – if she'd been in charge of Cinderella that night at the ball, there's no way she'd have been out past midnight.

Neale was, as was usual these days, sitting on JB's lap. Since they'd confessed to me, they'd decided to go public with the rest of the crew, and as soon as they were in a private place, somewhere safe from paparazzi and stray mobile phone photographers looking for a scoop, they were all over each other.

He caught my eye, and I raised my bottle to him, giving him a jaunty little salute. At least I hoped it looked jaunty – that was what I was aiming for.

Neale immediately jumped up from JB's knee, and scooted over to sit with me.

'I think you've forgotten how to use a chair, Neale,' I said, grinning at him as he settled beside me. 'You seem to be surgically attached to JB's lap these days. I'm a bit worried you're turning into Siamese twins.'

'Well,' he said, gesturing over to his boyfriend, 'can you blame me?'

I took a moment to look JB over, admiring his muscular arms and wild hair and sexy tattoos. He noticed my scrutiny, and gave me a saucy wink that, if it could talk, would have said something along the lines of: 'Like what you see, sister?'

'You make a fair point,' I replied, holding my hand up for a high five. He did so enthusiastically.

'So,' said Neale, pointing at my bottle, 'I see you're opting for the heavy stuff. You need to be careful with that, you know. Too much water can have dire consequences.'

'You're telling me! I've already been for about seven wees tonight! Vodka definitely takes longer to chug through my system.'

'Nature's way of telling you you're a born piss-head . . . So, anyway, we have a few days off now, before Los Angeles, don't we? What are you planning?'

'Oh, I don't know,' I replied, staring off into the distance. 'Maybe I'll go and visit some vineyards. Or drive to Big Sur. Or maybe . . . just sleep. I'm not sure yet. What about you?'

Normally, I'd be able to count on Neale to be my partner in crime during our downtime, but these days, I didn't want to take it for granted. His head – and other body parts – were definitely elsewhere, and I didn't want to get in the way of that.

'Bit scary actually,' he said, peering at me over his glasses. 'I'm meeting JB's parents.'

'Wow! That's huge! How are you feeling about it?'

'Terrified,' he replied firmly, his toes tapping on the floor nervously as he thought about it. 'I've never been taken home to meet the family before and, as you know, I've certainly never taken anyone home to meet mine.'

'You have absolutely nothing to worry about,' I said, reaching out and patting his hand. 'They'll see how happy you are together, and they'll love you for bringing such joy into their son's life.'

'You think?' he asked, almost shyly.

'I don't think, I know. Just be yourself. You two are perfect together.'

'Thank you, Jessy . . . and . . . well, I did have a suggestion. About what you could do on your days off.'

'Oh yes?' I asked, sounding cautious. I really didn't want him to be feeling so sorry for me that he suggested I come with them. I mean, I liked hanging out with JB and Neale, but that would be taking it a bit too far.

'Yes. I think you should go home. Just catch a flight, tonight if you can, and go home. Spend some time with Daniel. Sort things out. You've not talked about it – and I know why, you're being a dear and you think you'll bring me and JB down from our love cloud! – but I know you too well not to see that you're upset. Just take the time, Jessy, and go home. It's nearly Christmas after all.'

I looked at him, and thought about it. I looked across at Cooper, and at Felicia, who was watching him like a mother bear, and at all the people I'd had so much fun with on this tour.

I liked them all, I really did. And I'd had an amazing time so far. But Neale was right: I was upset. I was feeling insecure, and fragile, and homesick.

I could do it, I told myself. I had the money these days. And nobody would need me until we were due to play LA, in three days' time.

Home.

God, that had such a nice ring to it.

Chapter 11

I landed in London feeling both exhilarated and exhausted. As soon as Neale had suggested I make a flying – literally – visit back home, I knew it was the right thing to do.

All my instincts told me that I needed to at least give it a go. I still loved Daniel, and was sure he still loved me. He was my fiancé, the love of my life, and I needed to see him. Anyway, the alternative was too awful to contemplate – spending three days loafing around California feeling sorry for myself. That would be too pathetic for words, even by my standards, and I've set some pretty impressive standards when it comes to being pathetic, believe me.

So I'd done the most sensible thing possible – and asked Cooper and Felicia for their help. Also, you know, it seemed only polite to explain to Cooper what I was planning. It was his parade I was running out on, even though I promised him I'd be back in time for the next leg of the tour.

'I know you will, babe,' he'd said, holding my hand and squeezing my fingers. 'I trust you. And I know you need to do this. I really hope it fixes things between you two.'

'Oh God, me too,' I'd replied, ecstatic and nervous at the prospect. 'I've just been so . . . I don't know. Worried. About everything. About the way I'm feeling, and the way he's feeling, and about Vella, all of it.'

'I know you have, and this is the right thing to do. But I have to say this, kiddo – I don't think you need to be worrying about Vella. Daniel would never cheat on you.'

I must have looked less than convinced by this statement, which made me feel ashamed of myself – what had Daniel ever done to deserve my mistrust, this lack of faith? Nothing at all. I was just being rubbish.

'Of course not,' I replied, aiming for confident but falling somewhere nearer to desperate.

'He'd have to be crazy to cheat on someone like you,' Cooper had said, obviously picking up on my insecurities. 'You're beautiful and funny and kind and talented and smart, and I'm sure he knows how lucky he is.'

I nodded my thanks, and was stupidly grateful for his attempt to boost my confidence.

'You're just saying that to make sure I don't jib off the rest of the tour,' I said, trying to smile my way through it.

'Nope. I'm saying it because I mean it. Anyway, let's go see Felicia. If anyone can get you home in a hurry, it's my Girl Friday.'

And – obviously – he'd been completely right. His Girl Friday was possibly the most awesome woman I'd ever met, I'd decided. Within an hour, she had me packed, booked on a flight, and in a limo to the airport. She'd even arranged for a car to meet me at Heathrow, and managed to lay her hands on a chunk of cash in sterling instead of dollars. Not only did she do all of this, she actively seemed to enjoy it.

She'd come back to the hotel with me to get my bag – not that it contained much but clean knickers and some snow globes – and gave me a quick hug outside as the car drew up to collect me.

'Good luck, Jess,' she'd said, opening the limo door for me. 'Not that you'll need it. It'll all be fine. See you soon, OK? I'll be in touch. Make sure you get some sleep on the plane.'

'OK, I kind of wish you were coming with me though, then nothing would dare go wrong!'

'Ha, that is *so* not true! And anyway, how would Cooper remember to take his vitamins without me to remind him?'

I wasn't sure if she was joking or not, until she gave me a little wink to show she was.

I'd waved goodbye to her as we drove away, smiling at the thought of her 'being in touch' – of course she'd be in touch. There would be a million things she'd want to make sure I was doing – mainly arriving back in Los Angeles in time for the next gig. I was so grateful for all her help, and part of me really did wish she was coming with me – I was sure life in general would always be easier if I had my very own Felicia around.

I slept on the overnight flight, which I hadn't expected. Right up until the moment when the nice stewardess lady turned my seat into a bed, I'd felt wired, too pumped up to rest. But the minute my head lay on the pillow, I was out like a light. And I stayed out for the entire journey, sleeping better than I had for ages; or at least since Daniel left after that one awful night in Chicago.

Maybe it was simply the fact that I'd made a decision – that I was taking action instead of sitting around waiting for things to get better on their own – that allowed my mind to relax. Or maybe it was just because Felicia had instructed me to, and I didn't dare disobey her.

Either way, by the time I arrived in London, I was ready. Knackered – because long flights will do that to you, even when you're asleep – but ready. Ready to go home. Ready to see Daniel. Ready to put everything right between us. Perhaps I was aiming high, but I felt bizarrely optimistic about it all. I was sure that there wasn't anything fundamentally wrong with what we had going, we'd just hit a speed bump, that was all. Looking at JB and Neale together, I'd been reminded of how much fun being in a relationship could be, and that's what we needed to rediscover.

My body was telling me it was the morning, but of course it was well after seven in the evening by London time. It was just about light outside, but the rain Daniel had mentioned was still going strong, and the driver who had met me at the airport held an umbrella over my head as we walked to the waiting car. A big minivan drove past us, splashing us both with a muddy puddle, soaking my bare legs and sandal-clad feet. Ah, England – how I'd missed it!

I switched off as we started the drive to the farmhouse, and had a small internal debate with myself about whether I should have told him I was coming. I hadn't, and I told myself it was because it all happened so fast, but really, nothing happens too fast for you to send a quick message, does it? 'On my way home – get the kettle on' – that kind of thing? It only takes seconds.

But for some reason I'd chosen not to. Partly, it was because

I wanted to surprise him. I wanted to see the look on his face when I walked through the door, and laid a great big smacker on his lips. I didn't care if he was working, or in the studio, or in the middle of some top-level music producer meeting with Pharrell and Jay-Z and the reincarnation of Elvis Presley – I was going to kiss his face off, simple as.

Partly, if I was totally honest, I also didn't warn him because I didn't want him to be able to tell me not to come. I didn't want to hear that he was too busy, or that he wouldn't be finished work until midnight so maybe I should stay in town, or anything like that. I knew that was selfish, that I was disregarding what he might have going on in his own life, and expecting him to fall in with my crazy plans, but I made an executive decision not to care. Sometimes, you just can't fight the crazy, and this was definitely one of those times. I needed the crazy, and I hoped he did too.

By the time we escaped the sprawl of London and started driving down the familiar winding country lanes of the South Downs, it was getting properly dark. It gets darker in Sussex than anywhere else I've ever been – once you're away from the neon glow of the cities, and the night sky is uninterrupted by street lights, it's almost entirely black. The car headlights shone on the hedgerows and small rows of cottages that lined the roads, occasionally settling on the big eyes of a startled fox, eating up the miles and taking me ever closer to home. To Daniel.

By the time we were in the nearest village, and passed the small farmhouse where our neighbour Pat lived, her Christmas wreath already out on the door, I was bubbling with excitement. Literally wriggling around in the back seat with glee. Every familiar landmark I saw – the postbox, the T-junction that led to the garage, the ruins of the old castle in the field next to ours – felt like a massive step in the right direction. I didn't think it was possible to get excited about seeing a hoarding advertising the county show, but it was – because it all signified that I was nearly home.

It all meant that before long, we'd drive through the gate that always needed oiling, up the gravel drive, and right to the farmhouse, with its big red door and its always-smoking chimneys. That I'd be able to see Gandalf and all the chickens.

Mainly, of course, that I'd finally be able to see Daniel again, and tell him how much I loved him, and how sorry I was that things had been so hard, and how much I wanted everything to go back to normal again.

We'd make love, and sleep in each other's arms, and wake up to an entirely new and improved reality – and by the time I had to leave again, to fulfil my commitments to Cooper, we'd be back on solid footing.

It would, I told myself as the gate-that-needed-oiling hovered into view, all be OK. Better than OK: it would be brilliant.

We drove through the gate, and I scanned the parking area outside the farmhouse. Daniel's black jeep was there, which I realized was a relief – I'd not consciously allowed myself to think about what I'd do if he wasn't there, which of course was a very real possibility. He could have been in London, or at his mum and dad's, or even abroad – which would have been something of a bummer after flying over five thousand miles to be with him.

Still, now I'd seen the jeep, I didn't need to worry. And there were no other cars parked up, which hopefully – fingers, toes and everything else crossed – meant that nobody else was there either. I knew it had been a possibility that the farmhouse would be full, and that our romantic reunion would be slightly less intimate when surrounded by a full band, technicians and Vella, but it looked as though I'd lucked out on that front as well.

It must be fate, I thought, as I tipped the driver, took the business card he handed me, muttered a few incoherent words of thanks, and climbed out of the car. The heels of my sandals immediately sank into the rain-soaked gravel, and I remembered why wellies were the preferred mode of footwear in the countryside.

I ignored my cold, damp feet, and tottered towards the door. I could see the lights on in the kitchen, and sure enough, there was smoke pouring out of the chimney. I could even hear Ruby mooing away in the barn, and the gentle rustling of the chickens in the coop. Everything was exactly as it should be.

I took a deep breath, fluffed my hair up a bit, and opened the farmhouse door. There's a big hallway just as you go in, with an ancient stone floor and masses of coats and boots and brolleys piled up in the corner. From there, there's a door that leads you into the huge farmhouse kitchen, where we spend most of our time.

I could hear some low-level R&B music drifting through, and could smell something freshly cooked – at a guess, I thought, wrinkling my nostrils appreciatively, spaghetti Bolognese. Yum!

I dumped my bag along with the other clutter in the corner, and shucked off my sandals, before walking through to the kitchen. I imagined him there, wearing his apron that says 'Kiss The Cook' on it, stirring away at the sauce, getting ready for a night in on his own. Ha, little did he know – he was in for a very different type of night! I kind of wished I was able to film his reaction as well as see it, but it would just be weird to walk in there with my phone out.

I opened the door, and a huge grin broke out on my face as I saw exactly what I'd been expecting. Sure enough, he was standing there, by the Aga, wearing his battered old Levi's and his Jack Daniel's T-shirt and his apron; his feet bare, his blond hair falling over his forehead as he concentrated on his cooking. God, he looked good.

I saw the pine kitchen table, and noticed that it was all dressed up with nowhere to go – a fancy tablecloth that I'd never seen before; our poshest wine glasses; bubbly cooling in a bucket, two places laid for dinner. There were even some gorgeous roses arranged in a vase in the middle of it all. It looked spectacular.

Someone, I thought, grinning, must have warned him. Probably, I decided, as I tiptoed into the room, Neale. Yep, that must have been it. Neale had told him I was on my way, and he'd got all of this ready for me – this lovely romantic dinner for two. I reminded myself to give Neale an extra-big hug next time I saw him, because although I'd planned a surprise, this was actually so much better.

I crept up behind Daniel, and slipped my arms around his waist. I nuzzled into his neck, kissing the sensitive skin beneath his ears, and whispered: 'Hi, honey, I'm home!'

Two things seemed to happen at exactly the same time after that, and I can't possibly say which one I noticed first.

Daniel shrieked, completely shocked, and threw his wooden stirring spoon up into the air. It somersaulted around the kitchen, sprinkling drops of bright red tomato sauce everywhere and making the place look like a crime scene, finally landing on the floor with a clatter.

At the same moment as the spoon was flying over the table, the door that leads upstairs opened, and Vella walked into the room.

Vella, with dripping-wet hair, completely naked apart from a very small towel.

Chapter 12

For a moment, we all froze, dead still. Apart from the cat, that is – she was busily rushing round the room, licking up all the stray spaghetti sauce.

I stared at Vella, and she stared at me. Daniel stared at both of us, his gaze flickering between her and me and the prettily laid out kitchen table.

Then, I don't know, something in my expression must have changed – probably reflecting the completely murderous thoughts I was now having. I was hurt – devastated – and shocked beyond belief at what seemed to be happening here. But mainly, overwhelmingly, I was furious. Totally and utterly livid. All this time I'd been ignoring my instincts, telling myself I was just being crazy, reassuring myself that Daniel wasn't like other men, that he would never, ever do this to me.

And now, I found myself standing in what was technically my own home, feeling like I'd just gatecrashed somebody's hot date. Daniel was just like other men, after all. He was no better than my ex, Evan, or that slime bag Jack Duncan. In fact, he was worse – because he claimed to be better. Jack, for all his many faults, never promised me anything – certainly not loyalty or love or bloody marriage.

Daniel had promised me all of those things, which made it so much worse when it was revealed as a big fat lie. Daniel, just like Jack, was clearly thinking with his dick.

All of this must have played out over my face, because Vella simply took one look at me, and disappeared back through the door she'd come from. All that was left was a small pool of water she'd dripped on the stone floor, and the wreck of my previously stable relationship.

By the time I turned my furious gaze onto Daniel, he was walking towards me, hands in the air in a gesture of surrender, like he wanted to avoid the violence that my look must have been promising.

'Jessy, just wait,' he said, pleadingly. 'This isn't what it looks like, at all, I promise.'

He reached out to take hold of me, but I slapped his hands away viciously. I was too annoyed – too broken – to let him touch me. Possibly ever again.

'Really?' I said, my voice much calmer than I felt. 'Because this looks to me like a romantic night in for two. You've made a lot of effort here. Plus, you know, there is a naked woman walking round *our* home!'

'She wasn't naked,' he replied, frowning – and right that second, I could happily have killed him. My hands were on my hips, and I was trembling with a strange combination of righteous anger, adrenaline and exhaustion. The contrast between how I'd expected this reunion to play out and how it was actually playing out was a tough gig to handle.

'Near enough,' I snapped back, staring at him in disbelief. 'I can't believe you've done this, Daniel. I loved you. I thought you loved me. I thought you were different. But you're not. . .you're just like all the rest of them. . .'

'That's not fair, Jessy!' he answered, again trying to approach me. I trotted to the other side of the kitchen table to keep him at arm's length. I didn't trust myself to be any closer – I'd either hurt him, or collapse sobbing into his embrace, and I didn't want to do either of those things.

'No?' I replied, feeling the tears swim up now, stinging the backs of my eyeballs and spilling onto my cheeks. 'Well, maybe you wouldn't feel like being fair if you'd walked in on this little scene, or maybe you wouldn't care, who knows? We both know things haven't been right between us, and now I know why.'

'You're not giving me the chance to explain! But yeah, you're right, things have been weird. Weird, but fixable, surely? We're supposed to be getting married – and I love you, Jessy, I do! Don't let this break us apart, please. . .'

I bit my lip, and took a few deep breaths to try to calm myself down. The tears were flowing freely now, along with some random snot and half my mascara, and I probably looked about as good as I was feeling.

'I thought it was fixable too, Daniel. That's why I'm standing here. That's why I flew five thousand miles to come home, just for a couple of nights – to try and fix things. But it looks like you're doing just fine without me, doesn't it?'

I strode off towards the hallway, having no idea what I was going to do next, but knowing that I simply couldn't stay there. I was too angry and too hurt and too confused – plus Vella was still there. Unless she'd shimmied out of the window and climbed down a drainpipe, the utterly gorgeous, almost-naked, dripping-wet Vella was still upstairs. In my house. Waiting for my fiancé to sort out the situation with this screaming banshee of a woman who'd randomly turned up and ruined their lovely night in together.

I had to get away. To find some breathing space. To escape. Everything here was suddenly too much – the familiar crackling sounds of the fire; the pictures of us together stuck onto the fridge door with magnets; the framed poster of the school show we were in together back in another lifetime, when we were teenagers. Everything felt too familiar, too well-loved, too comfortable – none of which matched the way I was feeling.

I was feeling unloved, and uncomfortable, and almost out of my mind with grief and anger. I'd trusted this man, and now I felt like a fool. Maybe it had started to creep in a while ago, when I found out he'd known about Jack joining In Vogue and hadn't told me. We'd papered over those cracks, but maybe they were still there, just waiting for the chance to widen and split and open up like the gaping chasms you see in earthquake disaster movies.

Just then, I was definitely trapped on the wrong side of the chasm from Daniel, and I couldn't see a way back. If I tried to jump over it, I could fall headfirst into a black pit of despair. The only thing I could do was get away.

I ran towards the hallway, and grabbed my sandals. I hopped around on one leg, trying to get my uncooperative feet back inside the straps, holding out one hand to ward Daniel off. He was still talking, apologizing, asking for the chance to explain.

'Come on, Jessy. At least stay and listen to what I have to say! Don't run off like this!'

'Stay?' I said, looking at him in disbelief. 'Stay here? What did you have in mind? Maybe me, you and Vella could have a nice dinner together, then maybe a game of bloody Twister? Are you mad? I can't stay here, not with her. Not with you. I need to leave.'

I rooted around in my bag, and after spilling out most of the contents – lipstick, perfume, keys, random packet of throat sweets – finally emerged with a snow globe. Weird, that, as it doesn't snow in San Francisco, but there you go. That was the least of my worries.

I thrust the gift into his hands, and scurried to throw everything else back in my bag. I looked at him, and felt my resolve crack, just a tiny bit. He was furrowing his hands through his hair so much he was leaving ridged patterns, and he had tears in his eyes as well. He looked desperate and pale and sick. Part of me felt sorry for him, wanted to reach out and make it better. But part of me was also thinking it bloody well served him right.

'Please don't go. . .Don't leave things like this. . .' he said, grabbing hold of my arm and holding on tight to try and stop me flouncing out of the door.

I laid my fingers over his, and peeled them from my skin. I sucked in some air, and tried to calm myself. I knew that the sheer emotion I was feeling just then wouldn't last for ever, and that there would, eventually, come a time when I had to face all of this like a grown-up.

'Daniel, let me go,' I said, quietly. 'We can talk at some

other point. Right now isn't the time, all right? I need to go. I need to be alone. I just can't deal with this any more. Please, *just let me go*.'

*

I was back at the airport again. This was starting to feel like my second home now – or maybe my only home, if things with Daniel didn't work out.

Even thinking that made my heart ache a little bit more, but I had to face facts – our relationship was nowhere near as solid as I'd thought. I'd been imagining our future together – one that stretched for decades, and lasted as long and as well as our own parents' marriages had – and now, I wasn't so sure. About anything.

I'd ended up walking for miles in the rain, in stupid strappy sandals, just to fill in time while I waited for the driver to make his way back to me. Luckily, I'd had his business card, and he was only about forty minutes away when I called and begged him to come back.

I could, of course, have done the sensible thing, and waited for him at the farmhouse. Or at the edge of the driveway, or even in the barn. But I wasn't feeling sensible – I was feeling like I needed to put as much distance between me and Daniel and Vella as I possibly could. I needed time and space and somewhere away from Daniel so I could regain my balance, and start to lick my wounds.

He'd followed me as far as the end of the drive, pleading with me to come back, but eventually I'd simply sprinted away as fast as my high heels could carry me, along the country lane that led to Pat's house, yelling at him not to come after me. I couldn't bear to be near to him, it just hurt too much.

By the time the driver found me, I was a wet, miserable lump of humanity, perched on the little wall at the side of the road. My hair was drenched, stretched in a dripping ponytail down my back, and my feet were blistered, and I don't think I'd ever felt so rotten in my entire life. It didn't help that every time I felt cold or wet or tired, I imagined how cosy and warm and relaxed I'd have been, back in the farmhouse, if things had gone to plan. If things had turned out the way I'd desperately wanted them to.

Instead, I'd left Daniel there, in our warm, cosy, relaxing farmhouse, with Vella – and maybe she was comforting him right now. Even if what I'd walked in on had been innocent – and I really couldn't see how – then maybe now, by being such a drama queen, I'd have pushed him into her consoling arms. Maybe her consoling arms had been joined by some consoling boobs, and a consoling vagina, and they were busily banging away on the kitchen table while I traipsed around the British countryside in December catching pneumonia.

That train of thought, of course, really didn't help anything – apart from my nervous breakdown, which was coming along quite nicely, thank you. In fact, by the time I clambered into the back of the car, I'd tortured myself so much with images of Dan 'n' Vella's sexy times that I was almost as soggy from crying as from the rain.

The driver met my eyes in the mirror, looking on as I dragged my bag behind me, and said: 'Are you all right, love?'

'Oh yes, I'm fine,' I'd replied, blatantly lying. I neither looked nor felt fine, but I also wasn't going to pour my heart out to a complete stranger, kind as he seemed. Then I'd just become a really truly pathetic Back of My Car story for him to tell his friends and family.

'If you say so. . .Where to, then? Do you have family I can take you to? Can I take you home to them?'

He was obviously concerned, bless him, and wanted to deposit me safely with someone who would look after me. He was probably worried I was going to ask him to drop me off at the nearest tall building so I could take a swan dive.

I pondered where I wanted to go as I shivered in the back of his car, wiping my eyes clean with shaking fingers. Family. Home. God, that sounded nice, and I couldn't think of anything more I wanted just then than to go home.

Back to Liverpool. Back to my mum and dad and sister, and even my annoying little brother. Back to the house where I grew up, to familiar streets and sights and smells. I'd been living in what felt like another world recently – Miami, New York, California . . . even London and Sussex. How long had it been since I'd actually been *home*? Too long, I decided. But this wasn't the right time.

It wouldn't be fair to them if I suddenly and unexpectedly turned up in a snotty heap at the front door, demanding immediate cosseting and attention. Not that they'd mind – I knew they wouldn't – but it just didn't feel right.

It was also, of course, the house I'd grown up in, living next door to Daniel, and I didn't need any more reminders about that, about how far our history went back. Not while

I was feeling so low. Besides, if my dad got wind of Daniel potentially doing the dirty on me, he'd probably go right down there and have it out with him. They'd known Daniel as long as I had, and they'd been delighted when we got engaged. I think my family would feel as betrayed and hurt as I did by what had happened.

Or by what I assumed had happened. Daniel had sent me several texts and left three messages, all asking for the chance to explain. Maybe, I had to acknowledge, things weren't quite what they seemed when I walked in, but I wasn't in any state to think about that. To think about anything at all.

I was veering wildly between hating him and never wanting to see him again, and wanting nothing more than to be proved wrong and to let him talk me down from my high horse. In short, I wasn't thinking straight at all, and one of the few sensible things I could do just then was to back off, and let the whole thing simmer down for a while.

Besides, one small part of me knew, even if nothing had happened with Vella, things still weren't right. The distance between us had grown, and our lives were pulling us in different directions – mine towards Cooper and America, his towards cosy nights in with a soul-singing slapper. Ooops, bitchy! Even if he'd not actually slept with her, they were clearly close – in an intimate way that upset me almost as much as the physical act would. He'd only ever talked about her professionally, but obviously there was a lot more to their friendship – a friendship he'd definitely kept quiet about; hidden away from me, making out she was just another client when she was clearly so much more.

He'd cooked for her – in our kitchen – while she showered – in our bathroom – and waltzed around practically starkers. That was not the way Daniel usually interacted with clients, believe me. That was something very different. While I'd been away, missing him and worrying about us, he'd been developing this . . . friendship? Relationship? Romance? I had no idea, really, but I knew it upset me.

In some ways, I thought, him hiding a close friendship would be harder to handle than a one-night stand – a drunken mistake I could understand, and possibly forgive. But ongoing deception? That would be so much worse.

Things hadn't been right when he was in Chicago, and I just felt like our lives were getting invaded by tiny secrets, building up, all around us, choking out the simplicity and purity of what our relationship used to be.

I'd had enough of him, and Vella, and myself. And I'd definitely had enough of the rain.

'Take me back to the airport, please,' I said to the driver, dragging my phone out of my bag. It was mid-afternoon in the States, so I fired off a couple of messages, one to Felicia, explaining that I'd be coming back early, and one to Cooper, saying pretty much the same.

He immediately replied with a series of question marks and a sad face.

'Explain later. May need hugs,' I'd replied, with even more sad faces.

'Ready and willing,' he answered. 'Don't be sad.'

Ha! Don't be sad. Excellent advice – but completely impossible.

By the time I arrived back at the airport, Felicia had leapt into action – she'd changed my flight tickets for me, and booked me into a hotel at Heathrow, as the next flight to Los Angeles wasn't until the next morning. I had to change in San Francisco, and wouldn't be in LA until night-time the day after – my body clock was going to be all over the place.

*

In fact, I thought, as I sat in the first class lounge sipping a way-too-early mojito, it was already all over the place. I'd cleaned myself up at the hotel, and was at least looking presentable this morning – which was a good thing, as someone had definitely taken my photo on the way in. But even though I might look all right, I felt terrible – jet-lagged, exhausted, completely wrung out and drained, both physically and emotionally. That, I decided, justified the way-too-early mojito, and the fact that I was looking like a complete pop star knob by wearing shades indoors.

I was keeping one eye on my phone – the messages from Daniel were still landing, but I was following a non-opening policy for the time being to allow me to stay sane enough to survive the journey – and one eye on the departures screen when I happened to notice a familiar face walk into the lounge.

He was wearing one of those smart-casual suits without a tie that look laid-back but cost a small fortune, and was carrying a sleek black leather manbag that I recognized of old. He strolled to the bar, his phone to his ear, and cracked open one of his most charming smiles for the pretty girl serving the drinks.

I wondered, as I tried to curl up into an invisible ball, if he'd even notice me – I was wearing shades, after all. I was trying to slink out of my seat – planning something mature like locking myself in the toilets until it was time to leave – when he turned round, and spotted me.

He looked momentarily uncertain – as though perhaps he'd prefer to lock himself in the toilets as well – and then waved, and walked over.

'Jess! How lovely to see you! Are you getting the flight to LA?'

I sighed, and forced myself to smile. I had bigger things to worry about than him, I reminded myself, no matter how awkward this felt.

'Yes, Jack, I am.'

*

This was not, of course, an ideal scenario for my flight back to the States. I'd just caught my fiancé cheating – if not physically, then definitely emotionally – with another woman, in the home we shared.

I'd walked miles in the rain and caught a nasty cold, as well as given myself humongous and very ugly blisters. And now I was trapped, for hours on end, sitting next to my ex – an ex who'd shattered my self-confidence by also being in a relationship with one of my best friends behind my back.

All things considered, I was more than happy to drink the posh whisky that Jack kept pouring out for us. He was lucky I hadn't just grabbed the bottle and starting swigging away on my own.

'You didn't need to change seats and sit with me,' I said, gulping down a few searing mouthfuls. I don't really like whisky, but at least it was alcoholic.

'I know I didn't need to, but I wanted to. I thought we could catch up, and . . . well, I hope you don't mind me saying this, but you look awful. What's wrong? I know you too well not to notice, I'm afraid.'

I kind of hated him for saying that – for reminding me of something that I'd dearly like to forget. For reminding me of the fact that much as it made me shudder to remember it, we had been a couple. We'd spent months together. Endless nights in bed; countless meals in restaurants; infinite trips to coffee shops and gigs. All done in secret, but still done.

We'd been a couple, and I'd completely fallen for him – which had definitely been one of my worst errors in judgement. Until now, at least – until my latest disaster. Coming home to catch Daniel shacking up with Vella was definitely going right up to the number one spot in the Jessy's All Time Low Hit Parade.

'Oh, you know,' I'd replied evasively, determined not to end up having a heart-to-heart with bloody Jack Duncan, 'life, the universe, everything.'

'Ah,' he said, topping up my glass. 'I see. Does the "everything" cover Daniel? Because I can't imagine you getting this upset over anything less than that. You can talk to me, you know, I'm a good listener.'

The funny thing is, he was actually right about that. He was a good listener. When I'd looked back on our relationship, such as it was, it had struck me how much he'd listened – and how little he'd talked. All that time together, and he knew everything there was to know about me. Literally everything.

I, on the other hand, still knew relatively little about him – I'd never met his parents, or heard stories about his childhood, or met any friends outside the music business, or found out the name of his first dog. None of that nice, normal stuff – the stuff that builds bonds of understanding, and layers of shared intimacy.

Partly it *was* because he was a good listener, I suppose, but partly it was because he was so used to secrecy, to subterfuge, that he'd learned to habitually play his cards close to his chest. The natural inclination of the serial cheat. By hiding himself away, he became an excellent person to talk to – and it was a skill he'd clearly not lost, I thought, as his deep brown eyes gazed into mine, looking genuinely sincere and concerned.

Maybe it was the whisky, or maybe I was just desperate for someone to talk to who wasn't emotionally entangled in all of this already, but I did find myself replying: 'Yes. Daniel. I . . . well. Something happened. Or maybe didn't. But none of it was good. That's all I'm going to say on the matter.'

'That's very mysterious, and we can leave it at that. I won't pry,' he said, nodding. 'But it sounds to me like you've just made a pretty shocking discovery, Jess.'

'What do you mean?'

'Well, it sounds to me like you've just discovered that Daniel's not perfect, and it's not really fair to expect him to be, you know, because none of us are.'

'Ha,' I replied, pointing my finger at him. 'Some of you are most definitely less perfect than others. And Daniel. . .Well,

I'm not going to discuss it any further, especially not with you. Why are you going to LA anyway?'

'I'm going for In Vogue. Three new acts to check out. One of which is quite exciting, so I told Vogue I'd check him out.'

'Oh, cool. Maybe you could send me the details, I'll take a look as well. How is she, anyway? Vogue? I mean, we've chatted a bit, exchanged messages and emails and done the odd quick Skype, but it's not the same as actually seeing her. I miss her.'

I realized how true that was as I spoke the words, and was horrified to feel my eyes going wet with tears. Again. Honestly, between the ridiculous levels of alcohol consumption and the constant crying these days, I was going to end up in hospital with dehydration.

'She misses you, too,' Jack said, patting my hand and looking slightly terrified at the prospect of me going full-on girl breakdown next to him. 'But you'll be back before you know it. Your tour ends in, what, a week or so?'

'Ten days,' I said, sniffling, and necking a bit more whisky. I think I was starting to acquire a taste for it. 'LA first, then a couple of days off, then Vegas to end with.'

'There you go. Then you can come home, and sort everything out, can't you?'

I nodded, but had no idea if that was true or not. Where was home, now? And what would be left to sort out? My career was going better than I'd ever dreamed of, on that rainy day when I'd first met Jack Duncan, dressed as Elsa from *Frozen* and performing for a group of bored kids at his niece's birthday party. But everything else felt like it was in tatters. I felt cut adrift from Daniel, from my family, from *Vogue* – cut adrift and floating, like an astronaut lost in space, flailing around, looking for something to grab hold of to bring me back to earth.

I was pondering this when I realized that Jack had slipped his arm around my shoulders, and was making soothing noises in my ear. I felt his other hand stroking my knee, and immediately felt uncomfortable. Uncomfortable, and also – if I force myself to be 100 per cent honest here – a tiny bit excited. I mean, I was with Jack for a while, and whatever problems he had with relationships, the sex wasn't one of them – he was good at it, and he knew he was. He also knew exactly which buttons to press with me. Plus, yet again, I was a little bit drunk.

'Don't worry so much, Jess,' he said, his hand edging onto my thigh, his fingers tracing familiar patterns. 'You're young, just starting out in life. You shouldn't take everything so seriously. You need to relax more . . . and I do have one suggestion about that, if you're interested . . . something that certainly always helps me to chill out when I'm feeling stressed. . .'

'Oh yes?' I said, sounding as suspicious as I felt. 'Are you about to tell me you've taken up meditation?'

'No. I was about to ask you if you fancied a trip to the loo . . . the Mile-high Club is so much more fun in first class. . .'

I rolled my eyes, and 'accidentally' knocked my whisky glass off the table. It splashed exactly where I'd intended it to – all over his groin. The liquid spread over his pale-coloured suit trousers, leaving an amber stain exactly where a man wouldn't want one. Frankly, it looked like he'd peed himself.

He jumped, and dabbed at himself with a tissue, and laughed out loud, all at the same time. He didn't even seem remotely embarrassed, the smooth bastard.

'I suppose I deserved that,' he said, still sounding amused. 'I'm sorry, I just don't seem able to help myself sometimes.'

'You did deserve that, and much more. Jack, I think you've got problems, you know? We've been there, done that, and it will never be done again. You're back with Vogue now, and there is no way on God's green earth I would *ever* have anything to do with hurting that woman. Ever. The worst thing is, she seems to be under the impression that you've changed. That you meant it when you said you wanted a second chance, that you genuinely care about her and want to make a go of it.'

'I did mean it!' he said, looking flustered for the first time. 'And of course I care about her – I love her!'

'Really? Because unless I'm very much mistaken, if I'd said "yes" a few minutes ago, by now we'd be humping away like a pair of drunken rabbits in the bogs!'

'Well, I prefer to think of it as reaching new heights of ecstasy, but OK, I take your point. And maybe you're right. I was serious when I said I don't seem able to help myself. It's like I've got some kind of sexual Tourette's syndrome, or, I don't know, a sex addiction.'

'I've never been sure if that's a real thing, sex addiction,' I replied, passing him some more napkins so he could carry on drying out his pants. 'Or whether it's just an excuse for men to be complete dicks.'

'Men don't need an excuse to be complete dicks. Most of us come by that status naturally. But. . .well, I'm sorry, Jess.

You're obviously vulnerable right now, and as you said, I'm with Vogue, and despite all of that, I tried it on. Even I can see that's not right. So I'm sorry, genuinely. And I promise I'll think about what you've said, and have a serious look at my behaviour.'

'Perhaps,' I said, smiling at the thought, 'you could even take up meditation. But if you do, make sure you do it with a male teacher, all right?'

*

By the time I got to the hotel in Los Angeles I was, to put it mildly, a little on the dazed and confused side. I stared out of the car windows at palm-tree lined streets, and people sitting at tables outside bars, and neon lights, and glamour. I knew I was seeing an extraordinary place for the first time – but not a lot of it was sinking in.

Between the long flight and the whisky and the emotional turmoil, I was battered and fragile, blowing around in the wind like a lost leaf. I felt unrooted, unstable, and incapable of imagining what my future might hold – a future without Daniel.

The hurt and the pain was like a living creature deep inside my chest, banging away and trying to escape. I tried to keep it trapped, because I knew that if I let myself think about it all too much, I wouldn't be able to function. It was too raw, too big – too dangerous.

I had things to do. Hotels to check into. People to see. Sell-out stadium concerts to perform. I had to stand in front of thousands of people and transform myself into Jessika – the pop star. I needed to be spectacular, for their sake, and for Cooper's sake. None of this was their fault.

Jessy, the girl, however, was feeling less than spectacular as she traipsed her way into the beautiful hotel lobby, and went through the now boringly familiar process of swapping passport details for a room key. A couple of people approached me for photos – I was becoming increasingly well known in the States, and this now happened all the time – and I did my best. I smiled and grinned for their phones, and signed autographs, and did all I could not to let them down.

My heart, though, really wasn't in it, and I was flooded with a sense of relief by the time I managed to navigate the lifts to my suite. I just wanted to crawl into bed, switch off the lights, and pretend I didn't exist for a while. Pretend that everything that had happened over the last few days hadn't happened at all. It felt like the only way I could possibly survive this.

Fate, though, had something different in store for me. I'd taken my strappy and now completely wrecked sandals off in the lift, and as I padded wearily along the corridor to my room, barefoot, I saw there was someone sitting outside it.

I checked the number written on my check-in card, and glanced at the number on the door again. Yep, this was my room, and I was fairly certain I hadn't ordered room service delivery of a man.

As I got closer, and I stared at the hunched figure sat on the floor, leaning against my door, I realized who it was. And I felt OK about it. I'd been waiting for solitude, but now company was offered, I realized perhaps that was what I needed. I needed a familiar face; a comforting hug, a kind listening ear. I needed a friend, perhaps more than I'd ever needed a friend before.

'Hey, you,' I said, prodding him awake with my foot.

Cooper looked up, and his handsome face broke into a huge smile. Even that made me feel better – at least someone was pleased to see me. He stretched, and clambered to his feet.

'Hey back at ya,' he said, reaching out to wrap his arms around me.

I melted into the hug, and immediately felt some of the tensions and strains fade away. He's tall, Cooper, and built like you'd imagine a hunky American pop star to be built. There was just something so comforting about being snuggled up against his chest, his hands stroking my hair, and letting myself relax – letting someone else worry about me. I'm guessing that's not in the big book of feminist rules, but it's how I felt – protected, and cared for, and relieved.

Obviously, being me, I started crying straight away. I'd been holding it together for the journey – for the flight changes, the endless routine at customs, the drive here, the check-in, the posing with fans. I'd somehow, through all of that, managed not to explode in a shower of grief and anguish. But the minute someone was kind to me, the minute Cooper whispered consoling words in my ear and held me so tight, it all started to flood out.

He just let me cry, murmuring soothingly, keeping hold of me and rocking me gently. All that time spent growing up surrounded by sisters had obviously taught him a thing or two about how to handle a weeping woman.

Once the worst of it was over, he carefully disentangled us from each other, moving my hair from his shoulder and peeling my soggy face off his now equally soggy T-shirt. He took the key card from my trembling hands, and opened the door.

'Come on now,' he said, leading me inside. 'Let's get you settled.'

I sat on the bed, and tried to pull myself together, as Cooper carried out small but sensitive acts around me – switching the overhead lights off so there was just one gentle lamp glowing; adjusting the air conditioning so it got warmer; getting a bottle of water from the fridge. I saw that the rest of my luggage had already been delivered to my room, and he rooted through the cupboards until he emerged, smiling, with a pair of my pyjamas. The old, over-washed ones decorated with pictures of tiny pugs; the ones my sister Becky had bought me for Christmas a few years ago. I didn't dare to think about this upcoming Christmas.

Obviously, I had more glamorous sleepwear, but he'd managed to find exactly what I needed – the fabric version of comfort. He held them up, and laughed lightly, before disappearing off into the en-suite bathroom. I heard water running, and bottles clinking, and left him to it. Sitting there, in the dim light, sipping on the water, was about as much as I could manage right then.

'OK,' he said, trailing back into the room. He'd kicked off his sneakers and socks, and was barefoot – which I've always had this strange weakness for. It always feels weirdly intimate, seeing a man's toes. I probably have some deep-seated issues I need to talk through in therapy sessions.

'I've run you a bath,' he said, taking hold of both my hands and pulling me to my feet. 'Go and relax, get cleaned up, and put on your super-cute jim-jams. When you're done, I'll be here for you. We can talk, or not talk, whatever you need. I'll stay, or I'll go – it's up to you.'

I nodded, and muttered a pathetic-sounding thank you, and did as he said. I was extremely pliable right then, and would probably have agreed to anything he suggested – I was in a state of near collapse, physically and emotionally, and was just grateful for someone taking charge.

I felt better after a soak, especially as Cooper had made the bath lovely and hot, and poured in all the lotions and potions he could find to create a bubble paradise. Definitely a man with sisters.

I emerged feeling tired but also refreshed, and undoubtedly smelling a lot better than I did a little while ago. In fact, I smelled of roses. I roughly towel-dried my hair, gave it a quick blast with the dryer, and climbed into my pug pyjamas. I hadn't worn them on the tour – I think I'd only brought them to remind me of my family – and they still smelled of the familiar scents of my childhood home; of Fairy Non-Bio and Lenor. It was exactly what I needed.

I emerged back into the hotel room to see Cooper sprawled out on the bed. His head was on the pillow, raised up on muscular arms, and his eyes were closed. I wondered for a minute if he'd fallen asleep, and paused in the doorway, but he immediately opened his eyes and smiled at me.

'That's better,' he said, sitting upright.

'I'm sure it is,' I replied, walking over to the bed and

hovering next to it uncertainly. 'I'm fairly sure I smelled like a distillery when you first found me.'

'Yeah, a little bit,' he said, grinning, 'but that's actually one of my favourite smells, so it's all good. Do you want to talk, or do you want me to leave you to rest?'

I climbed under the covers – not for warmth, but for comfort, I suppose – and wondered how to answer that question. I didn't really want to talk – I didn't actually feel capable of it – but I also didn't want to be alone.

Neale was away meeting JB's parents, and my mum and dad would be fast asleep, and Daniel...Well, who knew what he'd be up to? That wasn't a thought worth pursuing. That left Cooper – who, on this tour, was definitely the closest thing I had to family.

'Can you stay?' I said, eventually. 'Just for a bit? I'm not sure I'm up for talking much, but it would be lovely if you could just be here?'

'Yeah, I can do that,' he replied. 'Need a hug?'

'Probably more than anything in the whole wide world right now.'

He nodded, and slipped under the covers next to me. He pulled me close, so my head was lying on his chest, and laid his hands on my head, stroking my hair. I put my arm around him and snuggled in closer, feeling the safest and most relaxed I had for weeks.

'I think,' I said, after a few minutes' comfortable silence, 'that it might be over. With Daniel. And I just don't know how to deal with that.'

'You think, or you know? Because there's a big difference, isn't there? What actually happened, if you feel up to it?'

It felt weird, lying there in the dark, talking to a man who I'd never met until a month ago, but it also felt right. Sometimes you just click with people, don't you? You know from the minute you meet them that you're going to be friends. That you can trust them. It was how I'd always felt about Neale, and Vogue, and . . . Daniel.

I explained what had happened, as quickly as I could, because I knew that if I lingered over any of the details, I'd start crying again. And I was really very, very sick of all the crying.

I felt Cooper's body tense next to mine as I reached the part about Vella appearing in her teeny-tiny towel, and he held me even tighter when I described how I'd ended up walking around on my own in the rain, lost in my own misery, waiting for my driver.

When I'd finished my sorry tale, he kissed the top of my head lightly, comfortingly, and said: 'So what do your instincts tell you?'

It was a good question, and one I probably needed to face up to.

'Well,' I replied, 'first of all, my instincts are usually crap. I have a long track record of crappy instincts – I'm always too gullible, too trusting. And maybe that's finally made me go the other way – maybe now, I'm being too quick to judge. I don't really know. To me, it looked like a romantic night in for a couple who were at the beginning of things. You know, that extra level of effort you make at the start . . . the way the table was set up, the cooking, the flowers. It felt date-y.

'But at the same time, it felt intimate. His feet were bare, he looked relaxed. And obviously, she was relaxed enough to be walking around practically naked. . .It felt like I'd intruded. Like I'd walked in on something I was never meant to see. I'm not saying they're definitely sleeping together – I still don't know for sure. But there's definitely something going on. Something close, that he's never told me about, never shared. I mean, I know I'm lying in bed with you right now, but I've never hidden the fact that we're friends. I've talked to him about you, he's met you. But seeing her there, like that, well, it felt wrong.'

I felt tired after that little speech, but also better. Somehow, saying it out loud to another person had made me feel clearer. No less hurt, but clearer.

'Jess, I'm so sorry, and there's not much I can say other than if you're right, the man is clearly an idiot. I've met Vella, and yeah, she's cute, but she's nothing compared to you. You're the real deal, and if he's too stupid to know that, then he doesn't deserve you.'

I felt my spirits lift as he spoke, and he couldn't really have said anything better. Because, you know, I'm all right. I'm not perfect. I can be annoying. I'm clumsy, and messy, and I always forget to put the milk back in the fridge. But I'm all right. And I didn't deserve this.

For the first time since the whole mess had blown up in my face, I felt a resurgence of strength – of fight. Of self-belief.

'Thank you,' I said, simply. 'That means a lot to me. And I've no idea how all of this is going to play out, but right now, that's made me feel better. You're a good man, Cooper Black.'

I looked up at him, and our eyes met. His fingers were tangled up in my hair, and my hand was lying on the flat muscle of his stomach, and neither of us spoke another word. We just stayed there, looking at each other, our bodies touching.

I don't know exactly when it was that something changed between us, but it did. Maybe it was the emotion. Maybe it was the dim lighting. Maybe it was the natural progression of the bond I'd always felt with him, but something changed, and we both felt it. What seconds ago had felt platonic and comfortable suddenly felt much more exciting – and much more dangerous.

He stroked the hair from the side of my face, never breaking eye contact, and my hand slipped beneath his T-shirt onto his bare skin as though it had a mind of its own.

We were both silent, both feeling it, both wondering what was going to happen next . . . both barely breathing as the moment built.

'Jess. . .' he murmured, turning my face upwards, angled towards his. I let my fingers trail over his tummy, his torso, feeling the heat between us, the soft skin over rock-hard muscle. He threw one of his legs over me, tugging me closer, until our bodies were glued together. Oh yeah, I thought, wriggling into him, he was definitely feeling it, and so was I.

Part of me knew it was wrong. That I was just reacting to the stress of everything that had happened. That I should pull away, and put a stop to this right now.

But somehow, I just couldn't. He was so strong, and so present, and so obviously turned on by me, even in my pug pyjamas. His hair was glowing in the lamplight, and his blue eyes were sparkling as he ran his gaze over me.

He leaned forward, and his lips met the sensitive skin of

my neck, my throat, trailing upwards to my lips. He paused, waited for me to object – I think we both knew we were reaching a point of no return.

I just nodded, once. I wanted this – I wanted him – so badly. Morning be damned, I wanted him.

He kissed me, so passionately, so intensely, that I lost all ability to think beyond the feeling of his lips on mine. His hands started to travel, slipping beneath my top, stroking and circling and edging their way towards my breasts.

I let out a sigh, and gloried in the feeling of his skilled hands all over me, touching me, arousing me, turning me to jelly.

I knew it was wrong. But it felt so right.

Chapter 13

When I woke up the next morning, I realized two things.

One, Cooper was gone. And two, it wasn't actually morning – it was two o'clock in the afternoon.

I could forgive myself the lie-in – I'd spent the last few days bouncing from continent to continent like a human pinball wizard, and it was understandable that I needed some rest.

What I couldn't forgive myself for quite so easily was the fact that when I saw the note Cooper had left on the pillow for me, my first thought was: *Oh shit!*

'Bye for now, Sleeping Beauty,' it said, scrawled on a page from one of those headed-paper notepads you always find in hotels and never use, 'thanks for an amazing night. Catch you later? Xxx'

I put the note down, and curled up into a tight ball under the duvet. The curtains were still closed, and even though I knew there would be blazing sunshine outside, it was blessedly dark in the room. I didn't want the cold light of day, and I certainly didn't want to have to look at myself while I was in it. I knew I wouldn't like what I saw.

I pulled the covers over my head, and waited out the waves of nausea that were rolling over me. It wasn't really physical, I knew that, it was emotional.

I'd been an idiot, and now I had to deal with the consequences – that I'd probably screwed up my friendship with Cooper; that I'd betrayed Daniel even if part of me thought he did deserve it, and that I somehow had to get through the rest of this tour dealing with a situation I didn't feel anywhere near up to handling. I even felt guilty about Felicia, because while we weren't especially close, I knew how she felt about Cooper, and I'd totally ignored any kind of girl code and slept with her man anyway.

I'd slept with Cooper. *Oh Jesus*! No matter how many times I repeated it in my mind, it didn't get any easier to deal with. What didn't help was the fact that it had been so good – because I hadn't just slept with Cooper once, I'd slept with him four times. Once could be an accident, the rest just made me an idiot. And a bitch. And fifty shades of stupid.

If it hadn't been me it had happened to, I could see the logic of it. I'd been hurt and vulnerable and scared. Daniel had made me feel unloved and unwanted. I'd been exhausted, and still a bit drunk, and completely insecure and off balance.

Cooper, bless him, had been there when I needed him. He'd been there as a friend – he'd been kind and thoughtful and supportive, and he'd effectively nursed me through a zombie-like state, providing a listening ear and gentle words and a rosy-smelling bath and pug PJs.

But Cooper was also – and maybe I'd somehow blocked this from my mind when I climbed into bed with him – drop-dead gorgeous. He was so good-looking, and sexy, and charming, and when you added all of that to the kindness and the thoughtfulness and the supportiveness, well, that was a pretty potent blend of manhood.

He'd told me I was beautiful when I felt ugly. He'd told me I was worthy when I felt worthless. He'd lifted me up when I was down. And, on top of all that, he had a killer body and incredibly effective kissing techniques. I could see why it had happened, but that didn't make it right. Nothing could make it right.

I was suffering from a self-worth hangover worse than any I'd ever had from alcohol. I'd turned to Cooper for support, and ended up getting a lot more – and now I was filled with regrets.

It hadn't been fair to Daniel, and it hadn't been fair to Cooper. I had no idea what he was thinking about it all, and for once in my life I was sincerely hoping that a man I'd just slept with would be happy to write it off as a one-night stand.

Because for me, that's all it could ever be. I liked Cooper, a lot. I enjoyed his company and respected him and yes, obviously, I fancied him. But I didn't love him, and I knew I never would – my heart was simply still owned by Daniel, whether he wanted it or not. I could only hope that Cooper knew that, and saw our night together as a passing moment, rather than the beginning of something more.

Probably, I told myself, as I geared up to getting out of bed, he'd be fine with it. I mean, Cooper Black was a mega-star sex symbol. He could have any woman he wanted, and had undoubtedly already had quite a lot. It would be just plain arrogant of me to assume that he'd be looking for a relationship – he'd probably write it off as a fun night, and we'd go back to normal. To joking around with each other, to sarcastic conversations, to performing, to being friends – but most definitely friends without benefits.

My worries about Cooper were, of course, only part of the emotional backlash. I was still in pieces about Daniel, and a quick check of my phone showed me that he'd continued to send messages. I'd been avoiding them, but look where that had got me – waking up in bed sore and naked after spending the night with another man.

I groaned, and forced myself to sit upright, and look at my phone properly. He'd left voicemails and texts and even an email. They basically all said the same thing: that he was sorry. That it wasn't what it looked like. That he loved me, and needed to speak to me.

Oh God, I thought, dropping the phone onto the bed and burying my head in my hands – what had I done? I wasn't anywhere near ready to forgive Daniel, it all still hurt too much, but what I'd done last night was a terrible mistake. Terrible.

All I wanted was a time machine, so I could take it all back. The stuff with Cooper at least. The rest – the turning up at the farmhouse, and seeing what I saw? No. I wouldn't take that back – painful as it was, it had forced me to face up to the fact that things between me and Daniel weren't going well. That there were cracks in our foundations that couldn't be ignored.

Hideous as it had all been, I needed to face up to that. And maybe – maybe – those cracks could be repaired.

Or at least, maybe they could have been before I jumped into bed with another man.

I got ready for my day, scrubbing myself as clean as I could, and wishing I could do the same with my brain. Everywhere I looked, there were reminders of what had happened.

My pug PJs, screwed up in a ball and discarded on the floor. One of Cooper's socks, which I found lying next to the bed. The empty bottles of toiletries that he'd used to make my bubble bath. The rumpled sheets that reflected a very busy night. The fact that Cooper had, thoughtfully, put the 'do not disturb' sign on my door before he left.

I felt overwhelmed and anxious and drained, and forced myself to eat before I left the room – a quick croissant and some coffee, just to keep me going. Felicia had texted to say she'd send a car to take me to the stadium for a rehearsal – one I would have missed if I'd still been in the UK, but would be good to do in advance of tomorrow night's gig.

Felicia. *Ah, shit*! Even seeing her name made me feel so much worse. Between her and Daniel's messages, I was really starting to hate my phone – almost as much as I hated myself. It pinged again, and I groaned as I looked at it through squinting eyes.

This one was from Cooper. 'Hope you're OK,' it said, 'can't wait to see you xxx.'

It just kept getting worse. I didn't reply to him or Felicia – I'd be seeing them soon enough – but I did sit down on the edge of the bed, and tap out a quick reply for Daniel. Because no matter what had happened – what might happen – there was no point in making things worse. We'd have to see each other eventually, and talk, and make some decisions, but not today. Definitely not today.

'I'm in LA,' I said. 'I know we need to talk but I'm not ready. Give me some time.'

I automatically typed kisses at the end of it, then frowned

and erased them. I had very mixed feelings about Daniel just then – I both loved him and hated him. Kisses, I decided, were most definitely not appropriate. I just wished I'd thought about that before I started snogging Cooper the night before.

I grabbed my bag and some water, and made my way downstairs to meet my driver. He was one of the chatty ones, and enjoyed giving me a guided tour of LA on our way to the concert venue. I tried to engage with him – I know how boring that job can be, and if you get a chatty driver, it's your duty to respond even if it's the last thing you feel like doing. Besides, who wouldn't want to have the giant white HOLLYWOOD sign pointed out to them? Even if I had enough drama going on in my own life to fill a dozen movies.

I was nervous as I arrived, posed for photos with a few fans, and made my way through security into the predictably concrete bowels of the stadium building. I kept my shades on, because I was so anxious, and suspected my eyes would be flittering around like drunken butterflies, looking out for Cooper and trying to gauge his mood and his reaction to what had happened between us last night.

When I finally did spot him, he was leaning up against a wall, trying not to look bored as Felicia lectured him about something. His eyes caught mine, and he straightened up immediately, waving in my direction.

I waved back, trying to look casual and smiley, while actually wishing that one of the lighting rigs would fall from the ceiling and cause a distraction.

When that didn't happen I walked over to join them.

Please, please, please, I said to myself, don't let Felicia

know, and don't let Cooper mention it. I was absolutely dying inside – of embarrassment, of anxiety, of good old-fashioned self-loathing – but I tried to look all perky and enthusiastic.

'Wow,' said Felicia, inspecting me like she would a piece of dented fruit in the supermarket, 'you look awful. Didn't you get any sleep at all last night?'

Well, she definitely didn't know – I suspected her tone of voice would be slightly more frosty if she did. Cooper gave me a cheeky wink over her head, and I bit my lip so hard it started bleeding immediately.

'Oh, you know, just jet-lagged. Thanks for sorting everything out for me. I really appreciate it.'

'No worries – that's what I'm here for,' she replied, patting me on the arm and walking away. She'd looked sympathetic as she'd said it, and I couldn't possibly have felt more like shit if Gandalf had come along and pooped on my shoes. I am a terrible, terrible human being.

'Hey gorgeous,' said Cooper, nudging me back into reality. 'You all right? You were crashed so hard when I left this morning, I wasn't sure if you were still alive. . .'

'Yep, still alive. Or at least fifty–fifty,' I replied, looking up at him. I was glad I'd kept the shades on – it meant I could examine his expressions without any fear of revealing my own.

'Well, 50 per cent Jess is better than 100 per cent most women,' he answered, giving me the kind of lazy grin that would have most girls swooning. And maybe me, once upon a time, but definitely not this morning.

I had no idea how to play this. On the one hand, he wasn't all over me, or coming in for a snog, so he clearly didn't want to 'out' us at this stage. But on the other . . . I could tell from the way he was looking at me that he hadn't woken up with a head full of shame and regret this morning, like I had.

It could be that we simply got on with our tour, and resumed business as usual, as though it never happened. That, I thought, was pretty much my perfect scenario – assuming the time machine idea wasn't a viable option.

'Look,' he said, in a voice low enough that only I could hear him, 'I know you're probably still tired. Still confused about Daniel. And I'm not sure that last night helped make you any less confused. But I don't regret it, OK? I don't regret it, but I think we need to talk about it. Can I see you later?'

I wanted to say no, desperately. I wanted to hide away in my hotel room and pretend I was someone else for the night. It was all too weird and complicated and horrible, and I needed to get my balance back.

But one look at his face told me that I couldn't say no. That whatever else had happened, Cooper was a friend, and he'd been a bloody good one. The very least I owed him was a chance to talk it through, and I didn't want to hurt him – didn't want to be the cause of pain to anyone else, despite how much of it I was feeling myself.

I'd meet him, and we'd talk, and I'd explain that it couldn't happen again, and I'd hope that Felicia never found out, and I'd not even dare think about Daniel, and it would all be fine. I'd get through it. Damage control.

'Yeah,' I said, trying to ignore the look of excitement that swam across his face before he had a chance to hide it. 'Of course.'

*

We ended up sneaking out to a little bar in a part of town that seemed mainly Hispanic. It kind of reminded me of Miami – the street cafés, the Latin beat of the music, the atmosphere – but a bit edgier, a little more 'real'. Cooper explained that it was one of his favourite places to visit in LA – that nobody here cared who he was, or that he was famous, and none of them ever listened to his kind of music anyway.

In other circumstances, I would have loved it – it's brilliant going to a big city and seeing a part of it you'd never expect to see. Liverpool's the same – there are so many hidden corners and unexpected secret places, places you'd never come across unless a local took you.

But just then, I was incapable of enjoying anything – even the ice-cold bottles of beer that had been delivered to our table, or the sultry heat of the night air, or the driving rhythms of the music. Just then, I was so nervous I jumped every time I heard a car backfire, or an especially loud peel of laughter.

'So,' said Cooper, leaning back in his chair, long jean-clad legs stretched out in front of him, looking a lot more casual than I suspect he felt, 'how are you doing today?'

'Oh, you know. Not bad. Doing the rehearsal helped – it was good to concentrate on work. Focus on something other than my pathetic love life.'

He raised an eyebrow at me and smiled, as I realized what I'd just said.

'Not that last night was pathetic! No, that's not what I

meant. I just meant that. . .' I stopped. I had no idea what I meant.

'It's OK, Jess. I know you weren't insulting my skills in the boudoir. Because I know they're impossible to insult.'

He looked part smug, and part amused, and I envied him that. Men are funny – no matter what else is going on they still need to feel like they're all-conquering heroes in the sack. And, well, he was – so I couldn't argue even if I wanted to. Even though I regretted last night, I couldn't claim that I hadn't enjoyed it. My body was a traitor.

'Yes. Well,' I replied, glad that it was dark enough to hide the fact that I was blushing, 'if you want me to fill in some kind of satisfaction survey to add to your sex website, just let me know.'

'Good idea. Something along the lines of "if one is for bored, and ten is for multiple screaming orgasms, how would you rate Cooper Black"? That kind of thing? I'm hoping you'd give me a ten at least. . .'

I sipped my beer, and looked at him. He was flirting. Flirting outrageously. This whole conversation so far was like an invitation to pick up where we left off, and I needed to nip it in the bud before I was tempted to give in.

A few more beers, a little more relaxation, some more charm, and maybe my mind would start to wander – maybe I'd start to remember more about the way it felt to make love with Cooper Black; remember how it felt to touch those muscular arms and that smooth, flat stomach; remember how it felt to be kissed by someone who so clearly enjoyed kissing me.

It would be far too easy to let that happen, and far too messy to allow.

'Stop flirting with me,' I said quietly, putting my bottle down on the table. Alcohol is not my friend in these kinds of situations.

'Why? It's fun!'

'It's. . .yeah, it's fun. Or it would have been fun, if last night hadn't happened. Now, it's just scary, OK?'

'What do you mean, scary?' he asked, frowning and looking genuinely confused.

'I mean . . . . Oh God, Cooper, I'm rubbish at this kind of thing! Can you please listen to everything I say and then run it through some kind of filter that makes it sound better? Like you'd do with a photo to make it look cuter – there really should be an app for that.'

'Jess, relax. You look like you're about to have a heart attack. Just say what you want to say, no filters required.'

I took a deep breath, and knew that I had to do it. That I could try not to hurt him, but I had to do it even if it did.

'Last night was wonderful. Cooper, you saved me, you really did. I can't tell you how grateful I am – you were so sweet, so kind, so thoughtful. And yes – before you start bleating about it – the sex was definitely a ten, all right? But, it was also a mistake.'

'A mistake?' he repeated, hiding any further response by taking a sip from his beer.

'Yes, a mistake. We shouldn't have . . . no, *I* shouldn't have . . . let things go that far. I was messed up, in all kinds of ways, and you were there for me when I needed you, and I . . . I feel like I took advantage of the situation. Of you.'

'Hold up,' he said, raising one hand to silence me. 'Stop

right there, Jess. Am I going crazy here – did I only imagine that we both wanted it?'

'No, of course not! We did . . . both of us. But I shouldn't have encouraged you. I'm a bloody disaster area, Cooper, surely you can see that? My body was with you – and honestly, my body loved being with you – but my mind? Well, my mind is still screwed up, still thinking about Daniel, still trying to figure it all out. It was a mistake, and I'm sorry, but it can't happen again. That wouldn't be fair to anyone, least of all you.'

He was quiet for a moment, looking thoughtful and serious – which was unusual enough for Cooper to make me worried about him. He ran his hands through his hair, and sighed.

'Christ,' he said, not meeting my eyes. 'I woke up this morning feeling on top of the world. And now I just feel . . . well, kind of dirty, to be honest. Kind of used. Which believe me are never words I expected to be saying about spending the night with a beautiful woman.'

I wanted to argue, wanted to say that I wasn't the kind of person who used someone. But the facts said otherwise, and I had to accept it, much as it stung, because I had used him. I'd used him as an ego boost, as a distraction, as a way of making me feel better about a truly shitty situation. And I'd certainly not paused to think about how any of that might make him feel.

I reached out and touched his hand, felt his fingers tense beneath mine.

'I'm sorry, Cooper. About all of it. And under different circumstances, who knows? You and me? It could all have worked out in an alternate universe. But not now. Now, I'm too messed up. I might always be too messed up, and I can't start something with you when I haven't finished things with Daniel.'

He looked up at me, eyes bright, mouth twisted into a bitter smile.

'Wow! The "it's not you, it's me" speech. I'm more familiar with giving it than receiving it, I have to say. Look, I get it. I kind of understand what you're saying, crappy as it makes me feel. But I think you need to reconsider. Because it's too late to say you can't start something with me – you already have! And Daniel. . .Well, Daniel is a dick. We both know he cheated on you.'

'I don't know that for sure. . .' I said, my voice trailing off at the end as I realized how pathetic that sounded.

'Yeah, all right. You don't know that for sure, but you knew it well enough to sleep with me, didn't you? Whatever happened between him and Vella, it felt serious enough for you to do that. So either it's over between you two because he cheated, or it's over between you two because you cheated. I suppose what I'm saying is that it's over. And I know the timing is off, with us – with what happened. But maybe, once the timing is better. . .'

His words felt harsh, but I reminded myself that I deserved them. That he was probably right. That even if he wasn't right, what I'd done was most definitely wrong, and it now looked like I'd added Cooper to the casualty list left in the wreckage of mine and Daniel's mess.

It would have been easy to agree with him. To say, *Yeah, you're spot on – so let's just wait a while and see what happens*

–*maybe this can all work out.* I knew that's what he wanted – for me to give him some indication that there was hope.

But while that would have been easier, it wouldn't have been right. Because Cooper was now so tied up with everything else, with the disaster of my life, that I couldn't possibly imagine a time I'd be able to see him as anything other than collateral damage.

'I don't think so, Cooper,' I said, as gently as I could. 'I think we need to draw a line under it. Under what happened between us. I made a mistake. I'm sorry. I like you, a lot. I respect you, and admire you, and I'm thankful to you. But right now, I can't ever see that growing into something more.'

He pulled his fingers away from mine, and smiled sadly.

'Maybe,' he said, downing the rest of his beer in one long gulp, 'for you, that's true. But maybe – for me – it's already grown into something more. Did that ever cross your pretty little mind? You can sit there and try and be logical, but maybe it's just too late. Maybe, Jess, I've fallen in love with you. . .'

Chapter 14

'Hello, Dad,' I said, so happy to hear his voice. The tensions between me and Cooper had been building, the messages from Daniel had carried on landing, and I felt terrible. So, straight after our first gig in LA, I'd retreated to my hotel room, and done what I needed to do – called home.

'Hello, love. I got your message, and waited up. Did a night shift, actually, so I'd be awake when you called. . .'

'Thank you. Did you have anybody interesting in the back of your cab?'

'Oh, you know, the usual – a few drunks, some airport runs, a couple of tourists looking for Penny Lane at three in the morning, one of those women from that soap opera . . . I always forget the name. Just an average night in town. Nobody puked up though, so I'm counting that one as a win. Now, what's up with you, Jessy? Your mum's been worrying past herself – I'm sure she'll come flying down the stairs in her nightie any minute now. . .'

I laughed at the thought, but hoped she wouldn't. It was eleven at night here, which made it around 6 a.m. there – way too early for her to be up and about when she had a shift at work to get to later.

I settled myself by thinking of them, at home, in their normal routines. My dad would have come in, and made himself a brew, and watched some sport on the telly with the sound off while he waited for me to call. Mum would be in bed, but, as he'd said, probably primed and ready to leap into mum-like action. Luke would be dead to the world. Becky, a few streets over in her own house, might be up with Prince Ollie, or still in bed with her boyfriend, Sean.

Liverpool itself would just be waking up as well – deliveries getting made, street cleaners out, ferries and trains and buses preparing to bring commuters into town for work. It would all be blessedly normal – and I so wished I was there. Or even remembered what it felt like to be normal.

'Nothing, Dad. I just needed to hear your voice. It's all a bit hectic here. The schedule's crazy, and I'm just a bit knackered, you know?'

'I can imagine. Luke keeps us up-to-date on where you're playing, what you're doing. For someone who spends most of the time when you're actually here winding you up, he's very proud of you.'

'I think he just uses my name to improve his chances with girls, Dad.'

'Perhaps,' he chuckled. 'So, everything's all right, is it?'

'Kind of. . .Well, no. Not really. Just a bit complicated, I suppose. Some stuff with work, and with Daniel.'

There was a pause, and the phone sounded weird. I knew he was covering it with his hand, which told me that my mother had arrived downstairs.

'Jessy?' she said, sounding worried. I pictured the look on

my dad's face, knowing she'd have just snatched the phone out of his hands. 'What's that about Daniel? Is he all right? I got a text from him yesterday, but when I called back it went to voicemail. . .Is everything OK?'

I wasn't surprised that he'd tried to contact her. I'd stayed incommunicado, apart from a few bland messages of the 'please let this lie until we see each other' line, and he must have been desperate. But knowing Daniel, he'd also have realized that it wasn't fair or right to involve them in this mess, and hadn't followed through. I was glad about that, but realized that it meant I needed to tell them. At least some of it.

'Look, Mum, Dad . . . don't freak out, all right? We're just having a few problems. A few issues we need to sort out.'

'Issues?' she repeated, sounding confused. It was early, after all. 'Issues? What does that mean? That's the kind of word they use on telly shows when someone's about to go psycho in a shopping centre with a machine gun! What's going on? And don't lie to me – I'll know if you do.'

She was right about that – she would know. So while I didn't lie, I also didn't tell her the whole truth – because what parent would possibly want to hear the whole sordid truth? That I'd walked in on my fiancé – a man they'd known since he was in nappies – with another woman? And that I'd responded to that crisis in an incredibly mature way, by shagging someone else? And that that someone else said he'd now fallen in love with me, and was showing it by refusing to speak to me in public? I felt humiliated even thinking about it, never mind saying it out loud.

'OK, I won't lie, but I'm not telling you everything, all right? I'm a grown-up, and I'm entitled to some privacy.'

She let that one pass, even though I could feel her pipping to argue with me – because phoning your parents at stupid o'clock to bleat about your love life wasn't that grown-up at all, was it?

'Daniel and me, we're kind of taking a break. Maybe for a bit, maybe permanently. I don't know. A few things have gone wrong. We've both done some stuff we're probably not proud of.'

They were both quiet for a moment, and I could picture them exchanging worried looks. Being a parent, I thought, must be a bloody nightmare – no matter how old your child gets, they still always seem to need you. It's like the crappy gift that keeps on giving.

'Right. Well, that doesn't sound good,' she replied, eventually. 'And, well, love, relationships are hard, aren't they? We know that, and we won't judge you, whatever happens. It's hard enough when life is normal, and neither me nor your dad can imagine how tough it must be when you have a life like yours. Like you said, you're a grown-up, but can I offer you some advice?'

Ha, I thought, smiling, as if I could stop her!

'Yeah. Of course,' I said, and meant it – she might not understand my lifestyle, but she'd probably forgotten more about life itself than I'd ever learned.

'Be kind to each other. Be kind to yourself. It's easier to stay angry than it is to forgive – but I know you, and I know Daniel. I've always thought you were right for each other, and I still do. I don't know what's gone on between the two of you, and maybe I'm better off not knowing, but remember this – he's loved you for a long time, Jessy. And there's no way that kind of love just goes away. It might get hidden behind some other nonsense, but it doesn't go away, and it's worth fighting for, all right?'

I nodded, feeling tears fall down my cheeks, and then realized that I was on the landline, not Skype, and she couldn't actually see me nodding.

'OK, Mum. You're right, I'm sure. And I'll try.'

'Good! I know you will – I didn't raise you to give up. But, Jessy? I also didn't raise you to do things you weren't proud of, did I? Again, I don't know what it is that you've done or think you've done, but make it right, make it better. We all make mistakes, every single one of us. We all hurt people, and we all mess up. Sometimes we don't get to undo those mistakes, and sometimes we don't get to be forgiven, but all you can do is try.'

'Yes, Mum. I know. I. . .Thank you. I miss you, you know.'

I heard a sharp gulp at her end, and knew she was crying too. I now felt guilty on top of everything else for upsetting them. I heard the clunking sounds of Mum passing the phone back to my dad, and tried to pull myself together.

'Your mum's always right, Jessy,' he said, sounding upset but obviously trying to hide it. 'About these things anyway. We love you, and we're proud of you. Don't ever forget that, will you?'

*

I was lying face down on the table, with my head poking through one of those round holes they have on massage equipment. Neale was mirroring my position on the table next to me.

We'd both just been pummelled to within an inch of our lives by a scary-looking Swedish bloke in the hotel spa, and were now at the part where we were left there for fifteen minutes, to 'relax'. I couldn't speak for Neale, but I was feeling more broken than relaxed, and the new-age tinkly-bell music that was playing in the background didn't help.

He'd arrived back the day before, but we hadn't had a chance to talk – it was literally all business, with him getting me ready for the show, the show itself, several more close non-encounters with Cooper, and then me hiding away in my hotel room for the rest of the night.

We'd promised each other a morning in the spa to catch up and, against all odds, I'd kind of enjoyed it so far. Probably because no phones were allowed, and I'd not seen Cooper at all that day. Our old routine – sharing casual breakfasts together, partying after the show, chit-chat while we sat around during soundchecks – had all gone out the window.

Cooper was cold-shouldering me, and I was chilled to the bone by it. I knew it was because I'd hurt him. And I knew I deserved whatever punishment he wanted to throw at me, but none of that made it any easier to deal with.

Even Felicia had noticed there was something wrong between us, and as she wasn't completely stupid, had probably figured it out. I was getting quite a lot of frost from her as well, all topped by her cornering me outside my room that morning.

'What have you done to Cooper?' she'd asked, hands on hips, her petite body trembling with anger.

'I. . .nothing. What do you mean?' I'd spluttered, clutching my bag in front of me, feeling like a caged animal getting poked with an electrified stick.

'I mean, there's something wrong with him. And he's not speaking to you unless he has to. So what gives?'

I stared at her, open-mouthed, not having a clue how to respond. I still felt awful about what had happened. Sleeping with him was bad enough, but then finding out that for him, it was so much more than accidental sex? That he was in love with me, and hoping for something I couldn't give him? That made it even worse. And there was no way I could possibly make it better – every time I tried to talk to him, to communicate, he blanked me. Now his guardian angel had me trapped in a hotel corridor, without witnesses, and looked like she might be about to kill me.

Eventually, after I'd spluttered and gestured and looked more and more hysterical, she'd just thrown her hands in the air in frustration.

'Right, I get it. You're not talking either. Whatever it is, fix it – I don't like seeing him hurt. It makes me angry. You understand that?'

'I know,' I replied, quickly. 'I don't want to see him hurt either. I'm sorry, Felicia.'

She stared at me, her huge brown eyes moist, and I was left in no doubt that she'd made her own assumptions. Probably the right ones. I don't think I'd ever felt so disgusted by myself.

'Yeah. Right. Me too – and I'm disappointed. I thought you were better than that. But hey, don't flatter yourself. He'll get over it. Do you think this is the first time I've had to watch while Cooper's had a fling on tour? As soon as you're gone, he'll forget all about you.'

She'd stormed off after that, and I couldn't say that I blamed her. And much as her words had been intended to hurt me, I also hoped that she was right – that as soon as I'd gone, Cooper would forget me, and get back to his life. That I wouldn't leave behind any permanent scars because of my selfish behaviour.

Just then, as I was staring at Felicia's angry stride as she marched away, Neale had emerged from his room, dressed in his kimono and already wearing a headband ready for his facial. Not that he had much hair to hold back, but the band, the kimono and the little brown specs definitely made for an interesting look.

'What was all that about?' he'd asked, closing the door quietly behind him – I guessed JB was still asleep. 'She looks like she's got her knickers in a twist about something.'

I'd puffed out the breath I didn't realize I'd been holding, and decided that the best policy for the time being was just to tell a very small fib. Or at least delay telling him the truth. A lot had happened while he was gone, and not much of it made for easy listening – and for once I wanted the day to be about somebody other than me.

'No idea,' I'd said, linking my arm into his and steering us towards the lifts. 'And anyway, come on! Spa day!'

'Yay!' he'd replied, giggling and clapping his hands. 'Just us girls!'

So we'd spent a few hours in here, getting rubbed and poked and creamed and oiled and exfoliated and prodded and massaged, chatting about nothing more important than shades of lipstick and what size bra we thought Vogue wore and the latest season of *The Vampire Diaries*, which had become something of a guilty pleasure for us both. He was a Stefan fan; I was Damon all the way. Which was good, because it meant we'd never fall out over boys. Even fictional vampire boys.

Now, after all our pampering, we were finally alone, and I genuinely wanted to hear how it had gone with JB's family. Neale seemed as happy and perky as ever, even with his face shoved in a massage table, listening to Tibetan monks chanting, so I had to assume it had gone well.

'So,' I said, from my side of the massage room to his, 'how was it? Did you love them? Did they love you? Was it lovely?'

'Oh it *was* lovely, yes!' he replied, wriggling around to get more comfy. 'We stayed in their house, and went out for dinner, and his dad took us to the nightclub he manages, and his mum took me to the mall, and it was lovely! I don't know why I'd been worried.'

'See, I knew it would be fine,' I said, smiling.

He grinned back. 'Anyway, I think I've had about as much relaxing as I can manage. I'm going to sit up. Avert your eyes, my precious. . .'

I heard him moving around and did as I was told, keeping my eyes closed while he arranged himself beneath the blankets. I then followed suit and sat up. Neale wrapped one of the sheets around his waist and trotted over to the sound system. He pressed about four buttons until he finally found a way to shut off the music, and I felt like hugging him. Nothing stresses me out quite so much as being told to relax.

He poured us both a paper cup of cucumber water – pulling a face that implied he'd be far happier if there was a triple vodka in that – and passed one over, before perching on the end of my massage bed.

'So,' he said, putting his glasses back on and screwing his eyes up as they adjusted back to the lenses, 'what's been going on here, then? And don't say nothing, because I'm not a complete retard. I have eyes – flawed as they are – and I can tell from your skin that you've been stressed. Plus, you know, Cooper is clearly pissed off with you. What happened?'

'Well. . .' I said, sipping the water and grimacing. Yikes! Whoever came up with idea of mixing cucumber and water? That was just weird. 'Let's see. . .I went back to the farmhouse and walked in on Daniel enjoying a romantic night in with Vella. Champagne and everything. Then I came back here, and shagged Cooper. Then Cooper told me he was in love with me, and I told him I didn't feel the same, and now Felicia wants to kill me, Cooper hates me, and Daniel won't stop telling me he's sorry.'

'Oh,' replied Neale, trying not to look shocked. 'I've not missed much, then?'

'No,' I said, deciding I'd rather dehydrate than drink more cucumber water, 'just your usual run-of-the-mill Jessy disasters. All things considered, I don't think any of them could possibly hate me more than I hate myself.'

Neale sat still and quiet for a few seconds, rubbing his hands on his knees and biting his lip.

'I'm actually really shocked and just trying to look cool about it, Jess.'

'Shocked about which bit?'

'All of it, but mainly Daniel, I mean. I know Daniel. He loves you. He's your JB but, you know, vanilla. Are you sure he was *with* Vella?'

I sighed, and threw the empty cup at the bin. Obviously, it missed by a mile, because I throw like a girl.

'I wish I could say yes, I'm sure. Which sounds weird, I know – wishing that I knew for sure that my fiancé had cheated on me, but. . .'

'Then you wouldn't feel so bad about sleeping with Cooper,' he finished for me. Of course, he understood.

I nodded, and stared at my hands. I felt embarrassed and ashamed and confused, as well as very oily from the massage.

'Well, I'm not one to judge, Jess. You're doing a good enough job of that yourself, anyway, you don't need my help. Let's just get through the rest of the tour, and see what happens. I like to think you'll sort things out with Daniel, and I'm sure Cooper will be all right in the end, but, well, who knows? All this deep and meaningful life stuff is exhausting. Do you want to go to the bar? They have pink champagne and a chocolate fountain and marshmallows you poke into it on sticks?'

I laughed, and nodded. Of course I did. Pink champagne and chocolate marshmallows would make everything feel better. God, it was good to have him back.

*

The gig that night was weird. The stadium was packed, and the atmosphere was electric. Normally, I'd have been soaring on the energy and adrenaline and the buzz from the crowd.

But everyone, it seemed, was in a strange mood – it swirled around us like a toxic cloud, infecting us all. I was unsteady because Daniel had had a huge bunch of flowers delivered to the hotel, with a card attached that said 'I love you. Don't give up on us, Jessy. Just call me, any time.' It had knocked me about a bit, imagining him dictating that message to a florist, and I thought I might explode with the sadness and confusion of it all.

I vowed to myself that I would call him, as soon as I'd got off stage. I did still love him, and I missed him, and the whole thing with Cooper had proved to me that my heart still lay with Daniel. Maybe we could work our way through the maze. I decided I'd tell him I'd come back as soon as the last gig was done, and that we'd sit down, and talk. Really talk.

It wouldn't be an easy conversation, because now, he wasn't the only one with secrets to confess. I was dreading telling him about Cooper – it might mean the end of us for real – but I knew I had to. We couldn't start our future together, our marriage, on a foundation of lies. We had to clear the air, and see if we could both move on. Yikes!

That, though, was an ordeal for another day. In the here and now, things weren't much better. Cooper was still being off with me, and I was trying to take it on the chin, but it was wearing me down. Felicia was in a grade A nark, rushing round like an angry hurricane, obviously stressed and furious about the fact that Cooper was upset.

The tensions seemed to seep down to the rest of the crew, and the rehearsal had been peppered with incidents: dancers falling over when they were usually graceful, backing singers missing notes they always hit, the tech guys fluffing their lighting cues and swearing like sailors, normally reliable equipment breaking down. Show business people can be superstitious, and I think we were all feeling the strain, imagining the worst.

I'd fully expected the concert to be a disaster – I think we all had – but somehow it all came together on stage; nothing set on fire, there were no earthquakes, and we all fell back into being professionals, managing to get through it unscathed.

OK, so Cooper didn't meet my eyes during our duets, and had made some impromptu changes to the dance moves that cut out most of our physical contact, but I could live with that. The last thing either of us needed was pretending to be all sexy together, I supposed.

Still, although it went well, I was relieved when it was over and looking forward to when we'd taken our final bows, Cooper had done his traditional bit where he thanked everyone involved, and we sloped off stage to the sound of a still-cheering audience, gulping down water and sweating after hours under glaring lights.

Tonight, though, was different. I had no idea what Cooper was up to, but as we stood together in the spotlight, preparing to leave, he paused, and picked up the microphone again. The crowd hushed, waiting to hear what he had to say. We all did, in fact – this tour was like a well-oiled machine, and spontaneous endings weren't what we planned for.

He turned to me, and whispered, hand held over the mic, 'It's OK – you're done for the night. You can go.'

I felt dismissed, and a little embarrassed, but tried not to show it. I gave the crowd one last wave, and did as I was told – I went. I lurked at the side of the stage, though, perched on the steps, waiting to see what was going on. I had a bad feeling about it, but that wasn't unusual. My whole life was one bad feeling these days.

'Now,' said Cooper, turning back to his people, 'I have a new song for you all. It's still a baby, so be kind. I only wrote it last night, and I've never performed it before, so bear with me. You guys don't mind if I make a few mistakes, do you?'

The resulting roar of thousands of eager fans echoed around the stadium, making it very clear that no, they didn't mind at all. They loved him – Cooper Black could probably stand on stage and recite the collected works of Enid Blyton, and they'd still find it exciting.

He nodded, and gestured to one of the roadies, who immediately walked on stage and passed Cooper his guitar. He didn't play much during the gigs – he always said he was 'just OK' on guitar, and he'd rather leave it to the band, who were 'beyond brilliant'.

He hooked the strap over his shoulder, and strummed a few notes to prepare. I noticed that the rest of the band had laid down their instruments and were looking on with as much curiosity as me – he was obviously going this one alone.

'OK,' he said, still strumming, tapping his toe in time to the chords. 'Now, I'm gonna do this one in a British accent, all right? I'm no actor, so forgive me, guys. Just imagine I'm one of those Harry Potter dudes, yeah?'

Everyone laughed – he really could do no wrong – and

when he spoke again, it was in an actually pretty good English accent. The kind of mock-Cockney that you see in crime films, where the roguish gangster might kill his rivals with a sawn-off shotgun, but always loves his mum.

'So – I hope you like it,' he said, sounding like he was in *EastEnders*. 'It's called "Screw You". And it's a love song – a love song about what happens when love goes bad. We've all been there, I know. OK, here goes nothing. . .'

The audience were quieter now, waiting to hear, and the band were sharing confused glances as Cockney Cooper started to sing. I sat on the steps, and felt a wave of sickness flood through me.

I knew what was coming, and it was going to be bad. I had the horrible suspicion that I was about to receive a musical boot in the face. I buried my face in my hands, and fought back the tears. There was nothing I could do to stop this, other than run screaming on stage – which wouldn't help anyone, and might result in me getting carted off by the enormous security guards.

Instead, I sat there and prayed. Tried to convince myself that I was being paranoid. That this was a coincidence. That there was no way Cooper would do this to me. He wouldn't, I told myself, he knows how things are with Daniel. He knows what a mess we're all in. Surely he wouldn't publicly humiliate me like that?

But as soon as the first few lines left his lips, I knew that I'd been wrong to hold out any hope at all. The Cooper I thought I knew was gone, and he'd been replaced by someone so hurt he didn't care who he took down, or how much suffering he caused. I knew then that whatever love Cooper said he felt for me had turned sour and bitter and angry, and this was his cruel and desperate way of showing me exactly how bad he was feeling.

'I had this girl in the back of my cab,' he sang, in his Mockney accent, 'and she looked so pretty.'

He paused, strummed a little more, and continued: 'Long blonde hair and big blue eyes, I showed her round my city. We shared so much, I thought it was love, but now I'm feeling shitty. . .'

I felt a hand on my shoulder, and knew it was Neale, trying to comfort me. I looked up at him, and saw his horrified expression.

'Oh no!' he muttered, looking as distressed as I felt. I nodded, and Cooper continued.

'She never *said* that she loved meeeee,' sang Cooper, emotion cracking his voice as the notes soared, 'but she showed me with her kisses. Beneath the sheets, we felt the heat, and that . . . that is what love is!

'At least for me, it meant so much, I felt my heart surrender. A love so rare, a love so raw, it left me scared and tender.'

I gulped as I saw him building up to the chorus, the audience swaying with him, thousands of phones held aloft in the darkness of the stadium. I clutched Neale's hand, and frankly, just wanted to die. I could see Felicia over on the other side of the stage, her eyes shining with tears, her fingers twisted into tight claws.

'So, what do I doooooo?' Cooper sang, obviously feeling every word he uttered. 'I'm so in love with you. I know you don't want me. I know you don't need me. It was gone in a flash, thrown out with the trash. So now, what do I dooooo?'

He stretched that last note out for ages, his voice more raw, more bluesy, than I'd ever heard it. If this song wasn't about me – if this song wasn't a hate anthem pointed in my direction – I'd have been moved. Thought it was beautiful. Maybe shed a tear, and empathized with his obvious pain. But it *was* about me – it was a weapon of mass destruction in musical form, and I felt devastated as he continued.

'So, what do I dooooo?' he sang, over and over, building it all up into a huge crescendo of anguished voice and furiously strumming guitar. 'What do I doooo?'

He paused, and cradled the microphone, and talked the next line in his Cockney voice: 'I say – screw you!'

He dropped the mic, ignored the screams and cheers, and disappeared off to the opposite side of the stage. I saw him brush past Felicia, and watched as she chased after him, and listened to the sound of a crowd that was now going well and truly wild.

I turned to Neale, who was still wide-eyed and shocked, and said: 'Did that just happen?'

'I wish I could lie, sweetie,' he said, stroking my hair with trembling fingers, 'but it bloody well did.'

Chapter 15

I knew I should leave him alone – knew I was the last person he probably wanted to see – but I couldn't help myself.

This man – this man who I'd thought of as a friend – had just stood on stage in front of thousands of people and destroyed me. It felt so unfair – I knew he was hurting, and I knew I'd caused it, but I'd tried to apologize. Tried to explain. He'd refused to listen, and instead done this, without ever giving me the chance to defend myself.

I caught up with him in the corridor, the fluorescent glowing lights harsh on our faces, revealing every crack in our make-up and every crack in our souls. He saw me coming, and held out one hand to shut an urgently chattering Felicia up. Neale trotted after me, his tiny feet flying to keep up, stopping by my side when I faced Cooper.

I stared at him, tears flowing freely now, so angry and hurt and confused.

'Why, Cooper?' I said, hearing the anguish in my own voice. 'Why would you do that to me?'

'Hey, don't flatter yourself!' he snapped back, throwing his empty water bottle down on the floor, where it bounced and rolled off into the distance. 'You're not the only English girl in the world, you know.'

'I'm not stupid, Cooper!' I yelled. 'It turns out I'm just a very bad judge of character! I thought you were my friend, I thought—'

'Well, you thought wrong,' he interrupted, his face twisted into an angry snarl.

Felicia stood in front of him, inserting herself between us as we screamed at each other. It wasn't much of an improvement – she looked just as aggressive. Neale moved in front of me, and faced off with Felicia, taking up as much of a fighting stance as he could manage. It was like they were our champions, both there to defend us in our times of need. My money was on Felicia – that point-cornered clipboard looked like it could be used as a lethal weapon in an episode of *CSI*.

The tense stand-off was being watched from a distance by random members of the crew, and some of the stadium staff. They were probably surreptitiously snapping photos already, but by that stage I just didn't care. I was totally shattered by Cooper's behaviour, and disgusted at the part I'd played in causing it.

I don't know what either of us would have said or done after that – probably nothing good – but we were interrupted by the arrival of JB, running towards us in a cloud of black hair, clutching his phone.

'What the fuck, man?' he said, ploughing through me, Neale and Felicia and getting right into Cooper's face. 'What the hell was all that about? It's already on the freaking internet!'

Cooper tried to stare him down, push him away, but JB was

bigger – and was one of the few people close enough to him to talk straight. There was history there, and it was probably only that history that stopped Cooper from punching his lights out.

'None of your business, JB! I'll do whatever the fuck I wanna do, all right?'

'No! Not all right! I get that you're hurt, but that doesn't mean you get a free pass on acting like a big fat baby, OK? This is a messed-up situation, and you've just made it a hundred times worse, for both of you. That little stunt is out there, online, and you *know* it's gonna go viral.'

I sucked in a deep breath, and felt like I'd been kicked in the stomach. It was online. It was going to go viral. Of course it was. One of the world's biggest superstars had just stood on stage and presented his bleeding heart to the world, and it didn't take a rocket scientist to figure out who he'd been singing about, even if he hadn't said my name.

Oh God – Daniel! I'd been planning on telling him about Cooper anyway, but now he might find out in the worst way possible. His parents might see it. My parents might see it. Everyone I knew and loved might see it. In fact, there was no 'might' about it: they would. I'd let everyone down, and there was no way to escape the consequences.

I thought I might actually be sick, there and then, splashing my guts all over Cooper's $500 trainers. I clutched my stomach, and felt the world swirl around me.

'Jessy!' said Neale, taking hold of my hand as I wobbled and staggered.

'Oh, no. . .' I muttered, trying to walk but finding that my legs were made of string cheese. 'I need to leave. I need to get back to my room. I need to talk to Daniel before he sees any of this.'

I glanced up at Cooper, feeling my face drain of all colour and my throat closing up like I was having an asthma attack. He was still glaring at me, but there was something in his eyes that hadn't been there before. Maybe it was regret. Maybe it was pity. I wasn't sure, and I didn't care.

'I will never forgive you for this,' I said, as Neale led me away, weaving us unsteadily towards the dressing rooms.

I leaned on him, and let him help me, because I wasn't capable of anything else just then. I was like a zombie as he gathered our stuff together, and wrapped me up in my jacket. I realized, as he tucked my hair away, that I'd been shaking uncontrollably; not from cold, but from the shock of everything that had just happened.

He laid a gentle kiss on my head, and murmured: 'There, there. It's going to be OK. Come on now, there's a car waiting.'

I was silent as we drove through the city back to the hotel, looking on as Neale checked his phone, his expression telling me everything I needed to know.

'How bad is it?' I asked, quietly, as the car made its way to the hotel drive. There'd be a party there tonight, but I would most definitely not be attending. The way I was feeling, I'd never go to a party again for the rest of my life.

'It's not brilliant,' he replied, tucking his phone away in his jeans pocket and helping me out of the car. We snuck in through the side door of the hotel – he knew I wasn't up to being photographed or quizzed, both of which could very easily happen in the main lobby.

By the time we made it back to my hotel room, I was feeling even worse, but I needed to know. I needed to know, before I called Daniel, and faced the music. Before my whole life imploded around me.

I sat on the bed, Neale by my side, his arm around my shoulders, fussing at me and making what he probably thought were soothing noises.

'Is it everywhere?' I asked, looking at him pleadingly. Part of me wanted him to lie, so I could ignore it for a little while longer – but the chances were zero to the power of infinity, I knew. He looked at me nervously, obviously worried about how I was going to react.

'It's all right,' I said. 'I need to know.'

He nodded, and pulled his phone out again. He tapped away for a few seconds, chewing his lip, and turned to face me.

'It's everywhere, Jess. Along with comments. Twitter, YouTube, Facebook, Instagram . . . the lot. A few gossip sites have already picked it up, and posted it with pictures of you screaming at him in the stadium. Thank you for that, popcorn-selling lady! Lots of speculation about what's gone on between the two of you. A photo of Daniel on one of them as well. It's been fast.'

Well, I thought, laughing bitterly, that's the internet for you. And nothing spreads quite as quickly as other people's humiliation, does it? We've all been guilty of it – reading silly stories about a Kardashian or a Lindsay Lohan or a Taylor Swift, and marvelling at the mess they seem to be making of their lives. Except now I was the click bait, and it felt a lot different to be on the other side, and to know how much damage it could cause.

'I have to call him,' I said, shaking my head and trying to clear my thoughts. 'I have to call Daniel.'

Whatever had happened back at the farmhouse – whatever may or may not be going on with him and Vella – he didn't deserve this. He was a private man, and valued his hermit-like existence. He'd always avoided the showbiz madness, and now I'd dragged him right into the middle of it – publicly humiliating him because I couldn't keep my legs closed. That thought sounded harsh, even to me, but it was true, and I had to face up to it.

I fished my phone out of my bag, and saw that there was already a message waiting for me. I hoped it was from him, but as soon as I opened the screen, I saw it was from Patty, back in the UK.

'What the hell?' it simply said, with a set of exclamation marks to show her surprise. Oh God, would all of this impact on In Vogue as well? Would Patty see this as a victory in the 'no publicity is bad publicity' vein, or would she be fuming with me? Knowing Patty, she definitely wouldn't care about the human fallout.

I deleted the message. I didn't have the time or energy to worry about things like that right now. There were more important people to worry about.

I dialled Daniel's number, and waited for him to answer. Except he didn't. It rang and rang and rang, and then I heard it briefly click in, before he obviously hit the reject button.

I rang again, and it went straight to voicemail. I tried texting, and waited nervously for a reply, my toes tapping on the floor and my heart in my mouth. I texted again, and again.

After ten minutes of this, I realized that he wasn't going to respond. That whatever I had to say, he didn't want to hear it.

I threw my phone down onto the bed, and scrambled to my feet, dashing wildly into the bathroom, so unsteady I bumped off a few walls on the way. I made it just in time to be violently sick in the toilet, ending up in a damp, crumpled heap on the cold tiled floor.

Neale appeared in the doorway, looking so stressed and freaked out I almost felt sorry for him.

He knelt down beside me, and started dabbing at my face with a bundled-up wad of tissue.

'It'll be all right, Jessy, don't worry,' he said.

But I knew he was wrong. I knew it wouldn't be all right, ever again.

*

I wanted nothing more, the next morning, than to pack up, give up, and fly home. I felt awful, physically and emotionally, and had no idea how I was ever going to unpick the mess I'd landed myself in.

I was still furious with Cooper, and the thought of carrying on with the tour made me feel like throwing up again.

Only two things gave me the strength to carry on, to face the day and see it all through.

One was a message from Vogue.

'Chin up, chica,' it said. 'We all make mistakes. Get through this, then come home to mama. We'll fix it all together. Love you loads.'

The other had been a tense conversation with my parents. Like they'd said before, they weren't judgey, but I could tell they were shocked, and disappointed. I'm not sure there's any feeling much worse than sensing your parents' disappointment, and them trying to hide it because they love you so much. It would have been easier to deal with if they'd sworn at me and said I was grounded.

But they were trying to be kind, even though they sounded weary, and that made it so much harder to bear. I really didn't want to make it any worse by turning up on their doorstep with my tail between my legs. They'd put up with a lot from me over the years – all the failed auditions and botched girl bands and endlessly supporting me through my ups and downs as a party princess children's entertainer.

They'd tolerated my awful behaviour when I first got famous, and put up with my dramas since, and they'd always been there for me. Now, I felt like I'd let them all down – I'd let everyone down.

'Just get through it, love,' my dad had said, sounding worn out by it all. 'Get through these last few days. You've always got us, don't forget that. Finish your tour, and see how things go with Daniel, and try not to crack under the pressure. You know we're still Team Jessy all the way, don't you?'

I did know that. I knew that I was lucky to have such a loving and supportive family. I knew I was lucky to have Vogue as a friend, and even more lucky to have Neale, who'd spent the night kipping on my couch so he could keep an eye on me and be there when I woke up.

I was lucky in a lot of ways, but not in love. I'd checked

my phone as soon as I woke up, but there was still nothing from Daniel.

I carried on trying throughout the morning, and throughout the awful journey to Las Vegas, where we were, blessedly, doing our last few nights of the tour. The tour that I now hated being a part of.

I'd decided that even if I could carry on with the gigs – be professional and fulfil my commitments – I definitely couldn't travel with Cooper. The whole idea of sitting on the tour bus with him was too much to bear. I might actually beat him to death with a vodka bottle, or smother him with a neck pillow. Possibly just shove him out of an emergency exit as we were speeding down the freeway.

Instead, Neale and I piled onto the second bus, with the tech guys and the crew. It wasn't quite so luxurious, but at least it didn't have Cooper Black's fake face plastered all down the side of it, or his real face inside it.

The crew were careful around me, polite but cautious, handling me as though I was some kind of human hand grenade that might explode with the slightest fumble. They may, of course, have been right.

They must have been wondering what was actually going on. The continued publicity around Cooper's impromptu character assassination had grown and grown and grown. I tried to block it out, but it was hard to completely ignore.

I knew from even a brief glance at the beast we call the internet that so far various stories had claimed I was his lover (technically correct, even if it was only for one night); that we'd secretly got married and now I was asking for an annulment;

that we were together but I was pregnant with JB's child; and that I'd broken his heart and Daniel's by revealing that I was actually having a lesbian love affair with Vogue.

I'd been ignoring calls from the few members of the media who had my number, and Patty had been refusing all requests for comments on my behalf. We'd cancelled the pre-gig press conference in Vegas – we really didn't need any more exposure – and, as a result, the rumour mill was going into overdrive.

In all honesty, I didn't care. I only cared about one thing – Daniel. He, understandably, was still refusing to take my calls, and ignoring my texts. I can't say I blamed him, but I still felt devastated. Betrayed, actually – because even when I found him with Vella, I did at least respond to his pleas and messages. Admittedly, I responded without warmth or regularity, but I didn't just shut him out. I felt that he deserved better than that, and better than he was giving me.

Both Cooper and Daniel had betrayed me, in fact, in different ways. My humongous inability to call anything correctly when it came to men was starting to convince me that maybe I should run off and join a nunnery, or go backpacking round Tibet on my own for ten years, until I was capable of functioning when it came to members of the opposite sex.

Neale remained by my side throughout it all, for which I will always be thankful. He sat by me during the long drive, and helped sneak me into the hotel, disguised as one of the tech crew in a baseball cap and an Iron Maiden T-shirt, and made sure I was all right before heading off to touch base with JB.

It was sweet, and kind, and one of the very few positives

to come out of the whole affair – I might have rotten taste in men, but I seem to have excellent taste in friends.

In fact, he and JB both were tremendous – especially considering the fact that JB was one of Cooper's oldest and closest friends. He must have had torn loyalties, but also had such a big heart, and such a non-judgemental approach to life, that there was room enough for both of us.

The two of them came round to my hotel suite for dinner, which we ordered from room service. I wasn't hungry, but I had to eat – we had two days off, and then a gig to get through. I wouldn't be doing anyone any favours if I had a physical collapse as well as mental, so I forced myself to get through at least a few bites of my pasta, even if it all tasted like cardboard to me.

The hotel suite was amazing: three huge rooms and a sumptuous bed set up on its own platform, dazzling views of the Vegas skyline from the floor-to-ceiling windows. I knew that downstairs, and in the other hotels, the casinos would be in full swing, full of noise and light and energy, and usually I'd be itching to get out there – to experience the party atmosphere, and throw myself into the vibrancy of the place.

But tonight, I didn't have it in me, and I think JB and Neale sensed that. Instead, we left the bright lights and the blackjack and the Cirque du Soleil to everyone else, and holed up in the suite with a nice bottle of wine.

'Cooper can be an ass,' JB said, as he poured me a glass. He was lounging back against the bed, looking like some kind of decadent rock sex god, and Neale was trying not to stare at his exposed midriff, bless him.

'Yeah, I noticed that,' I replied, cautiously. I was furious with Cooper – hurt as well as angry – but I didn't want to go too far in what I said to JB. He was his friend, and it wasn't fair to trap him in the middle of this.

'But usually, he's only an ass when he's in pain. The time he split up with his girl, Jeannie?'

'The one who was training to be a teacher?'

'He told you about her, did he?'

'Yes,' I said, sounding a bit on the bitter side, 'back when we were friends.'

'Yeah, well, he was the world's biggest jerk when that happened. Took it out on everyone around him. Same thing when he had issues at home, after his sister Eloise got divorced. Most of the time he's super laid-back, such a cool guy, and so much fun to be around – one of the most genuine people I've ever met, and especially in this business, where the bullshit factor is so high. But when Cooper hurts? Oh boy, then everyone hurts!'

I nodded to show that I understood. And I did. Cooper's behaviour hadn't sprung out of nowhere – it had its roots in the pain that I'd caused by being so selfish. By using him when I was low, and dragging him down with me. I knew that, and it lay like curdled milk on my stomach, making me feel queasy. But I was still angry, and still felt like I'd been double steamrollered by both him and the still-silent Daniel.

It was a huge mess all round, and knowing that I'd played a part in making it all happen didn't help.

'I know,' I replied, sipping some more wine, 'and I also know it's my own fault. But I'm just wrecked by it all, to be honest. Everything feels like it's turned to shit, and I'm sick to death of all of it. I'd just like a day without disasters. A day without drama. A day where I could stop obsessing about my own life, and just enjoy.'

I saw JB and Neale swap glances – one of those significant glances that close couples have, where they're asking each other a question without using any words. JB raised his eyebrows, and Neale nodded.

'What?' I said, excited. 'What is it? Tell me! For God's sake, I need some good news!'

'OK,' said Neale, folding his small hands on his lap and grinning at me. 'We were going to tell you when we decided, but then Cooper did his revenge song, and everything just went to hell.'

'What? Tell me what? Come on, the suspense is killing me!'

'We're getting married – here, in Vegas!' he squealed, unable to keep the glee out of his voice.

I didn't talk much after that – just whooped and hollered and hugged them both to within an inch of their lives. I was so very, very happy for them – just thrilled. It couldn't have cheered me up more. They were such a great couple, and Neale had waited a long time for happiness like this. For literally minutes, I was able to leave my own shoddy life behind, and focus on theirs.

'Oh God!' I said, once I'd stopped shrieking and leaping around like a madwoman. 'This is brilliant! When? Where? Can I come? Neale, we need to go shopping. . .'

Chapter 16

The chapel they'd chosen was perfect. For them, at least. I'd been expecting some flamboyance, some showbiz, maybe an Elvis impersonator or at the very least a fake Tina Turner complete with fright wig.

Instead, it was decked out tastefully in flowers blooming in a million shades of pastel, with the sounds of gentle classical music playing in the background, soothing and calm.

The minister holding the service looked to be about 108 years old, with a raisin-like face that had been dried out by the constant sunshine, and white hair that was bouffed and primped into an impressive helmet.

In front of him, at what was used as the equivalent of the altar, stood Neale and JB. They both wore baby-blue suits with matching silk ties, and they'd scrubbed up beautifully. I could tell that Neale had added a bit of subtle make-up, but JB, for once, looked like pure class instead of pure rock – his ears were free of rings, his face was free of stubble, and his thick black hair was combed and tamed into a well-behaved ponytail. Only the hint of his tattoos curling along his neck gave any clue to his usual wild boy image.

The only other people in the chapel were me, and Cooper.

That, as you can imagine, had been awkward at first. I knew he was going to be there, so I'd had time to prepare myself, and so had he.

He was dressed in a darker blue suit, and I was in a navy sheath dress – we'd both been given the colour code beforehand, and I expected nothing less from Neale. He wouldn't want us ruining the photos, after all, by turning up in flamingo pink or leopardskin.

I stood at Neale's side, and Cooper stood at JB's, as we all waited for the music to come to a close, and for the ceremony to begin.

JB and Neale only had eyes for each other, which is exactly how it should be – but even if they had been looking at us, they wouldn't have encountered anything to distract them from the fact that they were making this wonderful commitment.

When we'd arrived, in separate cars, I'd been worried. I was determined to behave myself, not to take any focus off the happy couple, but was concerned that Cooper might not have got that particular memo. His behaviour had been erratic to say the least, between the beat-down song and the screaming match and the stony silences that followed, and the last thing I wanted was for him to start kicking off in the middle of my best friend's wedding.

Luckily, he was obviously also planning on being a good boy. We'd nodded to each other when we all walked through into the chapel, and we'd both even managed a small smile. There wasn't much warmth there, or real happiness, but that was to be expected – neither of us was in an especially happy place right then.

But it said something about us both, I think, that whatever our differences, however much damage we'd done to each other, we were willing to set it all aside to celebrate the union of our friends. Maybe we'd both go back to being selfish arseholes as soon as it was done, but for the time being at least, we seemed capable of getting along.

The music finished, and the minister started the ceremony, talking about how we were gathered here in the presence of love, surrounded by love, to celebrate love. He talked for a while, but seemed sincere – he must have done thousands of these, and it was impressive that he still seemed to mean every sentence. He used words like 'joy' and 'commitment' and 'eternity', and it was very, very moving – even JB, usually the first to throw a cynical bomb, seemed enraptured by it all.

It was the part where the two of them spoke their own vows that really ruined me, though. Ruined me to the point where my mascara didn't stand a chance, and the tears flowed freely. It was so beautiful, and so emotional, and so genuine – the exact opposite of my life at the moment.

Neale didn't even look nervous as he spoke, which was proof of how confident he felt in this relationship. He looked on as JB talked of the way that Neale had changed him as a person, made him into a better man, and they held hands through it all.

When it was Neale's turn, he simply smiled, and said: 'JB, I love you. When I first met you, I loved the way you looked, your sense of humour, the way you made me feel.

'I loved the excitement of our relationship, the fact that it was a secret, and the fact that it was fun. Since then, I've grown to know you, inside as well as out.

'Now, I love everything about you. I love the way that you stay strong when normal people would feel weak. I love the way you behave towards your family and your friends. I love the fact that you are, completely and utterly, yourself. You live by your own rules, and those rules are simple: they're about integrity, and kindness, and honesty.

'Before I met you, so much about my life was wrong. I was hiding from myself, from my family, from who I really am. You've seen through all of that, you've seen me, really seen me, and you still love me.

'You've given me confidence and courage and conviction. You've given me the strength to be who I want to be. I've never in my whole life loved anyone the way I love you, and I know that I'll feel like this for ever.

'I love you here, in this chapel. I love you late at night, dancing at a party. I love you first thing in the morning, when your hair is a mess and you've stolen all the sheets. I love you while you sleep, while you're awake, and everything in between.

'Alone, we will survive, but together, we will truly live. I promise to always love you, always respect you, and always cherish you. JB, I'm honoured to have you by my side, as my husband.'

JB was also crying by this point, and Cooper was swiping at his eyes with the cuff of his suit jacket. Even the wizened old minister had gone a little teary-eyed. It was just so, so perfect.

They shared a long, loving kiss at the end of the ceremony, and then we all hugged each other – even me and Cooper. I had no doubt at all that I'd just seen something very special, and I felt privileged to have been part of it.

'Right!' said Neale, once the photos were done, the paperwork signed, and his beautiful ring well and truly admired. 'Now, it's time to celebrate!'

We made our way back to the hotel, where the ever-reliable Felicia had organized a party for the whole of the crew. As we walked into the lobby, cheers and catcalls and screams erupted in a volcano of sound, and a surge of humanity rushed towards Neale and JB, surrounding them with their congratulations.

There was food, and drink, and a cocktail fountain that seemed to be filled with ever-cascading pink champagne, and a table stacked high with shiny, wrapped gifts. It was amazing, and they both deserved it.

I hung back a little, watching my friend disappear beneath a tidal wave of well-wishers, and felt so happy for him. Happy, but also exhausted. The day had gone well – so much better than I expected – but now I felt drained. The stress of being with Cooper, of setting aside everything else that was going on in my life, had left me feeling like a dishrag. Seeing their love – their commitment to each other – had made me realize even more how set adrift I was. And, of course, how much I missed Daniel.

I decided that I'd stay and join in with the party for an hour or so, then once Neale was well and truly smashed and too drunk to notice, I'd sneak away. Back up to my hotel room. To solitude, and to checking my phone, and to trying to sleep even though I knew my busy brain wouldn't let me.

I was thinking all of this through when I became aware of Cooper hovering next to me. He was holding two glasses of the pink champagne, and held one of them out to me. He looked nervous and tense, as though he expected me to knock it out of his hand or throw the contents over his head.

Instead, I took the glass, and nodded my thanks. Now I came to think about it, a drink wouldn't go amiss at all.

'So, that was beautiful, wasn't it?' he said, gesturing towards the happy couple.

'It was,' I replied, sipping the champagne and almost sighing with relief as the fizz hit the back of my throat. Nothing improves your sense of well-being quite like a glass of bubbly. 'Very beautiful. And I feel honoured that we were there. I wouldn't have blamed them for giving up on us both, and going it alone.'

'I know. That was brave of them,' he said, managing a small smile. 'I guess they had more faith in us than we had in ourselves.'

That, I thought, wouldn't be hard – I didn't have faith in my own ability to cross the road, never mind anything more demanding.

'Look,' he said, standing closer, so we formed our own little bubble in the middle of the happy chaos, 'I wanted to say that I'm sorry, OK? For the song. The way I've been behaving. Everything. Seeing those two today . . . well, it made me realize what a shit I've been. I say I love you, but then I treat you like that – and it's not fair. I can't make you love me back, and doing what I did, I was just lashing out, you know? I was in so much pain. What happened between us meant so much to me, and so little to you, and I couldn't bear the thought, so I lashed out. It's childish and petty, but, well, I do that.'

I bit my lip, and for once tried to think before I spoke.

Part of me wanted to tell him to stick his apologies where the sun doesn't shine, but another part knew that this was an opportunity to make at least one relationship in my life better. To make peace, and move on. God knows I needed some peace.

'I know,' I said, quietly. 'And I'm sorry too. I shouldn't have let things go that way, when I knew I was still in love with Daniel. It wasn't fair to anyone. In fact, it was cruel, or it would have been, if I'd known then how you actually felt about me. I didn't know, though. I thought it was casual for you, and I'm so sorry I wasn't sensitive enough to realize what was happening. I was so wrapped up in my own problems I didn't even notice.'

He nodded, and gulped down his champagne – it seemed like we both needed a bit of chemical help to get through this conversation.

'Yeah, well, we both fucked up then, didn't we? Let's just leave it at that for now. I don't want things to end badly between us, Jess, I really don't. Right now, I feel terrible, but that will pass, and maybe one day, we can even be friends again.'

'I'd like that,' I said, sincerely, 'I really would. I'll be going home soon, and we'll both have some time and some distance, and . . . yeah. Maybe we can. Maybe it'll all be all right.'

'So,' he replied, looking on as the party started to kick up a gear – Felicia had supplied a karaoke machine and one of the tech guys was doing an impressive rendition of 'Black Betty' – 'what do you think will happen when you get home?'

Good question, I thought. And one I didn't have a clue how to answer. Seeing Neale today, so in love and so secure, had been both wonderful and torturous for me. I was thrilled for him – and, at the same time, I wanted what he had. I wanted to go back to feeling in love and happy and secure. I wanted to go back to Daniel, but I had no idea if that was even possible – if we could heal our broken relationship, or if too much had gone wrong.

'I don't know,' I said simply. 'I'll do my best to get through it, whatever happens. Anyway, Cooper, I'm glad we had a chance to talk. And I do hope that things work out all right for you. I know you think you love me right now, but to be honest, you don't even know me that well. Seeing what Neale and JB have together, that's the real deal – that's what we all want, isn't it? Someone who knows us inside and out, all our faults and bad habits, our stinky breath in the morning and our bad hair days and the times we act like idiots?'

'And loves us despite it all,' he replied, nodding to show he understood.

'Yeah. Well, it's none of my business, but I think you already have that. I think it's right under your nose, and you haven't even spotted it.'

He looked confused, frowning at me, and I pointed over to Felicia. She was dressed in her usual skinny jeans and T-shirt and Converse, still clutching her clipboard, still wearing her earpiece, but smiling away with the rest of the crowd. She looked like she was having fun, and had relaxed as much as she ever did, her face pretty and alive, her dark hair shining down her back.

'Really?' said Cooper, disbelief in his voice. 'Felicia? No way! She doesn't feel that way about me, does she?'

God, I thought, men could be so dense sometimes.

'She does, Cooper,' I replied. 'Believe me, she does. That woman knows you inside and out, and she still loves you – she'd do anything for you. And you'd be a fool not to think about that.'

I swallowed down the rest of my champagne, and left him, staring in bewilderment at Felicia, hopefully seeing her in an entirely different way. I made the most of his temporary befuddlement to pat him on the arm and leave.

I needed to be alone; I had a lot of thinking to do.

Chapter 17

'Daniel,' I wrote – resorting to an email – 'I'm writing this while tipsy, so forgive me if I make a few spelling mistakes. Today, I watched Neale and JB get married in Vegas. It was amazing, just so beautiful – and not an Elvis impersonator in sight. I wish you'd been here to see it.

'Anyway, I don't know if you'll even read this, or if you'll delete it as soon as you see my name. Maybe I should have set up some kind of fake email account so you wouldn't know it was me. Isn't it terrible that this is what we've come to?

'If you are reading this, then please know how sorry I am. About Cooper, about everything. I don't know what happened with you and Vella. You said it wasn't what it looked like, but what it looked like was so upsetting. Even if you weren't sleeping with her, it was too much. I felt like you'd left me, distanced yourself from me, and become close to her instead.

'Seeing the two of you together like that – seeing her walking around my house almost naked – pushed me over the edge. It's not an excuse. I'm not saying it to justify what I did – just to try and explain why I did it. And to tell you how much I regret it. It was a huge mistake, for so many reasons – the main one being that I love you so much, I feel physically sick at the thought of being with another man ever again.

'I love you, and my only hope is that we can find a way through this mess. Not so long ago we were planning on getting married – we loved each other that much. If any of that is left for you, then I hope you'll listen, and believe me when I say this: we can work this out. It might not be easy, but what in life is easy, when it's worth having?

'With all my love – Jessy xxx'

I deliberately didn't read it through again, because I knew that if I did that, it would all look wrong. That I'd start rewriting it, or fiddling with it, and I'd end up so frustrated with my lack of ability to communicate that I'd at best not send the email, or at worst flush my phone down the toilet. Instead, I just pressed 'send', took my make-up off, fell into bed – and slept. Dream-free, and soundly.

It was the first time I'd slept properly since everything kicked off, and perhaps that was because I'd come to a decision – that however it might end, good or bad, I was going to do everything I could to save our relationship. To get my Daniel back. To make it work.

It could all end in tears and humiliation and possibly a restraining order, but at least I had to try. I didn't want to look back on this in a few decades' time – when I was an old lady living with seventeen cats and talking to a cardboard cut-out of Leonardo DiCaprio for company in my kitchen – and regret the fact that I hadn't given it everything I had. I'd always been determined and single-minded when it came to my career, I'd never given up on that dream until I made it come true, and this was even more important. Without this, I knew, everything else was meaningless.

*

I woke up the next morning still determined, still convinced that I needed to try harder. Push further. Find out for sure whether our relationship was salvageable.

The concert tonight was to be our last of the tour, and a huge party was planned at one of the casinos later – the one with all the posh multicoloured dancing fountains outside it, that I vaguely remembered from watching *Ocean's Eleven* years ago. There would be celebs, and media, and I knew Felicia and the sound and vision guys had put together a showreel from the whole of the tour – hopefully just catching the highs, and carefully editing out the lows.

I was sure it was going to be amazing, and part of me wanted to stay and enjoy our last hurrah together. These people – the crew, the singers, the dancers – had been like family to me. I'd travelled with them and eaten with them and partied with them, and there is a certain intimacy you get from being on the road. Shared experiences, memories that nobody would ever really understand unless they'd been there. In ordinary circumstances, I would have loved to have said goodbye, and gone out with a bang.

But these were far from ordinary circumstances. The party would just have to cope without me, and I'd have to catch up with the showreel at a later date. I'd already decided that as soon as the show was done, I'd be leaving for the airport and heading back to the UK. Where, hopefully, I could begin the rest of my life.

I packed all of my gear up, astonished at how much crap I'd accumulated, and realized that I was going to have to buy a new suitcase from the hotel shop to fit everything in.

Between the packing, and the rehearsals and the sound-checks, it was a busy day – which was probably for the best. At least it stopped me furiously checking my phone every five minutes.

I had a quick dinner with Neale, and explained my plan to him, asking him to say goodbye to everyone on my behalf.

'Are you sure, honey?' he said, looking concerned. 'Don't you want to tell them goodbye yourself? Leave in the morning?'

'I don't think so,' I replied, chasing my food around my plate with my fork, 'it'd just be too hard. Things ended OK with Cooper last night, and I don't want to give them a chance to go wrong again. We're only ever a second away from Armageddon these days. I'll message him once I'm at the airport so he doesn't call the FBI and report me missing or anything. But, I just need to get home, Neale, you know?'

'I know, babe,' he said, reaching out to pat my hand. 'And I can only wish you well. I'll be back in the UK in a couple of weeks, but, in the meantime, stay in touch, won't you?'

Neale was heading off to Tahiti for a fortnight's honeymoon with JB, and I didn't want to sour the prospect for him.

'Of course. Though you'll be too busy bonking to talk to the likes of me, I suspect!'

Neale blushed, and laughed. 'Well, I certainly hope to be

busy bonking, yes – but, Jess, I'm never too busy for you, you know that, don't you?'

'I know,' I replied, giving his hand a squeeze. 'And I know how lucky I am to have you, Neale. But I'll be fine, I promise. I'm tougher than I look.'

He raised one eyebrow at me, and I had to laugh – it was a fair point. I was currently rocking a set of blonde hair extensions and wearing neon Lycra – I probably didn't look that tough at all.

'OK, OK! But look, I mean it. I'll be all right, I know I will. If I can't fix things with Daniel, I'll survive. I have a good family, and brilliant friends, and I'll survive.'

I hoped I'd reassured him, but I think he was still worried, and maybe feeling guilty because he was going off on a shag-fest while my life was in tatters. There was no need for him to feel like that, and I hated the fact that I was bringing him down at a time when he should be focusing on enjoying the good things in life.

So I spent the rest of the day trying to look bright and breezy when I was around him, all smiles and jokes and giggles, to try and ease off his anxieties. I wanted him to jet off to his sun-drenched island paradise and bliss out with an ocean full of pina coladas – not be concerned about me.

Very soon, it was time for us to go and start on the lengthy process of beautifying myself – or, to be more precise, of Neale beautifying me while I bitched and moaned and whined about the whole ordeal. I like the end result, but it's not so much fun while he's poking and prodding and tugging at my hair as though it's not actually attached to my body.

Just before we were about to go out of the dressing rooms and head to the side of the stage, my phone beeped. At first I ignored it – I was focused and in the zone and ready to rock the shit out of this last gig – but for some reason, an instinct told me to check.

It was an email. From Daniel. I had a scary few moments where I thought I might pass out then, seeing his name on the screen. And then a few more moments when I tried to decide whether to read it or not, my finger hovering over the message – if it was good news, it would definitely make the night go with more of a swing. On the other hand, if it was bad news, I'd be devastated, and quite possibly incapable of performing.

In the end I sat back down, got myself a bottle of water, and took a deep breath. No matter what kind of news it was, I had to know – there was no way I could get up on stage and carry on as normal, still wondering what he'd said. The not knowing would almost be as bad as being told it was all over.

I skimmed the email through narrowed eyes, as though it was an especially scary scene from one of those films like *Insidious,* where you spend half the movie not watching, because you know it's going to give you a nasty jump-scare.

Ah, I thought, as the words sank in. It wasn't really any news at all.

'I'm sorry I've ignored you,' it said, 'but it's all been too much for me. First of all, nothing did happen with Vella, but if I'm entirely honest, it might have, if you hadn't turned up when you did. I don't like facing up to the truth about myself, but it was possibly heading that way. You were gone, I was lonely and she was there. It started off as work, but grew into something more – but I'm sure you know how easily that can happen.

'I still feel hurt and humiliated and confused. I love you, but I don't know if we can fix this, or if we should even try. I'm going to stay with my parents for a while. Let's talk when you're ready. Daniel.'

Hmmm. It wasn't good news, but it wasn't bad, either. I could completely understand why he felt hurt and confused, and why he was switching off from it all and staying with his parents, away from our home and everything there that would remind him of our life together. We'd both behaved badly, and obviously both had regrets, but, ultimately, part of me thought that this could still work. That if we did get through this, and managed to forgive each other, then we could emerge from it all stronger than ever – we'd have learned some valuable lessons, and made mistakes we wouldn't ever make again. If nothing else, all of this had taught me how much I did love him, and how hard I was willing to work to put all the pieces back together. Daniel wasn't perfect, and I was a million miles away from it, but I still loved him. Still wanted him.

I only had a few minutes before Felicia would start sending out a search party, so I quickly tapped out a reply – which is harder than it sounds when you've just had your nails done.

'Last gig tonight,' I said, simply. 'Please watch.'

There was still a chance, I felt – that email had done nothing to persuade me otherwise. He said he still loved me, and where there's love, there's hope.

It was that thought that got me through the gig – gave me

the strength to dance and prance and sing and smile, enduring the spotlights and the noise and the heat, giving it my all for one last night. Setting aside all the personal problems, the tour itself couldn't have gone better. I was selling records in the States, In Vogue was getting global attention, and Patty informed me that my social media following had skyrocketed. Possibly not all for the right reasons, but she seemed happy.

More than that, I'd grown so much as a performer – gained so much valuable experience, picked up so much wisdom from Cooper and the crew and the other artists. They were veterans of this game while I was still a novice, and working with them had been a huge boost. I knew that when all this was over, and I was planning a tour of my own, I'd be so much better prepared for it.

In some ways, I was sad it was ending. I'd definitely miss the crowds and the cheers and the indescribable buzz of being on stage in front of a packed stadium of blissed-out fans.

But the rest of my life was more important than a few hours in a spotlight. I was finally old enough and wise enough to realize that, and to know that, now, I needed to set aside the showbiz, and concentrate instead on what really mattered – getting my life back on track.

By the time we'd done our last encores, and taken our last bows, I'd formulated a plan. Or at least a bit of a plan. OK, I'd formulated a few random sentences, but hopefully random sentences that would do the trick and help get Daniel back home, where we could start the long and probably painful process of picking through the rubble of our relationship, and, if we were lucky, building some new and far more solid foundations.

Cooper and I were standing next to each other on stage, in the spotlights, waving at the crowd as we prepared to leave. I met his eyes, and whispered: 'Give me a minute?'

He looked confused, and momentarily scared, and I realized that I was almost re-enacting the scene when he'd decided to kick me in the guts with that 'Back of My Cab' song of his. Perhaps he thought I was about to launch into a catchy ditty about a mean man with a small penis and a big ego, and trash him live on stage like he'd trashed me. I smiled to reassure him, and added: 'It's OK, don't worry.'

He nodded, and took a few steps back, into the shadows, where the band sat silent, waiting to see what would happen next. Wow! We must have been like a living soap opera for these guys, with all our crazy spilling onto the stage.

'Hey, everybody!' I said, waving into an audience that looked like a giant blob of nodding black shapes, pierced by the light of phones and video cameras illegally capturing the moment. Just then, though, that's exactly what I wanted – for once I was counting on the power of the internet and all those phones as a force for good.

'You probably all know that this is the last night of Cooper's tour, and I think you'll agree it's been amazing, right?'

I paused and, sure enough, a huge cheer rumbled through the audience.

'Yeah, I think so too, but now it's time for me to go home, back to the UK, and back to some of my favourite things. And that includes a goat called Gandalf, a couple of chickens – and someone else very special.'

I hoped that Daniel would be watching, that he understood that I wanted to give us a chance.

'Anyway, this is my last night here. I've loved being in the States and seeing your beautiful country, and you've all been so welcoming. But, like Dorothy says, there's no place like home – and as soon as I leave the stage tonight, I'm going home. So, America, goodnight, and God bless!'

Cooper stepped forward when he realized I'd finished, looking no less confused, but a bit more relieved. Together we took one more bow, gave a few more waves, and walked off stage to the sound of a screaming crowd.

I dashed off down the corridor as soon as we came down from the steps, not wanting to have to talk to Cooper again. I needed to get ready, and make my escape.

I'd sent my message. Now all I could do was hope that Daniel had been in the right frame of mind to receive it.

Chapter 18

It was early evening by the time the driver pulled up outside the farmhouse. I'd been met at the airport by the same guy who'd picked me up on my last disastrous visit, and he looked slightly concerned when he saw me. Probably worried I was going to have another full-on girl meltdown in the back of his car.

I stayed chatty and smiley throughout the journey, partly to reassure him, partly to take my mind off things – and the constant nagging fear that maybe I hadn't done enough. That maybe it was too little, too late. That I'd be returning to an empty home, surrounded by the ghosts of happiness past.

'One of these for the drive, love? It being Christmas Eve and all.' He passed a box of jumbo-sized candy canes over to me in the back seat.

I smiled and thanked him, taking one to be polite, even though I was too nervous to eat anything.

'Are you working tomorrow?' I asked, trying to take my mind off what I was headed towards.

'No, love, thankfully. I've drawn the short straw for the Christmas shift before, believe you me. But this year I'll be spending it with the family. Just the way it should be.'

Blinking back tears, I smiled, nodded and said how happy I was for him.

*

It was a beautiful winter night, the fields and hedgerows dappled in frost, robins perched in trees. It was exactly how everybody thinks of the approach to Christmas in an English village, and somehow that would make it so much worse if this all went wrong. If Daniel wasn't there. If that happened, I'd prefer grey skies and rain and possibly one of those *Twister*-style cyclones that would pick me up and carry me away.

The driver unloaded my cases for me and, as we said goodbye, patted me on the hand.

'Good luck, love,' he said, kindly. 'I'll keep my phone on just in case there's a change of plan.'

'I hope not,' I replied as I tipped him. 'But that's really sweet of you – drive safely!'

He gave me a jaunty little mock-salute, and got back in his car, the door thudding shut as he prepared to leave.

I stood there, for a moment, trying to get my bearings. This whole jetting around the world and stamping across time zones thing was definitely getting old for me. I'd be happy never to leave England again for the next ten years.

I'd flown overnight from Las Vegas, texting Cooper on the way to the airport to explain.

I meant what I said on stage. I have to go home. Thanks for everything, and enjoy the party. Speak soon?

There'd been no reply – and maybe that was too much to

hope for. Sure, we'd ended things on a better note than they'd been for days, but perhaps it was still too soon to expect friendship, and clearly too soon to expect him to respond.

I was, after all, dashing home to try and rebuild a relationship with another man – a relationship he'd hoped was well and truly over. But maybe, I told myself, one day, we could be friends again. And maybe, one day, he'd get his act together and realize that he and Felicia were made for each other. Right now, though, I couldn't worry about that – I had to focus on Daniel, and me, and finding a way for there to be an 'us' again.

In a rare and possibly first-time ever move, I'd refused all alcohol on the flight, and instead just tried to rest. It hadn't been easy – my brain was running around like a hamster on an exercise wheel, constantly going over things, imagining all the possible outcomes for when I finally saw Daniel again.

When we finally landed, I wasn't feeling especially refreshed, and had spent a good twenty minutes in the first class lounge trying to restore myself to human status. I'd brushed my teeth, applied fresh deodorant, brushed my hair and sprayed perfume on my wrists and neck.

The time difference was weird – I didn't think I'd ever get used to the way it messed with your head, but at least I was home. I'd debated going back to my flat in London first, dumping my cases and having a shower, but decided against it. If I did that, there was always the chance that I'd sit down for a minute, and fall asleep for forty-eight hours. Or that I'd just chicken out completely and wake up in the morning back at square one.

I had to push onwards, and hopefully upwards, I decided, whatever the outcome.

I watched as the driver made his way slowly back down the gravel driveway and back through the gate that always needed oiling, and hoped that this time, I wouldn't be making an emergency call asking him to come back and scrape me up from the side of the road.

I looked around, trying to re-familiarize myself with everything. I couldn't spot Gandalf, which meant he was either in the barn or on the other side of the paddock, but I could definitely hear the chickens clucking away in their shed. My heart sank when I realised that Daniel's jeep wasn't in the drive, but I told myself he might have put it in the garage. Except, of course, he never put it in the garage – the garage was full of spare sound equipment and boxes he'd never unpacked and random parts of drum kits.

But you never know, I'd been gone a while – maybe he'd cleared it out. I bit my lip so hard I tasted blood, and picked up my handbag. The rest of the cases could wait, possibly for ever.

I walked towards the building, gravel crunching under my feet, and put my hand on the door. I pushed, and was relieved that it wasn't locked. I knew there was a spare key hidden under the flower pots, but the fact that it wasn't locked must be a good sign – surely that meant he was here, even if his jeep wasn't?

Except, again, I knew, it didn't necessarily mean that. It could mean that Pat had been popping round to care for the animals, and nobody round here ever locked their doors in the countryside anyway.

I walked into the hallway, seeing the same familiar stone flagging, the same higgledy-piggledy pile of coats and boots and brolleys in the corner. It smelled like home. I paused, and listened – no music. No TV. No kitchen sounds. Nothing at all to indicate there was anyone else in the house.

I went into the kitchen, hoping to find Daniel sitting at the table with his headphones on, maybe checking some emails or messing around on his laptop. But the chair was empty. I felt tears sting the back of my eyes and blinked them back. If I let the floodgates open now, I'd never stop.

Instead, I went and poured myself a glass of water from the tap, and sat down at the big old pine table while I sipped it. People always get given a glass of water on TV shows when they need to calm down, but it wasn't really working for me. I noticed that my hands were trembling, the glass shaking with them, and I was making a terrible mess. I tried to steady myself, but my body wasn't interested in being steady, and there didn't seem to be much I could do about it. So I just sat there, at the table, on my own, spilling water.

I'd been running on adrenaline for so long, and now that I was finally here, in this empty house, I didn't know how I could ever move again. Every last ounce of hope suddenly drained out of me. My limbs felt like elastic bands, and my face was numb. Everything was numb.

I wondered whether Daniel had even seen my message at the concert. Or worse, whether he'd seen it and decided to stay away. A huge wave of tiredness washed over me and I lay my head down on the table, closing my eyes against the world.

I was still in that position, cheek squashed against the wood, when I heard the sound of the door scraping open. I lifted my head up and stared at the kitchen door. Oh God, I thought, please let it be him. Please, please, please, let it be Daniel and I'll never take him for granted ever again. Just give me one more chance. One more chance to make this right, to fix things.

After what felt like an eternity, the door finally opened. And it was him. It was my Daniel, and he was holding two enormous Christmas stockings.

I stood up, my legs wobbly beneath me, and ran towards him. He'd just about managed to offload the stockings onto the countertop before I threw myself into his waiting arms. He wrapped himself around me, and I buried my face in his T-shirt, breathing in the smell of his washing powder and his shower gel and everything that made him *him*, clutching hold of the material as though I would never let go.

He stroked my hair and kissed my head, and, for minutes, neither of us said or did anything else. He was here. He was home. And so was I.

He pulled my face away from his chest so he could finally look at me, and I stared into his blue eyes, feeling my own fill with tears.

'I'm so sorry!' I said, desperately. 'I've missed you so much! I don't want to be away from you ever again. Please, please, say you'll give this another go, Daniel! I'm so very, very sorry!'

'Shhh,' he said, running his fingers over my cheeks, my jaw, my shoulders, as though he was touching every part of me to remind him how it felt. 'I'm sorry too. It's OK, you're home. We're home. We'll figure it out, Jessy, don't worry. I love you, all right?'

I swiped tears away from my eyes, and replied: 'OK. I love you too. I can't believe we let things go so wrong.'

'There's time to discuss all of that later. We'll have the rest of our lives to talk about what went wrong. But right now, let's focus on what's right.'

He leaned forward to kiss me, and I don't think I've ever had a kiss like that in my life.

I was home. In Daniel's arms – exactly where I belonged. This was the best Christmas present I could ever ask for.

Chapter 19

Six Months Later

I stood poised with my back to the crowd, feeling the ever-increasing sense of anticipation building behind me. I'd performed a lot of concerts, and stood before a lot of audiences, but I'd never felt quite this sense of mounting excitement.

They were all there, waiting. Waiting for me to finally do it. I could hear their giggles and nervous chatter and the sounds of people jostling against each other.

'Come on, Jess, get a bloody move on!' someone shouted.

I laughed, and finally did it – I threw that bouquet as hard and as fast and as far as I could over my shoulder, launching it skywards and hoping it survived the journey back to earth.

I whirled around to see where it went, the taffeta of my beautiful white dress swirling with me, and wished I could capture the scene in my mind for ever. Or at the very least that the photographer managed to capture it for me.

The bouquet – a bundle of pink and white roses – was tumbling and turning through the air, making its way towards the crowd of women who were waiting for it. Sensible women. Career women. Intelligent women. Strong, independent women, who I admired.

Strong, independent women who, at that exact moment, looked as though they might happily attack each with rusty bayonets if it meant they might be the one to reach up and pluck those magical roses from the sky.

Patty was there, wearing a leopard-print bodycon dress and biker boots, her long-taloned hands reaching upwards. My old school friend Ruby was there, sturdy and intense, looking focused. Yvonne, the In Vogue receptionist, was there, looking way too young to be interested in such things. And, of course, Vogue herself was there – and, by all rights, she should definitely have this one boxed off. She was around three feet taller than all the other women, and had the build and reach of one of those super-athletic beach volleyball women you see at the Olympics.

I kind of wanted Vogue to catch it, just to see the look on Jack Duncan's face – because he was there, too, off to one side, dressed in his stylishly crumpled linen suit, pretending he wasn't looking but definitely keeping an eye on where that bouquet was going to land. He'd probably start sprinting for the gate if Vogue snagged it.

Despite her height advantage, though, Vogue just didn't quite have the eye of the tiger when it came to bouquet-wrangling. That particular crown went to probably the shortest woman in the crowd – Felicia Diaz. What she lacked in height she made up for in ferocity and elbow-shoving skills, and I looked on as she pushed everyone else out of the way, and performed a majestic ballerina-like leap into the air, arcing and curving against the sky until she finally grasped the flowers.

She landed back down on her feet – still Converse-clad, but

glittery ones to mark the occasion – and waved the bouquet triumphantly in the air, doing a little victory dance as she went, everyone cheering her on.

I burst out laughing, and immediately looked around for Cooper. Sure enough, there he was, standing off to one side, holding a glass of champagne. He was fully suited and booted, and looked wonderful. He also looked happy – happy about being here, on this blissful English summer's day; happy about being among friends; and mainly, happy about seeing Felicia do her little victory dance, waving her roses around and giving him meaningful looks.

His days as a free man were most definitely numbered, and he couldn't have looked more pleased about it. He met my eye, and raised his glass to me. We shared a smile, and I was thrilled all over again that we'd managed to stay friends. That time and patience and understanding had allowed us to move on. That Daniel was a big enough man to accept that. That Cooper had finally realized that he didn't love me – he'd never loved me – and instead opened his eyes to the woman he did love: Felicia.

I hitched my dress up slightly so I could walk better, and walked over towards my family. They were all there, including my ancient nan, and it was such a treat to have them close. We'd decided to hold the wedding reception at the farmhouse, and a giant marquee had been set up in one of the fields, filled with tables and chairs and trestles full of food and drink.

The service itself had been at the village church, with my sister Becky and Vogue as my bridesmaids, and Neale and JB as the ushers. I think Neale would definitely have been happier as a bridesmaid, but I didn't want to start my wedding by giving the vicar a heart attack. Bad karma!

It had been relatively small, just our close friends and immediate family, and incredibly beautiful. The church was tiny, and ancient, all pale stone and quiet spaces and sunshine pouring through stained glass and painting us all in shades of the rainbow.

Daniel, with his dad as his best man, had looked suitably stunned as I walked down the aisle on my own father's arm, and seeing the expression on his face was enough to make all the dieting and the dress fittings and the constantly getting stabbed with pins completely and utterly worth it.

And now, we were here, having a party in a field in the countryside, in the middle of nowhere. Apart from a few members of the guest list, it wasn't very showbiz at all – which was exactly how we wanted it. There would be no paparazzi, no gossip, no deals with *Hello!* magazine to share our 'special day' via a photo spread. It was our day, to be celebrated with people we genuinely cared about, in a way we genuinely enjoyed.

My dad was standing at the edge of the paddock with Becky, looking on as Prince Ollie – wearing a sailor suit that made him look like Baby Bluto – stroked Gandalf's nose. Sean, his dad, was holding him, ready to snatch him away if Ollie tried to grab the goat's ears. So far, so good – Ollie's chubby toddler face was gleeful, and Gandalf himself seemed perfectly content, having been plentifully bribed with hay earlier in the day.

Becky was pregnant again and clearly couldn't wipe the smile from her face. Who could blame her? If I'd ended up with a happy, chuckling baby like Ollie, I'd have wanted another one too.

My mum was back in the farmhouse, where she'd taken my nan for a 'little lie down' – which was code for the fact that Nan was rather merry on champagne, and had reached that stage where she might start taking her false teeth out or threatening to twerk, or maybe even both at the same time.

Luke, my little brother, appeared to be pestering Yvonne, who he seemed to have decided he was in with a shot with. Callow youth!

My dad saw me coming, and his face broke out into a huge smile. He put his arm around my shoulder, and kissed me on the head.

'Ugggh!' he said, wiping his mouth with the back of his hand. 'You taste like a chemical plant looks. Is that your real hair?'

'Yes!' I said, laughing. 'It's just had a bit of help from Neale, and maybe three cans of hairspray. We can't all be blessed with Bald Eagle good looks, Dad.'

'Aah, I know, love. It's been a curse, what can I say? Anyway, have I told you yet how beautiful you look?'

'Yeah,' I replied, nudging him and smiling, 'only about three million times.'

'Well, if a dad can't go overboard at his daughter's wedding, when can he? It's been a smashing day, Jessy. A really happy day. To be honest, a bit of a bloody relief as well. There were moments. . .'

'I know,' I said. 'Moments when you thought it would never happen. Me too. But it has, and I couldn't be happier, Dad. Last year . . . what we went through . . . well, it just made us stronger. Made us realize how right we were for each other. Made us . . . I don't know, just better all round!'

Dad nodded, looking like a wise, bald owl, and replied: 'It did. And I'm thrilled for you both. You need a few knocks in life to realize what really matters. Now we'll just be waiting for the next bit.'

'What do you mean, the next bit?' I asked, confused.

'You know, the *next* bit!' he said, miming a pregnant stomach and pointing at Becky. 'The bit where we get even more gorgeous grandchildren to spoil!'

'Don't do it,' said Becky, even though I didn't even notice she'd been listening. 'Your bladder won't forgive you, and taffeta will never be your friend again.'

She gave me a quick grin to show she was joking, then went back to watching Ollie.

'Not just yet, Dad,' I said, shaking my head. 'Maybe one day, if we're lucky. But for a little while at least, we want to concentrate on being married. On having each other, and work, and life. And besides, we've got all our animal family to look after as well.'

Dad frowned as he looked out into the paddock.

'Yeah, what is that thing again?' he said, pointing at a new four-legged friend, who stood shyly grazing on the far side of the field. She was a relatively new addition to the menagerie, and hadn't quite overcome her stage fright yet.

'It's an alpaca,' I replied. 'She's called Holly.'

Holly had been a gift from Daniel – for my birthday, which I was celebrating today in the best possible way I could have ever imagined. We'd chosen her name because it reminded us of Christmas and for that moment we both realised our love was worth fighting for.

Dad was frowning. He still wasn't completely comfortable with all this countryside stuff, and would probably have been more in his comfort zone if he was inching his cab round Anfield on match day.

'And are you sure that Gandalf and Holly won't get together and, you know, produce a little goatpaca or something?'

I burst out laughing at that one. A goatpaca! 'No, Dad. Not a chance of that, they're different species!'

Becky was sniggering away in the background, her hand placed protectively over her tummy, where Prince Ollie's new brother or sister was busily getting baked, ready for delivery in a few months' time.

'I'm off for a top-up,' I said, pointing to my empty glass and waving my goodbyes to Ollie. I walked back over through the gardens, past the marquee, enjoying the sensation of the sunlight on my bare shoulders.

I glanced at all my friends as I passed them, feeling as warm from them as I was from the sun. Vogue and Jack were, against the odds, still a couple. Felicia and Cooper were going strong. Neale and JB were as loved-up as ever. My family were happy and together and blooming. And I was married – to the most wonderful man in the world.

A man who I loved, who loved me, and who I was going to spend the rest of my life with. I looked around, scanning the garden and the meadow and the marquee, trying to locate him. He'd never liked the limelight, my Daniel, and that was fine with me.

I had an idea where I might find him, and made my way to the studio at the side of the house, tottering on my heels. Very soon, I promised myself, I'd be kicking those off and getting ready to dance.

I pushed the door open, a long, thin streak of sunlight pouring into the dim space of the studio, and saw that I was right.

There he sat, in his beautifully tailored suit, his tie tugged down for comfort, his blond hair flopping across his forehead. He was messing with something that had buttons and lights, and frowning in concentration. I paused for a second, drinking in the image, and matching it up to all those memories I had of this man.

Us as kids, when I'd be busy putting on a show for my parents in the living room, and he'd be the one operating the boom box in the background. Us as teenagers, when I was the star of the college end-of-year show and he was hiding away, doing the sound and lighting in the tech booth.

Us as adults – different in so many ways, but the same in all that mattered.

He realized I was there, and looked up at me. The blue of his eyes was shining, and his face was creased with a delighted smile. I squashed my big skirt through the door, and walked over to him.

'Hey, you,' I said, reaching out to stroke his hair back. 'Last-minute technical difficulties?'

'Nah, not really,' he said, patting his lap and indicating that I should be sitting on it. 'Just wanted to check the playlist for the party later.'

I snuggled into him, and he wrapped his arms around my waist, the dress ballooning around us.

'Needed a break from the spotlight?' I asked, grinning at him.

'Yeah. You know me so well.'

'I do. I know you, and I love you, Daniel.'

'And I love you too, Jessy. Happy birthday, Mrs Wells!'

Acknowledgements

Huge thanks to Debbie, Becky, Katie, Charlotte and all the team at Mills & Boon.

LET'S TALK
Romance

With new books out every 2 weeks,
Mills & Boon has a romance for every reader!

From Historical romances that will sweep you off your feet, to modern day love stories filled with passion and romance, you're guaranteed to find your happily-ever after.

millsandboon

@millsandboonuk

@millsandboon

For all the latest titles and special offers, sign up to our newsletter:
Millsandboon.co.uk